a *Songbird* novel

Troublemaker

MELISSA PEARL

ISBN: 1523312025
ISBN-13: 978-1523312023

NOTE FROM THE AUTHOR

I will never forget where I was when I came up with this story. It was in 2006 when my husband and I were traveling around the USA and Canada in a Chevy G20 van. It was the best year of my life, and many stories came to me as we toured the continent.

We were hiking through Arches National Park in Utah when Marcus and Kelly's story came to fruition. I'd been listening to the song "Just the Girl" by The Click Five, and I really loved the premise of a lovesick guy chasing after a girl who didn't really want him. I thought it'd make a fun story, having this girl think she was above him. But the best things can sometimes come in the most surprising packages, right?

As we trekked through this amazing, rocky terrain on a blue-sky day, my mind buzzed with ideas, and by the time we got back to the van, Kelly and Marcus had a story. The book has been added to and adapted since its initial birth, but I love that it all started with one song.

I hope you enjoy the story...and the music.

xx
Melissa

TROUBLEMAKER SOUNDTRACK

(Please note: The songs listed below are not always the original versions, but the ones I chose to listen to while constructing this book. The songs are listed in the order they appear.)

UPTOWN FUNK
Performed by Mark Ronson & Bruno Mars

BROKENHEARTED
Performed by Karmin

SEXY LADY
Performed by Jessie J

ABSOLUTELY (STORY OF A GIRL)
Performed by Nine Days

NEW SHOES
Performed by Paolo Nutini

ARE YOU GONNA BE MY GIRL
Performed by Jet

JUST THE GIRL
Performed by The Click Five

TROUBLEMAKER
Performed by Olly Murs & Flo Rida

HEY, SOUL SISTER
Performed by Train

GOOD TIME
Performed by Owl City & Carly Rae Jepsen

STITCHES
Performed by Shawn Mendes

WORK THIS BODY
Performed by Walk The Moon

DOWNTOWN GIRL
Performed by Hot Chelle Rae

LIVE WHILE WE'RE YOUNG
Performed by One Direction

EPIC
Performed by We Are Leo

SHUT UP AND DANCE
Performed by Walk The Moon

BETTER WHEN I'M DANCIN'
Performed by Meghan Trainor

SHE'S NOT AFRAID
Performed by One Direction

BENEATH YOUR BEAUTIFUL
Performed by Labrinth & Emeli Sande

THIS IS WHAT IT TAKES
Performed by Shawn Mendes

KISS YOU
Performed by One Direction

GIVES YOU HELL
Performed by Glee Cast

UPTOWN GIRL
Performed by Westlife

BACK FOR YOU
Performed by One Direction

ONE STEP CLOSER
Performed by Shane Harper

MARVIN GAYE
Performed by Charlie Puth & Meghan Trainor

EVERYTHING YOU WANT
Performed by Boyce Avenue

NO GOOD FOR YOU
Performed by Meghan Trainor

NEXT TO ME
Performed by Tiffany Alvord & Gardiner Sisters

HAPPY
Performed by Never Shout Never

LET HER GO
Performed by Jasmine Thompson

DEAR FUTURE HUSBAND
Performed by Meghan Trainor

To enhance your reading experience, you can
listen along to the playlist on Spotify.

Troublemaker Playlist Link:
https://open.spotify.com/user/12146962946/playlis
t/5hw1ZuKSJu1PhrJ1DKKRbH

For

Olly Murs
&
Meghan Trainor

You both have a playful charm and sexy style that always gets me singing and dancing. Thanks for making me smile and brightening my day.

ONE

MARCUS

Overwhelmed.

No, that was wrong. I didn't want to buy into that.

Under pressure.

Closer.

Stressed out of my mind.

Most definitely.

I stared at the long line of little red flags in my inbox and drooped my head with a heavy sigh. College had been a breeze. Exam time brought its own kind of pressure, but I'd thrived on it. The real world—a real job with intimidating bosses to answer to and a shitload of cash to deal with—that was something else entirely.

I was out of my depth, like a duck sitting in a pond, seeming to have it all together, but my legs were going a hundred miles an hour under the water. Somehow I had to stay afloat and prove to Torrence Records that I wasn't too inexperienced for this job.

At twenty-three I was the youngest manager in the company. Chaos was my first gig. I'd been employed during the filming of the reality TV show *Shock Wave.* For the first time in the company's history, Torrence Records had aligned themselves with a music-based television competition and agreed to take on the band that won. I was the guy who was going to take them under my wing and make sure they made Torrence proud.

Thanks to Jimmy and Nessa's romantic drama, I nearly screwed up my very first assignment. They'd made it damn hard on me…and themselves. I didn't think we'd recover from Nessa losing her hand. Thankfully, the new drummer, Jace, was a perfect fit, and we'd finally found a home for Nessa, too. They were in the throes of prepping for their first tour while their first single "Agility" was set to be a chart-topper.

I scanned my inbox, deciding which emails were the most urgent. It was ten o'clock in the morning. I'd already been at work for four hours and I'd only just started clearing my mail. Not the kind of life I'd envisioned for myself when I was in high school.

I rolled my eyes, grinning at my naiveté. The countless hours I'd spent dreaming about my future—a nice house, a flashy car, Kelly DeMarco in my bed every morning. If only I'd known that a nice house actually meant a paralyzing mortgage—which is why I'd invested in a small two-bedroom bungalow, three blocks from my parents' modest house in Culver City...and why I drove a 2001 VW Jetta. As for Kelly DeMarco, well, that had always been a pipe dream.

Being a band manager was intense, especially since I'd been given two new artists to take care of. Dion Bonnet would be a breeze. The guy was easygoing and already had an established following. The pianist had nearly finished recording a Christmas album, and it would no doubt be in the Top Twenty on iTunes within a week of its release. He was nice, polite, and after the crappy experience he'd had with his last record company, he was willing to do anything Torrence asked of him.

And then there was Caris.

My brow bunched. Clicking on the email with her as the subject line, I reread Everett Torrence's reply with a frown. He was expecting big things from the eighteen-year-old wild-child. She was a talent. I'd be an idiot to think anything else. But the pampered girl who'd been raised and preened to become a mega-star was going to give me a mental breakdown.

I wished they hadn't put her in my charge, but

after the way I'd dragged Chaos out of the mud, they felt I was the best man for the job.

Bryce, my irritating coworker, had smirked and sniggered beside me as I sat shell-shocked in the meeting. Everett, CEO of Torrence and self-made millionaire, had given me his stern look and said, "Time to prove yourself again, Chapman. Everyone else here said I shouldn't hire someone so young. Make this work and we'll see who's laughing, huh?"

I'd forced a tight, uneasy smile then nodded and told him I wouldn't let him down.

"Idiot," I insulted myself while squinting at the screen.

I slid my reading glasses on and wanted to whine when the words became that much clearer for me to read.

Marcus,

I know Caris is being stubborn again, but tell her she doesn't have final say on the album selection. Make her think Torrence will ditch her if she doesn't comply, but don't let her call our bluff. We want this girl. She's only just starting to get noticed, and we are going to be the ones who explode her career. She has to believe that we are the only record company for her.

Smooth this over by the weekend.

Everett
CEO ~ Torrence Records Ltd.

It wasn't often I received a personal email from the big-man, but I'd had to alert him to the fact Caris was demanding two songs that would not cut it. Just because she could sing and shake her booty didn't mean she could write decent music. When I politely told her this, she flipped out and threw a hissy fit that could have rivaled a two-year-old's.

Unfortunately, Everett Torrence was convinced that Caris had the potential to be the next big thing on the tween scene, and that meant mega-bucks. It pissed me off to no end that he was probably right. Torrence was willing to spend rich on this girl because she was a guaranteed investment…as long as we could keep her in line. I had to make this work, or I'd be costing the company a few cubic tons of greenbacks.

My fingers danced on the keyboard as I composed my reply.

No problem, Mr. Torrence. Consider it done.

Thanks for the opportunity to look after such an important artist.

Marcus

Lies, lies, lies.

"Brown-noser." My upper lip curled as I clicked SEND and moved on to my next email. I'd instantly disliked the uppity teen when I first met her. Caris thought the sun shined out her ass, and after hanging out with Nessa and the guys from Chaos, I knew firsthand what awesome rock stars were supposed to be like. Caris, as amazing as her voice was and as hot as her little body moved, was not one. Grooming her for the media was going to be a tough job, but it was mine and I had to do damn well. Or all the underlying messages exec kept sending me would float to the surface and become real: *You're not cut out for this job, Marcus. I'm sorry, but we're going to have to let you go.*

I snatched the headphones out of my top drawer and slipped them on, pressing shuffle play on iTunes. "Uptown Funk" started up. The familiar "Doh" then the clap made me feel instantly better. A smile spread over my face and my foot started tapping. Turning down the volume, I bobbed my head while dealing with the rest of my overflowing inbox.

I mouthed the words as I worked, the de-stress tactic I'd used throughout college working like a charm. Music could get me through anything. I couldn't necessarily sing in tune, but I could mouth the shit out of any song on the planet. I wasn't a bad dancer, either.

The red flags in my inbox gradually decreased as I worked through nearly a hundred messages. It was a time-consuming task, but so far, my friendly, personal touches were winning me points. If I hoped to have any kind of career in the music industry, I wanted to set myself up as the nice guy everyone could rely on. I was counting on the fact that my hard work would eventually pay off, and when people needed something done, Marcus Chapman would be the first name they'd think of.

Out of the corner of my eye, I glimpsed a figure moving toward my frosted glass door and pulled off the headphones before they knocked.

"Come in." Taking off my glasses, I rested them on my daily planner and grinned. "Good morning."

"Only just." Marcia smirked.

I glanced at the time and cringed. Eleven-thirty already?

The receptionist for the management floor walked across the polished wooden boards with a manila file in her hand.

Great. More work.

She stopped in front of my desk, hugging the file to her chest. Her kind brown eyes sparkled with humor, her faint dimples ready to appear.

I made a face at her. "What did I forget?"

She giggled. "Our song." She made a pouty face. "We didn't get our song this morning."

"Oh crap!" I jerked in my chair, scrambling for my mouse and quickly attaching "Uptown Funk" to my daily group email. It was probably the world's stupidest ritual, but I was determined to make what Bryce referred to as "the underlings" feel appreciated. I sent them a song every morning, something to brighten their day.

My nose wrinkled sharply as we listened to the whoosh. "Sorry it's late."

Marcia tittered then tipped her head to the side, looking at me like she no doubt assessed her young daughters when they came home from school with their grumpy faces on. "Are you okay?"

I nodded. "Just busy. You know how it is."

"Well, this should help ease your load." Dimples appeared in her heart-shaped face as she held out the file in her hand.

I gave her a bemused grin and reached for it.

"Remember a few weeks ago when exec accepted Bryce's request for another assistant? They said yes as long as her workload was shared between the managers."

Taking the file with a nod, I tried to act like the news was more than just a vague memory. "I thought Bryce was taking care of this?"

"Didn't we all?" Marcia rolled her eyes. "Thankfully, he's been held up in Memphis with Cardinal Sin and won't be back until Friday. Since you'll be sharing the assistant, he's happy for you to conduct the interview."

I placed the file on my desk. "Only one candidate?"

"She made the mistake of including a photo of herself." Marcia's dark eyebrows arched and she gave me a look that said it all. I held my sigh in check. I didn't know much about employment law, but I was pretty sure hiring based on beauty was a big no-no. But we were talking about Bryce Fisher, and the guy only thought with one appendage.

"I still have the other applications if this one turns out to be a bust." Marcia pressed her hands together like she was about to start praying. "Please make sure this one's intelligent. She's going to be working right next to me."

"I'll do my best to let my head do the thinking

on this one." I winked.

"Thank you. She should be here in about fifteen minutes. I've printed out a list of standard questions to ask her. It's in the top of the file." She headed for the door, her sensible black pumps tapping on the wood before she stopped and pointed at me. "I'm trusting you, Marcus."

I grinned. "This is the first time I've ever been asked to employ someone. I'm not going to screw up this interview. Exec doesn't need any more excuses to kick my butt out the door."

Her smile was kind and warm, her expression telling me not to worry.

The door clicked shut and I blew out a sigh, reaching for my glasses while flicking the file open. I slid the rectangular frames up my nose...and then my chest deflated.

My lips parted as I stared down at the image of the woman I was about to interview.

Aw, shit.

There was no way in hell I couldn't screw this up.

TWO

KELLY

My fingers were sweating. I didn't even know fingers could do that.

"Brokenhearted" by Karmin was blasting from my stereo, but no matter how many times I turned up the volume, it did nothing to calm me.

Clearing my throat, I steered my car into the underground parking lot and paused to grab my ticket. I clutched it between my teeth and started looking for a spot. I never did like public parking and was still annoyed that all the visitors' spots outside Torrence Records had been taken. My wheels squeaked on the concrete as I turned down another layer. I was going to kill Scarlett and Isla for this. One drunken dare was not supposed to lead to a job interview.

"You have to apply!" Scarlett shrieked at me. "You might get to meet Chaos!"

I sipped my Merlot and wrinkled my nose at Isla's laptop. "Who is Chaos again?"

Scarlett had practically jumped me for that one, and Isla had started filling in my application, pretending to be me. She even attached a photo and sent it from *my* email account.

It had been a joke! I was a college dropout! I'd expected my application to be snickered at then thrown in the trash. When I called and told Isla I had an interview, she'd burst out laughing. I'd hung up on her unsympathetic ass.

"So-called friend," I muttered, the ticket sticking to my glossy lower lip. I threw it onto the seat with a disgusted humph. The only way to get out of this with my dignity still intact was to nail the interview.

Shit, I was nervous. I'd never had to sit through an interview before...not one where I actually wanted something at the end of it. No bulbs would be flashing, my parents' arms wouldn't be wrapped around me, and I wouldn't be talking to a camera. I'd be sitting in a chair all by myself, looking at a real person. There would be no barrier of dazzle to protect me.

I spotted a set of taillights and accelerated toward them, tapping my finger on the steering wheel while I waited for the car to reverse. I ducked into the free spot and flicked off the engine but kept the music pumping while I gripped the wheel and sucked in as much oxygen as I could.

This was insane.

If my parents found out I was going for a personal assistant job with a music company, they'd both have seizures.

"But you're Kelly DeMarco, the heiress to Echelon Fashion!" Dearest mother's snobbery would leach out of every word as she stated the obvious, and then Daddy would jump in. "My angel, I thought you were going to work with me."

How did I tell him that was the last thing I could handle?

I might have spent the last six months living in one of their apartments, and yes, I was sponging off them financially, but that didn't mean I wanted to spend my days at the Echelon offices in LA. I couldn't bear the thought of working alongside my father, not after what I'd found out.

A shudder twitched my spine, and I killed the music. I flicked down the shade and checked my appearance. If I was going to have any kind of luck, I needed to look good. Beauty was the one thing I had going for me.

I gazed at my blue-gray eyes, made vibrant by the chocolate-brown shadow I'd added to my eyelids. I ran my fingers over my thick strands of shiny dark hair, flattening the couple of stray hairs that had popped up on the drive over. I smeared some more gloss over my crimson lips and smacked them together. With a nod, I flipped up the shade and forced my brittle legs out of the car.

I smoothed down my jet-black skirt and straightened the chic blouse my father's top designer had made for me a few weeks earlier. It had a lustrous white pinstripe that made the fabric shimmer when I moved. Thanks to my mother, I had the perfect figure for the catwalk, and since Daddy's designer loved me so much, I was often his guinea pig for new designs. Happy to be. I'd barely spent a penny on my Echelon wardrobe.

My satiny heels were loud and sharp on the cold concrete. I hustled to get out of the dingy parking garage. The exit stairs smelled foul, and I nearly got attacked by a piece of gum and two dead cigarettes on my way up to the sunlight.

"Ugh!" I checked the soles of my shoes to make sure they were still clean, then gripped my Prada bag and crossed the street. The Torrence tower loomed before me, and I had to remind myself to breathe as I pulled back the door and smiled at the guard.

My heels echoed on the high-polished wood. I glanced around the shiny lobby, keeping an eye out for Chaos—Scarlett would expect nothing less. All I saw were a couple of suits on the square black couches having an animated conversation while they sipped from their Starbucks takeout cups.

The woman at reception smiled and asked for my details. I signed a book and was then handed a pass.

"Eighth floor," she murmured then turned away to answer the phone. "Torrence Records…"

I rode the elevator alone and in hyperventilating silence. By the time I reached the right floor, my hands were sweating again. I rubbed them on the back of my skirt and tried to step out confidently. The office space was open and bright. Two charcoal sofas cornered a bean-shaped coffee table. I headed past them to the rounded reception counter and was greeted by a dark-haired lady with a bright smile.

"You must be Miss DeMarco."

"Kelly." I nodded.

"Take a seat. I'll let Mr. Chapman know you're here."

"Thank you," I squeaked and headed for the couches.

The woman grinned at me again as she walked past in her navy fitted pantsuit. The jacket was too wide for her narrow shoulders and needed to be brought in at the waist.

"You must accentuate your best features," I could hear my father saying.

I could tell from one glimpse what that lady's body type was and how to make her look better. I closed my eyes, willing the judgmental thoughts from my mind. Growing up with a fashion guru and a model for parents, I had no chance of not judging everything anyone ever wore. It was like permanently living on the set of *Fashion Police.*

College had been such a nice reprieve.

Then Fletcher had happened.

My throat thickened and I gripped my fingers together. I couldn't go there, not moments before

24

an interview. If I had any hope of pulling this off, I had to stay focused.

Wasn't it his fault I was even here?

I had to succeed. I had to prove my mother wrong. I couldn't spend another six months wallowing. My friends were right—it was time to woman-up and figure out what I was supposed to do with my life. None of my plans had played out the way I thought they would. My dreams for the future had been twisted, torn apart, and trodden on by the people I'd trusted the most.

"Kelly." The receptionist's voice caught my attention. "He's ready to see you."

Standing tall, I pulled my shoulders back and lifted my chin.

It was time to prove everybody wrong.

It was time to be more than just Kelly DeMarco, heiress to Echelon Fashion.

THREE

MARCUS

I stared at the door. My throat felt like sandpaper. Leaning against the back of my desk, I gripped the edge and hoped I could get out a sentence without sounding like Donald Duck.

This couldn't be real. I hadn't seen Kelly DeMarco since the day I graduated. I'd never forgotten the first time I saw her. It was my second day of sophomore year, and she'd been gliding past me with two girls. They were giggling and looking a touch nervous, the way all freshmen did in their first week. I'd stuttered to a stop and just stared at her. The earth stood still and a chorus of angels sang in my head until I was thumped on the shoulder by my big brother, Griffin.

"Get your sorry ass to class, little bro." He'd grinned then messed my hair, and I'd floated through the rest of my day.

I patted my reckless locks, wishing I'd taken the time to style them. If I'd known, I would have put in a little more effort after the gym. My fingers skimmed my glasses and I whipped them off, throwing them on my desk just before she appeared.

"Hi." She stood in the doorway smiling at me, looking a million times hotter than the last time I saw her.

It'd been graduation day—over five years ago.

Her smile was still the same, though. My heart did a weird little hiccup.

"Hello," I squeaked then cleared my throat and strode toward her with my hand extended. "Hi there."

Her long fingers wrapped around mine, her squeeze firm and confident in spite of the slight dampness of her skin. The towering heels she wore made her taller than me, and I felt every inch of the difference. I swallowed and let her hand go, still gazing at her perfect face. The faint dimple in her chin appeared as she tipped her head and smiled at me again. She was probably trying to figure out why I was acting like a mute fool.

"Mr. Chapman, right?" Her full, pouty lips pulled into a stunning smile, and all I could do was nod.

She didn't remember me.

Disappointment flashed inside. The way I'd dogged her in high school, I would have thought I'd left a permanent impression, but…

My eyes narrowed at the corners.

Wait a second.

She didn't remember me!

Yes!

I didn't have to be nerdy Marcus Chapman anymore, the weird guy with pimples and a goofy grin. For the first time ever, the dynamic between us had shifted. For the first time ever, I had something she wanted.

I stood a little straighter and beamed at her.

"Please come in." I pointed to the couch in the corner of my office. "Would you like a drink of something? Coffee? Tea?"

"No, I'm good." She smiled and drifted onto the couch like a swan gliding on a lake. Everything about her was elegant and beautiful. She really was the goddess I remembered.

Her blue gaze dressed me down, her shaped eyebrows rising as she waited for me to find my voice and start the damn interview.

"Right." I cleared my throat…again.

Pull it together, man. Not many people get to make a first impression twice!

My red-hot reprimand gave me the boost I needed. I switched into work mode.

"Right, okay, let's do this." I smoothed down my tie and took a seat opposite her. Flicking open her file, I scanned the information and decided one last test was in order. "I see you went to Beverly Hills High School."

"Yes." She nodded, clasping her hands together.

"Did you enjoy it?"

"It was okay." She shrugged then dipped her head with a chuckle. "Actually, high school was a breeze."

Her smile faded and she pressed her lips together. Her knuckles went a little white and I had to ask, "How about college?"

She shuffled in her chair then picked a little nothing off her sleeve. "College wasn't for me."

"I see you did three years of business studies at Stanford." I gazed at her file. Curiosity sizzled as I tried not to be affected by the flash of sadness I caught in her eyes. "What made you quit?"

Her delicate nostrils flared, and she glanced down at the coffee table between us. "Personal reasons, which I'm sure are not pertinent to this interview."

"Of course." I gave her a light smile, hoping to ease the angst radiating off her. If she got the job, I'm sure I could siphon out the real story.

If she got the job, who was I kidding? She was totally getting the job.

Yes, she was underqualified.

Yes, Marcia would be pissed.

Yes, if exec found out, I'd be a fired man.

But come on, it was Kelly-Freaking-DeMarco.

She was getting the job.

It had to look legit, so I ran through the rest of the questions. Most of her answers boosted me with confidence while only a few had me gulping down my doubts. I wanted to tell her that hiring her was a huge risk and that she'd really have to prove herself, but I didn't want to put her off. I'd offer her the job, then once she'd signed the contract, I could give her that spiel. We chatted for about half an hour, and I went into detail for some of the things she'd be doing. She had no questions for me, so I slapped the file shut and dropped it on the coffee table.

"Well, this all looks pretty good to me. How'd you like a job with Torrence Records?"

Her head shot back while her smooth calf muscles flinched. "Really?"

"Sure." I nodded. "I think you'll be great."

"Wow." Her laughter was breathy. "I, um…okay." She nodded. "I didn't think you'd…" Her head shook while her lips did that fish thing. No noise came out.

It reminded me of that time in high school when she and a mousy freshman were caught sneaking in late by Assistant Principal Higgins. That woman could terrify anybody. Kelly had goldfished for a minute, while the other girl blinked at tears and started sniffling. Kelly, a junior at the time, had put on a charming smile and lied, taking full blame in an effort to save the new freshman. Higgins wouldn't give an inch, issuing after-school detentions on the spot then clipping away. I'd flashed my hall pass when she glared at me, then I'd turned to head back to homeroom, but not before spotting Kelly flipping the bird at Miss

Higgins' back. The sniffling girl gasped then started giggling. "Thanks. Sorry you got detention, too."

"No big deal." Kelly had shrugged at the girl she obviously didn't know.

The freshman scampered off to class while Kelly's unchecked smile flashed in the empty corridor. It'd been a glimpse of something she never showed anyone, and only validated my unwavering infatuation for her. There was a ton of spunk hiding beneath the show she put on for everyone, and I made it my senior-year mission to try to unearth it. Too bad it was an epic fail.

I swallowed, the memory excavating my old high school insecurities. "Do you…not want the job?"

"Yes! I mean—" She scratched her temple and let out a nervous titter. Her nails had that French manicure thing going on. It looked pretty. "I just wasn't expecting such a quick offer. I have no qualifications. I mean, I…" She opened her mouth to say more then pressed her glossy lips together.

"We've all got to start somewhere, right? I'm the youngest manager here and yeah, it's daunting sometimes, but I know I can do it. I am determined to be the best manager this company's ever seen, and I wouldn't be able to say that if someone hadn't given me a shot."

Her hesitant smile grew to full bloom, making her eyes sparkle.

Damn, she was the most beautiful creature this world had ever seen.

I slapped my hands on my knees and stood before she caught me drooling. Turning away from her, I wiped my mouth then slid my hands into my trouser pockets. "Right, well, I'll get Marcia to email you the contract. You can look over it tonight and give me a call in the morning with your final decision."

"Sounds great."

Unable to help myself, I beamed at her, feeling like the freaking man as she rose from the couch and moved toward me. I wanted to skip to the door and do a little twirl, but reined myself in before complete humiliation. I had to play it cool. She didn't know I was the geek from high school. She only knew me as Mr. Chapman—her soon-to-be boss.

I walked her to the elevator and tried to subdue my smile by a few shades. I didn't need her remembering my goofy grin from five years earlier. The elevator doors dinged shut, and I ambled back to Marcia's desk. "Could you please email a copy of the contract to Kelly so she can look over it tonight. She'll call in the morning with her final decision."

"So, you don't want to look through the other applicants then?"

I shook my head, struggling to control my grin.

Marcia's jaw worked to the side, her expression anything but impressed. "You didn't let your head do the thinking, did you?"

My cheeks grew hot as I squeezed the nape of my neck.

She rolled her eyes. "Since when did you turn into Bryce?"

"I didn't." I held up my hand, slightly insulted by the idea. Bryce was a dick...and proud of it, for some weird reason.

Marcia's dimples appeared as a hot blush worked its way up my neck. "Oh, so the fact she looks like a Milan model had nothing to do with it?"

I adjusted the knot of my tie before smoothing it down my chest. "She'll be fine. We've all got to start somewhere, right?"

"You know, she's the daughter of Enrique DeMarco. That girl doesn't need to start anywhere. Her family owns a fashion empire."

"How do you know that?" If my memories from high school were correct, Kelly tended to keep that info pretty low-key.

Marcia's lips pursed then grew into a cute little smile. "I Googled her. Something about her name sounded familiar."

I grinned and leaned my arms against the desk. "Fashion empress or not, she obviously wants this job or she wouldn't have applied, right?" I glanced at the elevator doors, wondering what had gone down at college to make a girl like Kelly walk into Torrence Records in the first place.

I was determined to find out, and I was going to do everything in my power to make sure the sad heartache that swept across her face never surfaced again. Kelly was looking for a new beginning, and she was going to find it at Torrence.

I'd make sure of it.

All I could hope was that she didn't remember my geeky high-school self before signing the contract.

FOUR

KELLY

I waggled the pen in my fingers and stared down at the dotted line on the bottom of the contract. Biting the corner of my lip, I poised the pen above the line and paused for the thousandth time since reading the damn thing.

I'd been pausing all freaking day.

After leaving Torrence Records, I stuttered my way to the car then hiccuped to the gym. I fumbled through Zumba class, screwing up most of the steps. The afternoon instructor approached me at the end to no doubt ask what my problem was, but I managed to slip out the door before she reached me. I finally stumbled through the apartment door at around four-thirty, only to knock over two of Isla's boxes.

I glanced at the stacked boxes in the living room, that familiar tug of dismay trying to pull me down. She was leaving that weekend. Moving in with her fiancé and abandoning me. I tapped my pen on the table, the rhythm growing fast and demanding as I imagined how empty and quiet the apartment would be without my roomie.

I threw the pen down. It rolled to the middle of the table, stopped by the glass fruit bowl in the middle. I didn't understand why my nerves were fraying. It was a personal assistant job, for crying out loud. I was capable of doing it. I just never expected to be offered the chance. With a sigh, I snatched the pen back and poised it over the paper again.

A key jiggled in the lock. I glanced up as Isla walked through the door. Her smile was bright and radiant. It had been since the day Logan proposed.

"Hey, lady." The tip of her tongue poked out between her teeth. It always did that when she smiled big. Dumping her book bag on the table, she slumped into the chair opposite me and frowned. "What's wrong?"

I made a face then pushed the contract across the table. Her eyes scanned the document before rounding large. "You got the job?"

"Okay, the magnitude of your surprise is actually insulting."

Isla giggled, tipping her head back and letting

out a loud guffaw. She was the most inelegant laugher I knew. When she really got going, the weirdest noises came out of her. I slapped my hand over the contract and snatched it back before she got that far.

Restraining herself—sort of—she giggled her way into the kitchen and pulled out the bottle of wine we'd started the night before. "Well, I think it's great. Have you told Scarlett?"

"Not yet. I want to wait until I've actually signed the thing."

Isla reached for two glasses, her green eyes sparkling. "Did you see Chaos?"

"No." I shook my head. "As if I ever will. The interview was conducted in a very sedate office. If I sign, I'll be working on the lower executive floor with the managers and marketing department. I won't be seeing any rock stars."

"You never know. Rock stars might visit their managers." Isla tipped her head in time with the wine.

The dark red liquid sloshed into the glasses and my mouth watered.

"So, tell me about it. What will you be doing?"

"Um." I scratched my right eyebrow and gazed at the contract. "I'd be working for a few of the band managers—travel arrangements, admin type stuff, just general assistant responsibilities...whatever they ask me to do really."

Isla placed a glass in front of me and sat down. "Sounds cool."

"Yeah, it could be okay. The guy who interviewed me seemed nice enough. He'd be one of the guys I'd be working for."

"Is he cute?" She waggled her pale eyebrows at me.

"Isla." I scowled at her giggling face and sipped my wine. It slid down my throat easily, bringing instant comfort.

"Come on, tell me about him."

I huffed and swirled my wine. "Okay, he was short with light brown hair and a nice smile. Hazel eyes. Decent suit. He was…" I shrugged. "I don't know. Not ugly, but hardly a looker. He's so not my type."

Isla's lips quirked, her eyes narrowing at the corners as she scrutinized my expression.

I widened my eyes and tipped my head, letting her know I was telling the one-hundred-percent truth.

"Name?"

"Marcus Chapman."

"No way!" Isla slapped the glass table. "Are you kidding me? Do you think it's the same guy?"

"What are you talking about?" I placed my glass on the coaster and started fidgeting with the pen.

"You know!" She twirled her hands in the air, her ginger curls dancing around her face. "The guy who couldn't leave you alone in high school."

She was way too excited about this. Her eyes were so large and dazzling, she looked like a Disney princess.

I wrinkled my nose, forcing my mind back to

high school. I had a lot of guys dogging me throughout my teenage years, but there was one guy in particular…

My breath caught in my throat as I pictured the pathetic puppy and his numerous attempts to ask me out. It had been totally humiliating. Oh man, his goofy smile and wild laughter…and his jokes that I couldn't admit to anyone were actually kind of funny.

But he'd been relentless.

An image of his hazel eyes, gazing at me with unchecked affection, crystallized in my mind.

"O. M. G." I dropped the pen and froze. Those hazel eyes. Those…he was…I couldn't…

"It *was* him?" Isla giggled.

I closed my eyes and rested my head on top of the contract. "How am I supposed to sign now?"

"Oh, come on." Isla lightly tugged my hair. "Sit up and stop being such a baby. Does it really matter if it *is* him? I'm sure he's moved on from his high school crush."

"Ugh!" I sat up and slapped my hand on the contract. "Do you think that's why he offered me the job?"

"No!" Isla brushed her hand through the air. "He can't hire you for your looks. His job would be on the line."

I made a face. "Then why did he offer it to me?"

Isla shot me a reprimanding scowl. "Because you're an intelligent woman who can do this."

Resting my elbows on the table, I covered my face and sighed. Being the wealthy daughter of a model made it really hard to read people's true intentions. The amount of times I'd been burned by my looks or status... People were assholes.

"Kel." Isla's voice was soft and serious. I looked up, letting her really see me. She and Scarlett were the only ones who were ever allowed to. "You need this job. Scarlett and I weren't kidding around. You have to start moving forward. In three days' time, you'll be living on your own. You can't spend it watching soap operas and shopping with your mother while she tries to organize your life. If you don't want to work for your dad, then work for someone else. Torrence is a cool company, and I know you'll be in the exec offices, but you may still get to meet Chaos." She winked.

I snickered. "If I did, Scarlett would shatter every window in this apartment with her screaming."

"For that reason alone, you must do this." Isla's serious expression made me laugh. She joined me and we were soon giggling like tweens. It took me back to high school and my laughter faded.

Isla shook her head. "This Marcus thing was years ago. He's probably totally over you and living with his girlfriend."

I sighed and slowly reached for the pen. "Yeah, well, he's definitely lost his geek factor, so him actually having a girlfriend is probably quite plausible."

Isla twirled the stem of her glass with a sly smile. "He was good-looking, wasn't he?"

I wrinkled my nose. "Not my type."

Her smile was all-knowing and I gave her a warning look that told her not to go there. Marcus Chapman was seriously not my type. He never had been. I liked tall, dark, and sophisticated, not short, scruffy goofballs. I waggled the pen again and gazed down at the dotted line.

"Trust me. You want to do this." My best friend's intense gaze held so much. She was the only one who knew the whole truth, the entire heartache...my utter disgust and despair.

I swallowed and she nodded again.

"It's *your* life, Kelly. It's time to start owning it."

FIVE

MARCUS

The back kitchen door jammed like it always did. I jiggled my key and used my shoulder to nudge it open. The second the hinges creaked I was greeted by two dancing kittens.

"Hey, guys." I chuckled while they scampered around my feet. "Slow down, I'll give you cuddles in a second."

Dumping my satchel on the kitchen table, I shrugged out of my jacket then crouched down to greet my little buddies. Pumpkin, an orange ball of fluff with blue eyes and the sweetest face in the world, nestled against my leg, purring softly. Flash, the dark gray streak of lightning, bolted between my legs then dug his claws into my trousers.

"I missed you, too." I petted between his ears and he meowed. "Hungry?"

He meowed again.

"Of course you are."

Standing tall, I collected one in each hand and let them play with my collar and sniff my neck while I walked toward the pantry. Nina, the housekeeper I shared with Chaos, had left my place immaculate as always. If only she wasn't happily married with grandkids. The way she looked after me, I'd snatch her up in a moment.

I laughed at myself, pulling out the kitty biscuits then placing my furry friends on the feeding mat. They pranced around me while I shook some food into their bowls. I'd been hesitant to get kittens at first. My job was insanely busy and I really didn't have time, but my sister, Felicity, volunteered at an animal shelter and she'd told me about these two strays that no one wanted. I couldn't resist and ended up adopting the two buddies who acted more like brother and sister the longer they lived with me.

Nina had promised to check on them daily, and so far they hadn't torn my house to shreds or peed on every exposed piece of carpet. The kids next door really loved them, and I'd given one of them a spare key so she could pop in and play with the kittens after school.

It was working out well, and it meant that I wasn't coming home to an empty bungalow every night.

My lips pulled into a pout. Was I pathetic?

Most probably.

I was twenty-three years old. I'd broken up with my college girlfriend, Allison, in my senior year, and I replaced that hole in my life with kittens.

"You are a sad little man," I muttered.

Shaking my head, I pulled out the leftover lasagna mom sent me home with the night before and set about heating it in the microwave. It was already eight o'clock, and I wanted to be at the gym by five the next morning. I had another full day ahead of me…including a meeting with Caris.

"Oh joy."

The microwave beeped. I snatched a fork from the drawer and perched on the kitchen table to eat. My leg swung idly as I stuffed my face and watched my kitties finish up their dinner.

It was in the quiet moments that I often wondered if I'd made a mistake breaking up with Alli. But she'd wanted to move to the East Coast to pursue her masters in psychology. She'd managed to score a really great opportunity working with some professor who liked her thesis proposal. I didn't want to head east. I wanted to stay in LA and find a job. Those student loans had no intention of paying themselves.

When the Torrence Records gig came up, I couldn't help wondering if it was a sign that I'd made the right decision…but I still missed her sometimes. She'd been a great friend, a good lover, and we'd had fun together. She'd never turned my insides to hot spaghetti like Kelly did, but at least she'd been in my league. I didn't need mush. I just wanted to love someone and have that someone love me back with the same passion.

I scraped the lasagna bowl clean then rinsed it in the sink. Pumpkin and Flash were back to dancing around my feet, trying to trip me up as I headed into the living room. Flopping onto the couch, I grabbed the remote and flicked on the TV. The kittens crawled up to join me, snuggling against my legs while I pulled the laptop out of my bag. This was our evening ritual. Some inane TV show would play in the background while I worked and the kittens fell asleep against me. I'd usually hit a wall around ten and drag my sorry ass to bed, falling into oblivion before a new day surfaced.

As I opened my inbox, my mind jumped to Kelly. It'd been doing that all day. The way she looked standing in my office door had been enough to paralyze me. She'd grown more beautiful…more unattainable.

I scanned the emails, checking for her name. Marcia had cc'd me on the contract email, and I was impatiently waiting for any kind of response. So far—nada.

Running my tongue over my upper teeth, I shook off the disappointment and got to work. There were five emails to do with Caris. Two were complaints from the sound techs, one was a vent from the songwriter she was working with, and two were freaking encyclopedias from Caris's mother waffling on about how sensitive her daughter was. The flowery prose was peppered with veiled demands that I would have to try to meet while also protecting Torrence. The Caris gig was going to be a real bitch.

I was tempted to slap my laptop closed and deal with it in the morning, but a ding sounded. The box popped up and my heart stopped for a second as I recognized Kelly's email address.

My eyes devoured the words of her message, a broad smile growing on my lips until I let out a loud whoop that scared the crap out of my kittens.

"Sorry, guys." I petted Pumpkin's head and ran my fingers down Flash's back. "She signed. She freaking signed! Kelly DeMarco is my new personal assistant."

Pumpkin blinked at me, her large eyes looking mystified. I smiled at my sweet little girl and scratched behind her ear.

"I haven't told you the story yet, but when Daddy was in high school, he fell in love with a beautiful girl."

Flash scratched the couch, his claws digging into the fabric.

"Hey, stop that." I grabbed his paw and gave it a rub. "I know you're not interested, but Pumpkin wants to hear." I winked at my ginger fluff-ball. "Anyway, this girl was a dream come true. She's got this magical smile that hardly anyone has seen. She grew up in the limelight so she's always putting on this show, right? But if you catch her off-guard and manage to glimpse the girl…the *real* Kelly…it's a thing of absolute beauty. She's strong and sweet and caring and fun…" I shook my head, that goofy grin spreading across my face again. "She's like dignified royalty with a bubblegum center. I tried everything I could to get her to open up to me—Valentine's cards, funny notes in her locker, goofy grins in the hallway. I even offered to help her study, not that she needed it. But I was a desperate mule, convinced I could be the one to truly make her happy."

I let out a loud, dramatic sigh and ran my finger around the corner of my laptop screen. "I couldn't do it, though. That girl has a knack for decorum. Breaking through that was like an impossible dream. See, she's cool by default—rich, beautiful—so of course she hung out with the dignitaries of Beverly Hills High, but…" I shook my head. "I always felt like she ended up with the wrong kind of guys. The good-looking jocks who were boring as hell. I just know, I mean I *know* I could be the right man for her. I could make her laugh and smile. She could be herself around me. I'd look after her."

I stared at the email, not reading the words. Instead, I was remembering Kelly at my senior prom. She'd been there with some good-looking dickhead who spent the night showing her off then groping her on the dance floor. She didn't smile the whole time. She was far too classy to be treated that way. Even she knew it. In the end, she'd left with her two best friends. I'd secretly followed them into a dance club and watched her face grow radiant as she spent the rest of the night partying with her girls.

"So beautiful," I whispered. "A smile to die for."

Man, I wanted a chance with her. But how was that even possible? She'd snubbed me so many times in high school. I'd trailed her around like the loser I was, hoping my witty charm would somehow win her over, but if anything, it simply put her off.

Why the hell did I think things could be any different this time around?

I shook my head with a wry grin that quickly faded.

"Man up, Chapman."

I was acting like I'd lost before I'd even started.

Kelly didn't remember who I was, and I'd changed since then. I didn't have to be the kid who tripped over his shoelaces trying to say hello to her. I was Marcus Chapman now, manager of artists like Chaos and Dion Bonnet. Kelly worked for *me* now. It was my chance. I couldn't let self-doubt kick my ass.

SIX

KELLY

My fingers were sweating again. Seriously!

I gripped the handle of my new light-oak satchel. I bought it a few months back but hadn't had the chance to use it. The chic Tory Burch bag matched my oatmeal skinny pants that tapered just above my ankle. I matched the fitted trousers with a scoop-neck top and a fitted black jacket that ended mid-thigh.

Isla had moved out on Saturday. She and Logan were all smiles and excited kisses while I helped in morose silence. After they left, I wanted to curl into a ball and cry, but Scarlett wouldn't let me. She opened a bottle of Pinot Noir and got busy designing the perfect outfit for me to wear to work come Monday.

"You want to say professional, yet sexy." Her long fingers spread wide as she presented her pitch like the marketing guru she was training to be.

I rolled my eyes. "Sexy? Really?"

My platinum-blond friend bobbed her head and jumped over to my computer, finding "Sexy Lady" by Jessie J. The music started pumping and she danced around my room, jumping onto my bed and mouthing the words while I stood on the floor trying not to laugh. In the end, I was pulled into her antics and hauled up on the bed with her. We hollered the words and shook our asses until the song finished, and we slumped onto the pillows in a fit of giggles.

Five minutes later, Scarlett's boyfriend called and she was out the door.

"He's mixing at the club tonight. Like hell I'm missing that."

She hadn't invited me, which meant she planned on spending the night up at his console, dancing and making out with him.

It took all my willpower to finish off the ensemble Scarlett started for me, but I played "Sexy Lady" until it was embedded in my brain.

I stepped into the elevator and glanced down at my nude pumps. They finished off the outfit perfectly, and I did look damn sexy. I needed to; it was the only thing giving me any kind of confidence as I walked into a job I was unprepared for. I hummed the tune in my head as I ascended to the eighth floor. It didn't help my nerves. My fingers were still slick as the doors dinged open and I strode into my new workplace.

"Kelly." The receptionist smiled at me. "Welcome."

"Hi." I shot out my hand, once again doing my best to put on a show of confidence. The woman looked me up and down before tucking a lock of hair behind her ear and reaching for my hand.

"I'm Marcia. I take care of the exec floors and you'll be working beside me...filling in during my lunch break, that kind of thing."

"Excellent." I nodded and smiled, but actually wanted to throw up all over her.

"Let me show you around."

My head was acting like one of those bobbing toys people put on the dashboards of their cars. I stiffened my neck to try to control it.

"Morning, Kelly." A pleasant male voice greeted me from behind. There was a familiarity to his tone that was almost comforting, but then it wasn't... because it was Marcus.

I spun on my heel and smiled politely. He was wearing black pants with a grape-colored shirt tucked into them. His tousled hair was a stylized messy that actually suited him. It was a far cry from the fifties comb-over he used to love in high school. I always thought he was trying to be quirky and different—he'd definitely achieved that goal, but totally missed it on the cool factor.

Gazing into his smiling eyes, I was transported

back to the hallways of Beverly Hills High. He'd often linger with his friends outside my homeroom, goofing off in the corridor like he was supposed to be there when really he was just waiting for a glimpse of me. It had been creepy and weird, yet…oh all right, it was a little bit cute, and on the days he wasn't there, I always noticed.

"Hello, Mr. Chapman." I went for formal, hoping to deter any weird advances from the guy. Tousled, stylized hair or not, I couldn't handle a repeat of the gooey-eyed Marcus Chapman era.

He grinned, his mouth a little lopsided. "You can call me Marcus if you like, everybody else does."

"Okay," I squeaked then cleared my throat. "I'm just gonna…" I pointed over my shoulder and turned away before he could say anything else to me.

Marcia had this curious smirk on her face but was nice enough not to say anything when I caught up to her. I pressed my lips together and kept my expression bland and unreadable.

I had no idea what Marcus may have said to her. Hopefully she didn't know anything about our history. Ugh. That would have been so humiliating.

Marcia spent the next half hour touring me around the lower executive floor. All the big wigs were on the floor above us—the CEO, Mr. Torrence, plus his team of talent scouts, the finance department, and of course his personal assistant. On my floor were the marketing department, legal, and artist managers. The company was sizable, but being the daughter of Enrique DeMarco, I was used to powerful people with lots of money. By the time I'd done the rounds, I figured I was on the "nuts and bolts" floor of the company. The people I was used to associating with were above me. Was it weird that I felt more out of my depth down here than I probably would have up there?

"Okay, so we'll share incoming calls." Marcia sat down at her station and spun her chair around to face me. I glanced at the area I'd be working in. My side was bland with a desktop computer, an empty set of trays, and a pencil holder with three pens and a highlighter in it. Marcia's was the opposite—a cluttered cacophony of stationery, papers, and photos pinned on the wall beneath the high counter. All the pictures were of her, a man who looked to be in his mid-thirties, and two little girls. I checked her ring finger and noticed a simple gold band. Funny, I'd assumed she was my age. She looked too fresh-faced and vibrant to be a working mother.

I took my seat and looked at the black phone with a million buttons on it. "Most calls are fielded by the main reception area on the ground floor. All the calls that come through to us are either from them, or the caller has specifically been given this number. Our job is to field the calls for our departments. We're kind of like the gatekeepers. If any of the departments are in a meeting, they'll let us know and we'll take a message. Your main priority is Marcus, Bryce, and Edie. Although, Edie's a really hands-on manager, so she's hardly ever here. She likes to stay mobile, so you'll mainly be working for Marcus and Bryce."

My head started doing that bobbing thing again. Marcia failed to notice my anxious stare as she pulled the phone toward me and explained how it worked. Different flashes meant different things. I had to press some hash button and then punch in a three-digit code to check if the person was free before putting the call through. No caller should get through without giving the receiver a heads-up first. Everybody in the office had a code for his or her phone.

"You'll learn them really quickly, but refer to the list as much as you need to. It's better to take your time and get it right than send someone through to the wrong person." I scanned the list of names and numbers, rubbing my slick fingers together.

"Hi there." A tall man with dark eyebrows and jet-black hair leaned against the reception desk. He looked like he'd wandered into work late. He had a superior air about him.

Hot damn, he was gorgeous.

His face was sharp and chiseled, his eyes a dark cyan. The immaculate charcoal suit he wore fitted him perfectly, and the midnight-blue shirt beneath told me that this man knew how to dress well and take care of himself. Attraction pulsed through me thick and strong.

I couldn't stop looking at him.

Marcia stiffened and cleared her throat. "Good morning, Bryce."

He gave her a cursory look before training his

gaze back on me. I met his flirty smile with one of my own, stretching out my hand. "You must be my new boss. I'm Kelly."

"It's very nice to meet you." He shook my hand, his eyes sparkling. "Once you're finished up here, pop into my office and I'll give you a little rundown of what I'm expecting from you."

"Sure." I smiled and he winked at me before ambling away.

I glanced at Marcia and mouthed, "Wow!"

She rolled her eyes and went back to talking about the boring telephone.

The lesson wrapped up and I stood, collecting my notepad and a pen.

"Where are you going?" Marcia asked.

"To Bryce's office. He wanted to see me."

Marcia studied my expression, her lips twitching like she wanted to say something, but wouldn't. I narrowed my gaze, daring her to be honest. The phone rang, making me jump. Marcia lifted the receiver like it was the easiest thing in the world. "Torrence Exec, Marcia speaking ... Sure, can I ask who's calling? ... Okay, let me check."

I watched her fingers carefully as she pressed the right buttons.

"Hey, Marcus." She grinned then paused, listening, before starting to laugh. "Don't worry, it's the arena. I think they want to talk Chaos logistics. Are you free?" She laughed again. "Yeah, that's the one. I'll put her through."

There was something so light and happy about the exchange that I almost felt jealous. It was completely insane. I studied Marcia's fingers again as she transferred the call then scribbled down the order she did things in.

"I'll let you get the next one if you want to practice."

"Uh-huh." I nodded but didn't mean it. I never knew a telephone could be so terrifying.

Spinning on my heel, I was about to make a dash for hot guy's office when a sweet girl with a pixie face and short hair blocked my way.

"Hi." I stared down at her.

"I'm just here to set up your email account and make sure your computer is working."

"Sure." I moved out of her way and she took my chair. Her fingers flew over the keyboard while she stared at the screen and set up my Torrence work account. I watched over her shoulder, trying to memorize as I went. For someone who had never worked in an office before, it was kind of overwhelming, but I was determined to hide that behind a confident smile.

"And you're set." The woman stood from her chair and told me to sit down.

I pulled it into the desk and rested my fingers on the keys.

"So, just choose a password."

I fumbled my way through the task, scoring a surprised look from both my coworkers. As the tech girl walked away, Marcia gave me another one of her scrutinizing gazes.

"What?" I snapped softly.

"Do you not know how to touch type?"

"Of course I do, I'm just…out of practice." I didn't want to admit that I'd spent the last six months on vacation, moping around and feeling sorry for myself. The closest my fingers had come to typing was controlling the television remote.

Marcia shook her head and turned back to her work, obviously annoyed. I had no idea why. I wasn't working for *her*. I was working for the managers. She wouldn't even be affected by my incompetence.

I thought of Bryce and was about to rise from my seat and go find his office when an email from Marcus appeared. I would have normally cleared it later, but the message was marked important, and because Bryce hadn't given me a specific time, I felt I had to deal with Marcus first.

Sigh.

I double-clicked the message and a song started blasting out of my speakers.

"This is…" some guy sang. I scrambled for the volume, nearly knocking my stationery cup over as "Absolutely" by Nine Days blared from my workstation.

Marcia started giggling and a hot anger rose within me. Why the hell would Marcus prank me on my first day at work? What an asshole. He'd always prided himself on being funny in high school, and I'd never bought into his goofy charm (well, mostly never). The point is, it was embarrassing and here I was, five years later, being humiliated by him once again.

I quit out of my email to shut the song up and

muttered, "Jerk."

"What did you say?" Marcia leaned toward me.

"Oh, nothing." I shook my head.

"Sorry, I should have warned you." Her smile was tentative. She'd totally heard me say 'jerk'. "If you see an important email from Marcus in the morning, always put your earphones in, because it's going to be a song."

"What?" My head snapped in her direction.

"Yeah." She giggled. "He does that, every day. We all get it. Like a little good-morning gift. He likes to send us something upbeat so we've got a catchy tune in our heads while we work. It really does help improve your mood."

I made a face. "He...sends a song to everyone in the morning?"

"Not everyone...just..." She shrugged, an affectionate smile glowing on her face. "Like, exec wouldn't get it. It's just for the, you know, people who have to work in an office all day, who don't get to go out and schmooze with the rich and famous."

I didn't know what to say. It was so...sweet and...ugh, typically Marcus.

The guy obviously hadn't lost his weird factor, but as long as he didn't embarrass himself (and subsequently me) with relentless, lame-ass flirting, then things would be fine. Knowing the email went out to everyone helped me forgive him.

Marcia turned to her work, and I glanced at the back of her head before reaching for my earphones. Plugging them in, I opened my email and double-clicked Marcus's message again. The song was a good choice—upbeat and cheerful. I just hoped he wasn't thinking about me when he picked it.

Cutting the song short, I pulled the plugs from my ears and grabbed my notepad. I had a meeting to get to. Working for multiple managers could prove to be challenging, but I had a feeling I was really going to enjoy working for one of them in particular.

A smirk tugged at my lips as I strutted down the hall to Bryce's office.

SEVEN

MARCUS

I'd managed to make Kelly smile five times in four days—not the full-beam version I used to live for, but flashes of spontaneous pleasure that made me feel like a million bucks. Keeping a tally was stupid, but I was doing it anyway. My dad always said that if you can make the woman you love smile each day, then you're doing something right.

I wasn't about to shout from the rooftops that I was in love with Kelly DeMarco, but I was happy to admit that I was crushing big-time. Being around her again reminded me of all the things I'd fallen for in high school.

All my friends, and especially my older brother, Griffin, thought I was completely insane for liking a girl who had no interest in me, but they didn't get it. All they saw was a rich snob. But I'd studied that girl, and I saw the sweet smiles she gave her friends, the way she stood up for that quaking freshman girl when Mrs. Higgins was going at them, the way she managed to hold her dignity intact when one of the guys she rejected started a flurry of sordid rumors about their antics in bed together. It'd all been lies. I'd happened upon her and her two friends—Scarlett and Isla—one day and hidden round the corner while she blubbered about her humiliation and what had really happened.

She'd never know it, but I tracked down that asshole and tried to beat the shit out of him. He was twice my size and cut my cheek open with one punch, but at least I'd given him a fat, bleeding lip before he downed me. We both got suspended for fighting and everyone assumed he'd been bullying me. He wasn't about to tell the school that shorty Marcus Chapman had gotten two solid punches in before he'd had time to react. He went into hiding and swooped back into the school with high-fives and fist-bumps. A freaking legend.

Idiot.

I ran my finger over the scar below my left eye. My mother had stitched it up with a grim frown. I sat in her doctor's office, my eyes transfixed to the wall as I tried to hide how much it hurt. Her long, hard looks were doing their best to wheedle the truth out of me, but I was taking that nugget to the grave. She never would have understood why I'd taken a hit for some girl who didn't want to know me. But I just couldn't live with the fact that no one else was willing to stand up and defend her honor. Sometimes, it felt like I was the only guy in the school who really gave a shit about her…about the real her.

Thankfully, Kelly seemed to be fitting in at Torrence. She looked pretty nervous on her first day, but her smile was growing more genuine as each day passed, and I was pretty sure she'd go into the weekend having enjoyed her first week.

The weekend.

Jitters went to town on my stomach as I picked up my phone and called Kelly into my office. I'd decided the night before that there was no point being in this position if I wasn't going to do something about it. Bryce had been flirting up a storm with her since Monday. As far as I knew, they hadn't gone out yet, and I wanted to get in before that happened.

Kelly knocked on my door.

"Come in."

She appeared, looking stunning in a fitted navy dress with a big belt accentuating her slender waist. Her shapely legs were made long and inviting by a pair of high shoes that had a thick strap around the ankles. As always, she walked with a supermodel quality that was hard to look away from.

"What can I do for you?" Kelly held an iPad in her arm, ready to take notes. I'd seen her walking around with a pen and notepad on the first day and arranged for tech to organize an iPad like Marcia's. Torrence was trying to go paper-free, but it was taking time to make that final change. Bryce was still old school, so anything to do with his work always had paper attached to it.

I slipped off my reading glasses and played with the arms, opening and closing them while trying to work up the courage to ask her.

"Uh, so I just wanted to check in and see how your first week is going?" I smiled, happy with my move to build slowly into the big question.

Kelly's tense stance relaxed slightly. She tipped her head, causing a thick waterfall of dark hair to cascade over her shoulder. "It's going well. I think I'm doing okay."

"As far as I can tell, you're doing great."

"It was good of you to hire me."

"Yeah, well, I know quality when I see it." I winked.

Her grin faltered and she looked to her iPad screen. "I..." Her perfect nose wrinkled, and she made a little face before sighing. "I remember who you are from high school. I wasn't going to tell you because I was worried that's why you'd given me the job."

I sat back, feigning surprise at the suggestion. Sweat beaded the back of my neck, and I lost the ability to speak.

"Anyway, I've had a great first week, and I can see myself enjoying this job, so thank you."

A smile grew on my lips.

Kelly tapped her nail on the edge of the iPad. "And I know that things were kind of weird in high school, and I really appreciate the way you've been so professional. I have to admit, I was a little worried that maybe you'd try to ask me out or something and I just... you know, that would be way awkward."

My smile faded. "Of course." I shuffled in my seat. "Yeah, that would be totally weird. I wouldn't, um, yeah..." I pulled a face. "Way too awkward, right?"

Kelly laughed, but it was a strained, thorny sound. "I just thought it would be better if I didn't date anyone from work."

It was a small comfort. At least she wouldn't be hanging out with Bryce.

Desperate to save face, I sat up and glanced at my computer screen, leaning forward as if the world's most important email just landed in my inbox. Reaching for my glasses, I held them up in a farewell wave and forced what I hoped was a genial smile.

"I'm glad things are going well for you, Kelly. I really hope you enjoy being here."

"Thank you. The morning songs are a nice touch." She pointed at me, her sparkling gaze making my stomach do a belly flop into my intestines.

She was trying to be nice and soften the blow of her preemptive rejection. I could see it in her eyes. I grinned and nodded, grateful for her effort.

"I'll keep sending them."

"Is there anything else you need?"

You, in my bed every morning, opening your eyes and looking at me like I matter.

"Uh, no, I was just doing the boss thing and making sure my new assistant was happy."

"Well, I am."

"Great." I didn't mean to accentuate the T. Thankfully she didn't seem to notice and spun for the door. I watched her leave, the stone in my throat sinking down and lodging in my gut.

How the hell was I supposed to make my move now?

I couldn't. She'd made it abundantly clear not to go there, and I had to respect her wishes or turn into Marcus the lovesick freak again. She didn't appreciate that in high school. She wouldn't appreciate it now.

I needed her to see Marcus, the "he's got his shit together" guy, and the only way to do that was to back off and let her go out with someone else this weekend. She'd no doubt have a hot date with some tall, dark, and handsome asshole who would admire her stunning beauty, but wouldn't see further than her crystal smile and luscious curves.

Slumping back in my seat, I stared at my computer screen and pictured what my weekend held—work, kittens, dinner with my kid sister and parents, work.

"Awesome," I mumbled before banging my head onto my scribbly day planner.

EIGHT

KELLY

Dinner with my parents.

Oh how I hated Thursday nights.

I parked my car in the turning bay and sat for a moment, psyching myself up for the weekly dinner date. "New Shoes"—the song Marcus had sent out that morning—was still playing around in my head. I smiled. It was a good one. I actually found the whole song-sending thing incredibly cute. I couldn't admit how much I liked it, though. Marcus didn't need any kind of encouragement. Oh yeah, I'd spotted his face when I told him I wouldn't be dating anyone from work.

It'd been a lie.

I'd be more than happy to have drinks with Bryce, but he hadn't asked me yet. My mother would be mortified if I made the first move. She was totally old school when it came to dating. Men were supposed to take the lead. I'd never actually had to ask anyone out because they always came to me first. I'd tried to find out Bryce's story from Marcia, but it was obvious my coworker had no interest in talking about the guy.

She was a happily married woman; she probably had zero interest in other men. I, on the other hand, was painfully single and, unlike Marcus, Bryce *was* my type.

Sucking in a breath, I clicked open my door and crunched across the pebbles to the house. My family lived in a mansion. Dad came from old money. His parents had immigrated to New York from Italy and brought their fortunes with them. They started up a boutique on Fifth Avenue sixty years ago, a little shop called Echelon Fashion. My grandmother designed and made the clothes while my grandfather ran the business. It had flourished quickly and soon expanded to different parts of the city, then across the States and eventually worldwide. With a team of top designers, the Echelon label had a regular spot on the catwalks of Milan and Paris. The DeMarco name was world-famous in the fashion circles and, being an only child, I was expected to inherit it all.

The idea terrified me. I was into fashion, sure, but owning an empire like that? I didn't know whether to slit my wrists or jump for joy. Thankfully, Daddy was still in his early fifties and had no intention of handing over the reins. More than anything, that man loved control.

I rolled my eyes and opened the door.

"Good evening, Miss Kelly," our butler greeted me as I entered the house.

"Hi, Stuart, how are you?"

"Very well, thank you, miss." I patted his shoulder and clipped across the polished marble into the antique parlor. Mom had adored the old-style home the second she'd laid eyes on it. My parents had been newlyweds, and Daddy had fallen all over himself trying to please the stunning model. Oh how times had changed.

My smile was tight as I approached my mother and leaned forward so she could peck my cheek. She was in her mid-forties now, yet still looked like a beauty queen. Her dark, shiny hair was cropped around her face in a stylish bob. Expertly applied makeup highlighted her high cheekbones and made her pale green eyes pop, while her slender lips were brushed in muted pink, which matched the champagne diamonds in her ears and on her wedding finger. She had a regal elegance that I imagined she'd been born with. I was positive she'd never dribbled as a baby. The very idea would have mortified her.

I smirked at my snarky thoughts then took a seat opposite her.

"So, Kelly, my darling. I haven't heard from you this week." Her pale gaze scrutinized my outfit.

Luckily, I'd remembered my dinner date so had been able to choose something I knew she'd approve of.

Crossing my legs, I laid my hands on my thighs and gave her a demure smile. "I've been busy."

"Oh, really? Doing what?" My mother had this soft, gentle voice that sounded so serene and elegant, yet every question out of her mouth was a live grenade. Casual chats with her were like negotiating a minefield in rollerblades.

"Uh..."

"Darling, please, don't use filler sounds like that. It makes you appear unintelligent. Just say what you want to say."

I cleared my throat. "I've been working."

Mom's face went blank. She blinked a couple of times then frowned. "Your father never told me about this."

"Daddy doesn't know." I rubbed my thigh then adjusted the sapphire ring on my middle finger.

"How can your father not know you are working for him?" Mom snickered. "He's in the office every day."

"I'm..." I went to say 'um' but quickly swallowed it and licked my lower lip instead.

"You're..." Mom twirled her hand, her eyebrows dipping with impatience.

"I have a job at Torrence Records. I'm the personal assistant to three managers there."

Mom's elegant mouth morphed into a disgusted frown. "A secretary! Are you out of your mind?"

"Mom—"

"No, I am not finished." She held up her pointer finger. "How could you do this, Kelly? You are the daughter of Enrique DeMarco and you have taken a job with some record company? It doesn't even have anything to do with fashion!" She spat out the last word before straightening in her chair and regaining her composure. "Explain yourself."

"It's not that big a deal. I just needed something to do with my time, and I'm not ready to join the business yet."

"You are twenty-two years old, and since college is obviously above you, I'd say you're ready to work for your father."

"I don't want to work for my father." I couldn't hide my venom.

Mom rolled her eyes, her hair not even rustling as she shook her head. "I should never have told you. I was simply trying to make a point...which you completely, missed by the way."

I gripped my hands together and looked at the ornamental fireplace.

"I just don't understand how you could lower yourself to this. A mere assistant. Honestly, what has gotten into you?"

"It's not long-term." I still had an entire meal to live through, so I went for answers that would appease. "It's simply a break."

"You've had six months to get over this," she quipped. "And if you ask me..."

Which I'm not.

"You should still be up there trying to win him back."

"They're getting married!" I glared at her, still flummoxed by her response to the Fletcher fiasco. I thought she would've been on my side. "He doesn't want me. He made that abundantly clear."

"You had an option, but you refused to be flexible, and now you've thrown away the best thing that has ever happened to you."

I let out a disgusted scoff and shot out of my chair. Flexible? Was she fucking kidding?

No, she wasn't. That was the scariest part of all.

My relentless mother kept barking at me. "Fletcher Winslow would have been the perfect partner for you. His family owns the biggest textile company on the West Coast. The two of you together could have—"

"Stop!" I spun to face her. "We're not together. We never will be. He made his choice, and I don't want to be *flexible*."

"It's not about love, Kelly." Her petite nostrils flared. "It's about securing the future of Echelon Fashion. You need to partner with someone who can make this company grow even bigger. That's always been the plan."

Stupid plan! I hated the plan!

"When you fell in love with Fletcher, it was so perfect. You're far better suited to him than Evangeline Prescott." She said the name like it was a bad taste in her mouth.

"She's your best friend's daughter. Should you really be saying her name that way?" I couldn't help a little snark. The wounds were still too raw and close to the surface.

"I never should have suggested you room together. You are far more than Evangeline could ever be. I didn't see her as a threat. It's clear Fletcher made the wrong decision, although you were the one to finally end it."

Her laser gaze made me look down at the plush cream carpet. The points of my shoes sank into the wool.

"And now, we're too late. He's going ahead and marrying her because you wouldn't compromise."

An image of me bending low and screaming in her face that I wasn't about to marry a cheater tore through my brain, but I'd never have the courage to do it.

"So now, we have to find you someone else."

"I'm not interested in finding someone else," I muttered. "I don't want what you have with Dad."

Mom's lips parted like I'd just told her I was gay. "Kelly Rosina, you are a woman of privilege, and there are certain responsibilities that come with that. You don't have the luxury of falling in love or flitting your life away as a single lady. This is a family company. We may be a powerhouse in the fashion world now, but that won't last forever unless we keep pushing and expanding. Honestly. Use your brain."

My eyes smarted and I spun to face the opposite wall before she noticed. "You loved Dad when you married him."

"Yes, but those feelings fade, and I am grateful that I married a man who can give me the life I want."

"A loveless marriage?" I choked.

Her voice was stiff and strained. "We both get what we need from each other, and we are good business partners."

"I can't believe you stay with him when you know what he's doing behind your back." I looked over my shoulder and glimpsed the way her jaw clenched.

With a regal sniff, she brushed the edge of her nose and rubbed her fingers together like my words couldn't touch her. "We all make sacrifices to get the things we need. I know what's important to me, and I don't need your father's monogamy to get it."

The sharp tap of business shoes could be heard on the tiles. I pulled my expression into line before my father entered the room. I had no idea if he knew Mom had told me about his infidelity, but I didn't want him seeing how I felt about it.

"*La mia bambina.*" He smiled, stretching his arms wide so I could step into his embrace. I wrapped my arm around his tailor-made jacket and inhaled his rich scent. Echelon had branched into perfumes last year. It had been Daddy's idea, and he'd been working to get the perfect combination of scents. Sovereign for Men was my favorite. The fragrance curled my toes. Thankfully, my father was wearing Emperor, which I didn't particularly care for.

I kissed both his cheeks before standing back and smiling at him. He held my arms out wide and quickly assessed my dress. He mostly approved, but I could tell by the dip in his brow that he would have chosen different shoes. I tried not to let the silent criticism bother me.

He turned to my mother and gave her an affectionate smile. *"Buona sera, mia cara.* Sorry I am late. I was talking to my father. Even in retirement, he cannot let the business go." Dad chuckled, but it was a forced, hard sound. He unbuttoned his jacket and turned for the dining room. "I am heading to Paris next week. We are expanding the branch there. I will not have time to socialize, but you ladies are welcome to join me if you would like to do some shopping."

Mom's eyebrow rose and she gave me a smirk that said, *"See! Shopping in Paris. This is the life you should be fighting for."*

I threw her a tight smile as my father continued, "Imogen, I will need you for the press conference, too. We will be announcing our part in Fashion Week later in the year, and I want you by my side. The press loves your smile."

"Of course, darling." Mom gave him a dazzling smile, ignoring Stuart as he pulled out her chair.

I sat down and smiled at our chef as she placed a bowl of minestrone in front of me. "Smells delicious, Abelie. *Grazie.*"

"Prego, Miss Kelly." She touched my shoulder and winked before bustling out of the room with the tray tucked under her arm.

Dad picked up his spoon and rubbed it with his napkin like he always did then looked across the table at me.

"So, you will join us?"

"Uh…"

I received two sharp looks—one for saying "uh" and the other from my father, who was preparing himself for whatever I had to say. A nervous smile flittered over my lips as I swallowed and launched into all the reasons why I should be working a low-level job with Torrence Records and not up at Stanford University finishing my business studies degree and winning back a man who would spend our married life cheating on me.

I didn't state it quite like that, of course. Dad's infidelity was obviously a taboo subject, and if I was going to win him over to my "let me have a year off to screw around" argument, then I needed to sell the lie as best I could.

Because that's what it was really about, right?

How to wrap the lies in pretty little bows so people only ever saw what you wanted them to.

NINE

MARCUS

Music blasted from the speakers of the huge arena as I stood in the empty rows of seats watching Chaos dance on stage. Nessa looked freaking hot as she pranced around beside Jimmy. Having her front and center was the best thing for the band. Opening night in LA had already sold out. Only three sleeps to go and my first band would be starting their twelve-week tour around the USA. I was Papa Bear proud and couldn't wipe the smile off my face as I listened to them rehearse. Friday night was going to be epic.

My phone buzzed and I checked the screen. It

was a text from Kelly, asking me to call in when I was free. It'd been two months since she'd signed to work as my personal assistant. We'd made it through the holiday season, and she'd returned with a bright smile. I had no idea what was driving her, but she seemed determined to make the job work. I was pretty sure she was enjoying it. She never told me otherwise, not that she would. It'd probably helped that I hadn't asked her out once. I'd held my tongue every time I was tempted, and we'd settled into a friendly work routine. After nearly ten weeks with me, she was relaxed and had the job pretty much down pat. I relied on her for a lot, and she delivered every time. It was a huge relief that I hadn't completely screwed up when hiring her. She was a smart cookie and capable of more than she realized.

I slid the phone into my pocket and decided to see out the set before returning her call. I had a sinking suspicion I knew what it was about, and I didn't have the stomach for any more Caris bullshit this week.

Jace smacked the drums in time with Jimmy's strum, and Nessa let out a whoop when the song finished. All five of them were grinning like chimps. I applauded as loud as I could, but it was a feeble comparison to the music they'd just been making.

"Thanks, Marcus," Nessa spoke into the mic and winked at me. Her skin glowed with a fine sheen of sweat and her smile was a megawatt triumph. Jimmy came up beside her, wrapping his arm around her before whispering something in her ear. Her cheeks bloomed red and she giggled then looked up at him.

Their gazes locked, held in place by some kind of mushy glue that would be impossible to dissolve. Those two lovebirds. I shook my head, trying to look disparaging, but I couldn't pull it off. Truth was, my insides were raging with yearning. I wanted what they had. I wanted Kelly gazing into my eyes and telling me she loved me without even uttering the words. I wanted Kelly to see what she did to me and how far I'd be willing to go for her.

Flick said something, trying to catch Jimmy's attention. He had to shout it twice before Jimmy even noticed.

"Huh?" The tall guitarist loped over to the keyboardist.

Nessa waved her stump at me before spinning to join the boys. She'd come so far since losing her hand. She'd discovered who she really was and put it all on the line to follow her dreams. It was damn impressive and made me feel like a bit of a loser for giving up on my desires so easily.

Once Nessa had finally found the courage to take that leap, she'd been the happiest version of herself. It was like a neon light had come alive inside of her, a passionate spark that couldn't be diminished. She'd fought to get everything she wanted—her man and a career in the music business.

Well, I had one of those things working for me, but I wanted a girl, and not just any girl. Kelly had cut me off at the pass before I'd even had a chance to show her the kind of guy I could be. I'd given in so easily, embarrassed by who I'd been in high school and desperate to show her how cool I was now.

Screw it.

I might not be Kelly cool, but I had my own way about me and I needed to own it. If Kelly would just give me a chance, I could prove to her how right we'd be together. She didn't need tall, dark, and handsome...she needed a guy who could make her smile.

Pulling out my phone, I walked up the aisle of the arena and headed for the back door. If Chaos started up again, the noise would at least be muted. I pressed the phone to my ear and listened to it ring four times before Kelly answered.

"Hey, thanks for calling back. I didn't want to hand out your number to this guy. He was pretty irate."

I sighed and waited until the heavy door clicked shut behind me before saying, "What did Caris do now?"

Kelly hissed. "Spent over five thousand at a music store downtown. She told the place to bill Torrence Records. When he sent his bill in and we responded that we had no intention of paying, he got pretty annoyed."

"You've got be kidding me." I groaned.

"Accounts wants a piece of you for saying she could do this."

"I didn't!" I threw my arm wide.

"That's what I told them, but her mother's claiming you gave her daughter a musical allowance. It's in the contract or something."

I squeezed the bridge of my nose and shut my eyes, anger coursing through me.

"I just wanted you to get ahead of this before Mr. Torrence finds out. I know how much he wants to keep Caris on board, but there's no way he'll want his record company looking bad. You'll be the first person he blames if this goes south."

"Yeah, yeah. I know. Thank you. Um…" I ran a hand through my hair. "Okay, can you set up a meeting for me with that new legal assistant, Justin, and get Lenny from accounts to join us. I'll see if we can't smooth this over without too much hassle."

"On it. I'll set it up for this afternoon."

I checked my watch. "Cool. I should be back by three at the latest."

"Great. Can I do anything else for you?"

A nervous breath caught in my throat. My insides were rumbling with the new crisis, but if anything was going to make me feel better, it would be looking forward to a date with my dream girl.

The air rushed out of my lungs and I said, probably way too loudly, "Yeah, let me take you out."

"Excuse me?" Her voice pitched high with surprise.

I curbed my excited jitters and spoke more calmly. "I want to take you out, for a drink or dinner or something."

Her pause was long and painful. I could picture her top teeth brushing over her full lower lip as she tried to think of the correct response. "Are you asking me out on a date?"

"Yes."

"But…" She sighed. "Marcus, please don't do this to me again."

My head jerked back with a frown. "Do this to you?"

"You know, hound me like a pathetic little puppy."

"I'm asking you out for a drink, Kel. I'm not wagging my tail or taking a dump on your front lawn."

A sweet laugh escaped her before she could catch it. I smiled, but the triumph didn't last long. She cleared her throat, her tone edged with a cool iciness. "Look, I'm flattered and everything, but no. Okay? No. We said things wouldn't get awkward at work, please don't change that."

I banged my head lightly against the concert wall of the arena. Pressing my forehead into the cool roughness, I stared down at my black shoes. "I guess I want to stop pretending not to like you so much. I'm not the guy I was in high school, I promise, but I still care about you and I want to take you out on a date."

Her reply was a soft sigh followed by a dagger to the stomach. "I had to cold-shoulder you in high school to make my point. Please don't make me do that at work. Just accept the fact that I'll never see you as anything more than my boss, okay? Let's not ruin a good thing."

She hung up before I could say more. I scratched my neck then adjusted my collar, trying not to feel like a fool as I headed back into Chaos's dress rehearsal. The music had started up again, but they were just goofing around while the sound guys perfected something. Jimmy was singing into the mic, making Nessa laugh as he sang, "Are You Gonna Be My Girl" by Jet.

The song, of course, made me think of Kelly. So many songs did.

I'd subtly tried to send some to her in my daily song email, but because it was to the whole office, I couldn't really make my message abundantly clear. Plus, over half the receivers were women, and I didn't want any of them to read into them...but I wouldn't mind if Kelly did.

Music had a profound effect on people. It'd won Nessa over in the end. She couldn't live without it, and she'd put everything on the line to ensure she could keep it as a central part of her life. Kelly had always loved music in high school. I could picture her on that club dance floor the night of senior prom. She'd never looked so happy.

It was time to up the ante. Yeah, she didn't want to go out with me, but only because she was afraid to really give me a chance. I needed to prove to her that I could see through her shiny veneer, and I wasn't afraid to dive beneath it.

TEN

KELLY

Marcus sauntered into the office just before his meeting. I'd set it up for three so he'd be rushing through the door and straight into the crisis room. He asked me to sit in and take notes, which I didn't mind doing. With two other people in the room, it was impossible for him to say anything else to me about the fact I rejected his invitation.

The meeting took nearly two hours. The first thirty minutes was a private bitch-session about the haughty artist (I didn't take minutes on that part), and the next ninety were spent problem-solving the dilemma. Justin had looked over her contract and said she was in definite breach, but Mr. Torrence would no doubt overlook the misdemeanor to keep the artist on board. Marcus hated the injustice of it, but in the end had to acquiesce and allow Caris to get away with her frivolity. Lenny helped him skimp from another untouched budget to cover the cost.

Marcus's indignant anger was kind of attractive, and I had to bite my lips together and avert my gaze a couple of times when he was really ranting.

He huffed and thumped the table before sitting back in his chair. "Just make sure this shop doesn't allow any artist to bill Torrence again without prior authorization. I'm not about taking money from justified budgets to pay for this princess."

"I'll-I'll organize that for you." Justin punched a note into his laptop. The guy had started up around the same time as me. He'd come fresh out of college and still hadn't lost his twitchy edge. From what I'd picked up through office whispers, he worked around the clock, always one of the last to leave. He was still finishing his law degree part-time while working here. It was a big ask and one I'd run the opposite direction from, but I guess if you're Mr. Torrence's son-in-law, you're out to make a good impression.

He looked up at me, and I shot him a reassuring smile. His grin was skittish, but he nodded. "All right, I-I better get going. Call me if you n-need anything else."

"Will do. Thanks, Justin." Marcus gave him a wave before slapping his hand on the table. He looked drained and in good need of a relaxing night out. A small part of me wanted to give him that, but I couldn't. He wasn't my type, and I didn't want to encourage him.

Besides, I had plans with Scarlett and Isla. I wasn't about to cancel those for a guy I'd never end up with.

*****

I rubbed my forehead and winced. One too many shots with the girls had left me with a splitting headache. My morning aerobics class at the gym had helped take the edge off a little, but I was ready for a strong coffee. I sipped my water bottle as I rode the elevator up to work.

Clipping onto my floor, I greeted Marcia with a sheepish grin and she chuckled. "You were just going for the dancing, right?"

I poked my tongue out at her then followed it up with a playful wink.

She'd ended up becoming a good friend over the last couple of months and we chatted about most things. I kept my warped family life to myself, but we talked about her girls and husband, plus my best friends.

"Coffee?" I placed my bag behind the desk and started heading for the lunchroom.

"Yes, please," she called after me.

My hips swayed as I briskly walked to the machine and poured two cups. It smelled like a nice, strong batch. Just what I needed. In the past, I would have stopped for a proper café-made coffee, but I hadn't had time that morning and the office stuff was actually growing on me. I sipped from my mug and let out a contented sigh before heading back to the main desk.

"So, a good night then?" Marcia took the cup from me. "Thanks."

I slipped into my chair with a giggle. "Scarlett's boyfriend is a DJ at this club in town and he was mixing last night, so we got free drinks. Bad idea." I pulled a face.

Marcia laughed. "At least you got home safely."

"Yeah, thank God for Uber, right?" My eyes bulged. "And thank God I don't live with my parents anymore."

Marcia winced, her nose wrinkling. "Oh man. No offense, but I hope my girls don't turn out like you. I'd be a worried wreck waiting for them to get home at night."

I lightly slapped her shoulder. "Everyone needs to have a little fun. A few drinks never hurt anybody."

"I know, I know." She waved her hand through the air. "It's just my babies are going to grow up and turn into these stunning girls like you…" She shrugged. "I don't know. I just hate the idea of leechy men trying to make a pass at them."

I rolled my eyes. "I don't go clubbing to find guys. I go there to dance."

"I was never into the clubbing thing. Those places petrify me." She shook her head. "Give me a Cherry Coke and a football game any day. A house full of passionate people watching the game and hanging out together. Snuggling on the couch with my man while my girls play Barbies on the floor. I love it."

Her cute expression made me grin. We came from two different worlds, but she was the most likable person. The entertainment I'd grown up with had been elegant dinners in classy restaurants or sitting on the side of a runway watching skinny girls strut my father's latest designs. I would never have been allowed to play on the floor. DeMarcos didn't sit on the floor. My nursery hadn't been filled with pink, plastic toys. I don't remember what it had been filled with. All I remember is spending my holidays and weekends following my parents around while they dragged me from one function to the next and forced me to smile when the cameras started clicking.

Clubbing for me had been a chance to let loose. I could get lost in a gyrating crowd that didn't give a shit who my parents were. A little alcohol running through my veins while the music throbbed through me—that was the kind of rush I was interested in.

I switched on my computer and sipped my coffee while it loaded. I started with my email, wondering what Marcus's song would be. I glanced over my shoulder and tried to glimpse Marcia's screen. She had her headphones on and was grinning.

I quickly plugged mine in as my inbox opened and a series of blue dots appeared for each unread message. I could see a few double exclamation marks but went for the top one from Marcus.

Into my ears popped a guitar riff I recognized immediately—"Just the Girl" by Click Five. My eyes bulged when the words began and my insides slowly disintegrated.

I closed my eyes, heat and anger bubbling inside me. There was nothing random about his song selection. He was making a point—a very clear one. I yanked the plugs from my ears and threw them down, but the music was still coming through them. I scrambled for the space bar and quickly paused the song.

Why was he doing this to me?

"You okay?" Marcia glanced at me.

"Yeah, I just…" I shook my head and swallowed down my disgusted sigh.

Marcia looked at my screen then smiled. "Do you not like his song this morning?"

"No, it's fine." I shook my head. "It's…it's fine."

Marcia's brown eyes turned a warm nutmeg as her dimples popped into place. "You pushed him in the pool in high school, didn't you?"

My mouth fell open, humiliation rising up my face like a heat wave. "He told you that?"

"No." Marcia giggled. "But you just did."

I covered my face with my hands. "Shit. Do you think anyone else will figure it out?"

"I'm the only one who knows you went to school together, and I only know that because I happened to have read both your résumés." She grinned. "He's never talked to me about you before. I…I don't know your history."

With a short tut, I crossed my arms and looked at my screen. "You don't want to know our history."

"Did you guys date or something?"

"No!" I spun my chair to face her. "Why do you think I pushed him in the pool? The guy was relentless. He tried everything to get me to notice him."

"Which you obviously did."

"Yeah, but not in a positive way. I thought he was a complete dick." I rubbed my temples, remembering that day—the surprised look on his face while his arms flailed and he splashed into the water. It'd been kind of mean. Everyone around us had laughed, including the guy who'd given him stitches. I'd never admit this to anyone, but I'd had two reasons for pushing Marcus into the pool, and saving him from a broken nose had been one of them.

"He was so embarrassing," I muttered the truth I *was* willing to admit. "Every time he approached me, people around us would stop and stare. I could hear the whispered snickers as I yet again had to come up with another reason to brush him off." I sighed. "And now he's starting up again and I just…I like this job."

"So, go tell him." She pointed in the direction of his office.

"I've tried. Seriously, this guy can't take no for an answer."

Marcia pursed her lips. She was a Marcus fan. I

didn't want to offend her, but she had to see that the guy wasn't faultless. "He must really like you."

"I don't know why." I rolled my eyes. I did, actually. It was because I was pretty and, to him, probably perfect. But he didn't even know me. I'd never given him a chance to see beneath the layers and I didn't want to.

Marcus and I were not a match. I had to make him understand that, or working for him would be a freaking nightmare.

Shooting out of my seat, I tugged my skirt straight and headed for his office.

"What are you doing?" Marcia called after me.

I spun on my heel to face her. "I've tried to be nice about this, but he obviously doesn't get it. It's time to put my angry face on and scare him off."

Marcia chuckled while I straightened my shoulders and marched toward his frosted glass door.

I knocked once and threw the door open, storming to his desk with what I hoped was a fiery scowl.

He countered my wrath with an easy smile. "Morning, Kelly. How's it going?"

"Don't." I pointed at him. "I know what you're doing and it won't work. If anything, that song is offensive, and I can't believe you would send it out to everybody like that."

"You're the only one who's ruffled by it, though, right?" He winked.

I crossed my arms. "Stop being a cocky little shit."

"No one knows. It's a private joke."

"Well, it's not funny! I don't want people figuring out our history."

"So, don't tell them." He shrugged. "It's just a song."

"You picked it on purpose. You're trying to rile me."

He leaned back in his chair, gazing at me with a soft sparkle in his eyes. Threading his fingers together, he rested them on his stomach, and I felt a tug of something sweet and tempting, which only pissed me off more.

I wasn't attracted to this guy!

"If you think this will make me change my mind about going out with you, you're wrong. All you've managed to do is irritate the hell out of me."

He made a clicking sound out the side of his mouth. "It's more entertaining than your polite rejection."

I jerked back from his cool response. I never would have gotten that from him in high school. No, five years ago, he would have mumbled an apology then shuffled his shame-faced ass away from me.

My scowl deepened, causing my forehead to wrinkle. I smoothed a hand over the offending lines before placing it on my hip. "I don't want to go out with you. Why can't you get that?"

"And why can't you give me a chance?" He leaned forward, his tone sounding sharper than I'd ever heard it before. He wasn't afraid of me anymore.

I swallowed. "I don't like you like that."

"That's because you've never let yourself see me in any other light. You think you know me, but you don't. All you see is a guy who doesn't fit into your perfect world." He stood, straightening his jacket. "Maybe I don't, or maybe you fit into mine."

For some weird reason, my mind flashed to the movie *Titanic* of all things. I pictured Jack sitting at a fine table with Rose and wooing everybody before taking the girl of his dreams downstairs to have a blast with the third-class passengers.

I blinked, trying to shake the images from my brain.

"I don't—of course, I wouldn't—" I didn't know how to finish the sentence without coming across like a first-class snob…and he knew it. I could tell by the playful smirk on his lips.

I narrowed my eyes and adjusted my bracelet before lifting my chin. "I'm asking you to respect my answer."

"And I'm asking you to be brave."

I waited for a suitable reply, but nothing came, so I spun on my heel and headed for the door. There was no way I would let him get to me. I was above his try-hard attempts. I just had to remain a cool, professional broken record. He'd get the message eventually, and if he didn't, I'd…I'd quit!

ELEVEN

MARCUS

Well, that had gone down like a cast-iron balloon. I tried to pretend her venom hadn't bothered me, but it'd taken every ounce of courage not to dip my head and apologize. I'd actually stood up to her. I'd never done that before. It had felt freaking fantastic, but it still hadn't gotten me what I wanted.

Her reaction was kind of sexy, though. The way her skin flushed pink as she snapped at me. Damn, she was hot. I grinned as I remembered her flustered face just before she pushed me in the pool at Tony McAvoy's graduation party. It had been

my last chance to ask her out before the summer—
one final act of courage before I never saw her
again. She looked at me like I'd lost my mind then
shoved my chest. I'd splashed into the pool fully
clothed and figured it was the last time I'd ever talk
to Kelly DeMarco.

I stayed in my office for the next hour or so,
fielding calls and emails. I had to check in with
Chaos around midday. Pre-performance jitters
were hitting them big-time, and I didn't want
anyone to lose it before Friday night. I was taking
them out to lunch then paying for them to blow off
some steam at Laser Strike.

Hell, I might even join them.

Running a hand through my hair, I grabbed my
empty coffee mug and headed for the lunchroom.
Unlike Bryce, I didn't expect the cleaners to clear
ten mugs off my desk at the end of the day. I also
didn't expect any of the female office staff to make
me a coffee.

Ambling past the front desk, I shot Marcia a
warm smile, which she reciprocated. I had no idea
why Kelly wasn't sitting beside her, and I struggled
to hide my disappointment. I'd wanted to greet
both women, acting like Kelly's vexation hadn't
bothered me.

Holding in my sigh, I made my way toward the
coffee maker but was stopped by the sound of
someone humming. I paused with a grin,
recognizing "Just The Girl." I loved it when my
morning song made someone sing later in the day.
Poking my head into the resource room, I spied

who was standing at the photocopier singing.

My lips parted while my heart skipped around inside my chest. The grin that spread across my face was so broad, I swear it touched my earlobes.

"Hey, Kelly."

She jumped and spun around, her face morphing with horror as she realized she'd been caught.

"Great song, right?" I leaned against the doorframe.

She pressed her lips together, her pale gaze warning me to back off.

"Some would say it was romantic." I grinned.

"Or pathetic." Her right eyebrow cocked, and her lips twitched like she was fighting a smile. She spun away before I could see it.

So she liked to joust. Interesting.

I banged my mug lightly on the wooden frame. "Well, I'm glad my pick of the day worked for you. It's great to have a positive effect on people, you know? That's why I do it, to really brighten people's day. To make a diff—"

"Would you shut up," she spoke over her shoulder then pressed the photocopy button with a loud smack. It buzzed and whirred, spitting out a pile of paper. It looked like new contracts. Must be one of Bryce's newbies, with that amount of paper involved. It was probably my cue to leave, but the view was pretty fantastic, so I decided to linger for one more minute.

Kelly kept her eyes trained on the photocopier, which buzzed, made a loud clunk, and went still.

She froze then tipped her hands to the sky. "Why did you stop working?" she said to the machine. "Why did..." Glancing over her shoulder, she saw me still standing there and pointed at the machine. "Why did it stop working?"

"Because it's a photocopier and they're a pain in the ass." I pushed off the frame and walked toward her.

"Well, tell it to stop being mean to me and start working again. Bryce needed this stuff twenty minutes ago."

I bent down to the look at the screen. The letters were slightly blurry, so I pulled back until they came into better focus.

ERROR 148

I had no idea what that meant.

"It's unlike you to leave a job until the last minute," I murmured.

"I wouldn't have if he'd given me a reasonable time frame. He only emailed me this half an hour ago and asked me to have it done by the time he got in, which was twenty minutes ago."

"Don't stress. We'll get it working." The phone in my pocket buzzed. I pulled it out as it started ringing. "Hi, Mr. Torrence, how's it going?"

"You got a few minutes?"

I glanced at my watch. I had to leave in an hour to meet up with Chaos. Meetings with the boss man tended to be of the long-winded variety. I winced, but nodded. I couldn't say no. "I have to leave at noon and I'm right in the middle of something I can't walk away from, but if you're free in twenty minutes, I can come up to your office."

"Try to make it ten if you can."

"Will do." I slid the phone back in my pocket and tried to ignore the double-kick my heart did every time I had a pending meeting with the CEO. Everett Torrence had a steely gaze that made me feel like a snotty-nosed kid with untied shoelaces and dirt on my knees. I'm sure he didn't mean to make me feel that way, but he did...no matter what we were talking about. In this instance, the quick chat would no doubt be about Caris. He must have found out about the five thousand dollar bill.

"Something you couldn't walk away from?" Kelly tipped her head. "You made it sound like something really important."

I looked at her with a bemused smile. "You need my help. It is important."

Crouching down, I opened the door, in search of a paper jam. I didn't spot anything obvious, so I snapped the door shut to see if that would kick-start things again. The machine buzzed but then the screen started flashing with the same message.

"Do you know where the manual is?" I looked up at her, not missing how close her legs were to my face. I could rub my nose against her thigh if I wanted to. Not that I would, but she smelled so good. The perfume she wore up top didn't overpower the sweet scent of her skin. She must have washed or moisturized with vanilla or something, because her legs smelled lick-able. The image of my tongue coasting the smooth terrains of her body twisted my stomach into a hard ball of desire.

I stood and hitched my pants while Kelly searched the shelves for the photocopier manual.

"Shit, I can't see it."

"No problem. We'll figure it out." I walked around the machine and noticed a narrow panel that looked like it could open. I ran my fingers around the edge until I found a small catch. Behind the mini door was a green lever that I figured I needed to spin. I started turning it and slowly pumped out a rumpled sheet of paper.

"Why doesn't it just say paper jam on the screen instead of being all cryptic with a number?" Kelly tapped her finger on her arm while I cranked the lever.

"I told you, photocopiers pride themselves on being annoying."

Her lips flashed with a smile, but she pulled it into line before it could bloom. I stood and yanked out the offending sheet, balling it up and throwing it into the recycling box.

"Okay, let's see if it works now." I snapped the door shut and pressed the green button with a hopeful smile. The machine whirred then paused.

We both held our breath, staring down at the display screen until the copier buzzed and started spitting out paper.

Kelly let out a sigh. I smiled at her relief then leaned my elbow on top of the copier and looked up at her.

"So, I'm going out to lunch with Chaos. Do you

want to come?"

Her glare was dry and unimpressed.

I put on my best "innocent" smile. "Didn't you say Scarlett was a die-hard fan? You could get their autograph for her."

"Don't try to woo me with good-looking rock stars," she clipped.

"I'm not." I grinned. "I'm trying to give you 'world's best friend' status. If memory serves me right, Scarlett will flip out if she gets something she really wants. She's still excitable, right?"

The corner of her mouth rose, but she brushed her finger over it, pushing it back down. "It's not going to work. I'm not going out with you."

Her eyes sparkled a little, like she was somehow enjoying our banter. I used to feel that way in high school sometimes. If I ever asked her out when no one else was around, her eyes would glimmer as she sent me on my way, like if I stopped trying she'd be disappointed.

Maybe that's what kept me coming back for more...maybe that's what kept driving me five years later. "Kelly, come on. Don't think of it like a date. It'll be a business lunch."

She shook her head and pressed her lips together. The little dimple on her chin was accentuated by the expression. Was she fighting a smile again?

I opened my mouth to continue the small repartee we had going, but I was interrupted by a deep voice coming from the doorway.

"Kelly." We both spun to see Bryce standing

there. His hands were in his pockets, and he looked particularly annoying in his expensive suit. He eyed the small gap between us before putting on his dazzling smile and being the perfect asshole.

"I'm nearly done." Kelly's cheeks flushed and my insides turned brittle.

"Great." He ambled over with a cocky grin. His long fingers rested on her lower back as he gazed down at the pile of pages spitting out of the machine. "Hey, so I was thinking I should take you out for dinner tonight."

Kelly stilled then looked up at him. I couldn't see her face from where I was standing, but the triumph in his expression told me all I needed to know.

"Sorry, Bryce." I tipped my head. "Kelly doesn't date guys from work."

Her head snapped in my direction, her dark expression warning me not to embarrass her. I was about to say, "It's what you told me," when she turned back to the towering guy and said, "I'd love to."

I tasted sawdust and then a little bile before swallowing down a mouthful of acid. It burned through my guts.

The way Bryce was eyeing her made me want to punch his face in. I spotted the clock on the wall. Everett Torrence was waiting. I didn't care. I wasn't leaving Kelly's side until I'd warned her about the consequences of dating Bryce. I'd found too many girls crying in the lunchroom over that chauvinistic ass-face. I wasn't letting Kelly become another one of his victims.

TWELVE

KELLY

I felt a mixture of guilt and jubilation.

Bryce asking me out had been providential. It served so many purposes. The main one being to get Marcus Chapman off my back.

The problem was, after Bryce eyed me hungrily, he strolled out of the photocopier room and Marcus stayed put.

"So, you changed your stance on the *no dating office guys*, huh?"

My shoulders tensed and I leaned against the photocopier, spitting out the truth in yet another attempt to deter him. "I never had a stance. I just said that to try to put you off as nicely as I could."

His pale eyebrows dipped together. "Have you guys gone out before?"

"No, I've been waiting for him to ask." I couldn't look at Marcus while I spoke. I didn't know why. I should have been eyeballing him with a vanquishing simper on my face, but I couldn't bring myself to do it. He had, after all, helped me with the photocopier, which was making him late for an important meeting. "Mr. Torrence is waiting for you."

He ignored my murmur and just stared at me like I hadn't spoken at all. "You can do so much better than a guy like Bryce."

I rolled my eyes. "Meaning you?"

He scratched the hard plastic top of the machine, his lips pursing to the side as he shrugged. "Yeah." He looked up at me, his hazel eyes beaming with an honest assurance that was held together by a touching modesty. "I can definitely treat you better than he will."

I turned to face him properly and placed my hand on my hip. "And what makes you so confident of that?"

"I know who I am. I'm not one of those guys who dates the pretty girls just to get them into bed. Bryce is."

His calm warning threw me a little. I knew men like that all too well, but I wasn't about to let Marcus get the upper hand. I was grateful for my four-inch heels. Sparring with him was kind of fun, and the added height somehow made it easier to drive home the fact he was wasting his time pursuing me. I raised my neck and looked down at him. "Maybe I want that kind of guy, or maybe I'm the kind of girl who flicks them off."

His eyes narrowed slightly as he scrutinized my expression. I kept it as unreadable as I could, yet I still felt bare when he whispered, "I don't think you are."

"Marcus." I clasped my hands together and took a step away from him. "We may have gone to high school together, but you don't know me."

"I'd like to get to know you." He stepped forward.

I took another step back and rolled my eyes. "Would you please quit while you're ahead?"

"I'm not ahead. You've never given me a chance to be anything more than a loser." He sighed and rubbed the back of his neck. "But I don't want to make your work life hell, so just tell me why you said yes so quickly to Bryce. One hundred percent, honest answer."

It was the last thing I expected him to say. One hundred percent honesty wasn't my forte, but if it meant he'd leave me alone, I'd give it a shot.

"Fine. I think he's very good-looking. He'll probably take me out, buy me some expensive wine and feed me some delicious food."

Marcus scoffed and shook his head like that was lame.

I pierced him with a steely glare. "In my book, that's a guy worth dating."

Marcus gently placed his hands on my

shoulders and looked straight up at me. "Bryce Fisher will take you out and buy you nice wine with the sole intent of getting you naked in his bed."

His touch was disconcerting—the soft pressure of his fingers kind of warm and inviting. That sweet, tempting sensation washed through me again. It put me on the back foot, so I shook him off me and forced a teasing smile. "Naked in his bed doesn't sound too bad to me."

"And then he'll dump you." Marcus's tone was scathing, and it made me bristle.

"I'm Kelly DeMarco. Guys don't dump me, especially after getting me naked in their bed."

His face pinched tight with disgust. "That's pretty arrogant."

"It's the truth." I crossed my arms and raised my chin, the way my mother did when she wanted to make me feel small and admonished.

Marcus didn't shy away from my haughty-rich-girl routine. Instead, he rubbed his hand across his mouth and stared at me like he was that micro-expression expert from that TV show, *Lie to Me*.

"You know, Kelly, I think you're lying."

I opened my mouth to protest but he cut me off by raising his finger.

"I'll tell you what. I'll leave you alone. I won't ask you out again, but if you sleep with Bryce and he dumps you, then I'm allowed one date."

"What?" I squeaked.

"One date."

"Forget it." My eyebrows rose. "This is like

sexual harassment in the workplace," I snapped, not really meaning it.

He rolled his eyes. "You know it's not like that. I'd never force you to do anything. All I'm asking is if you're brave enough to play my game." His eyes sparkled. "If you're as confident as you seem to be, it'll never happen anyway, right? Because you're Kelly DeMarco and guys don't dump you." He put on a mocking voice, but then followed it up with a wink, so it was really hard to get mad at him.

I bit back my smile and shook my head. Why did he have to be so charming? There had always been a sweet playfulness about him. I didn't want to like it.

Marcus kept watching me as I gritted my teeth and fought a little war inside myself. "And in case you're wondering, I'm not asking you because you're drop-dead gorgeous. All I've ever wanted to do was hang out with you and make you smile."

My heart tripped up for a second, confused by the sweet look on his face.

He stuck out his hand. "One date."

I gazed down at his fingers, my jaw clenching tight as I resisted the urge to turn and walk out the door. With a short sigh, I snatched his hand and shook. "If by some miracle this does happen, I want to be clear that it is one date, and after that you never, ever ask me out again."

Marcus gripped my hand. "Not unless you want me to."

"I won't."

"Okay." Marcus grinned like he didn't believe

me then let my hand go. Closing the gap between us, he whispered in my ear, "Enjoy your expensive wine."

He sauntered out of the room before I could formulate a comeback. My senses were too busy tingling and trying to find themselves again after a luscious whiff of Marcus's aftershave.

He was wearing Sovereign for Men by Echelon.

*****

Bryce took me to Devil May Care—a chic restaurant in Hollywood with fine dining and expensive wine. He ordered a rare steak while I picked at the salmon fillet with steamed vegetables. It was delicious. We finished off the meal with a shared bowl of Baileys ice cream. It was all very civilized, and my mother would have been highly impressed.

I could foresee myself mentioning the date to her on Thursday. She'd ask for details, and I'd spin the story to make it sound like everything she'd need it to be. Bryce was tall, good-looking, and had an aloof class about him…just like Fletcher did.

I'd never forget the first time I saw Fletcher Winslow. I was a college freshman. Evangeline and I had just finished setting up our room, our parents had left, and we were heading out to explore campus. I'd spotted Fletcher across an open quad, and my heart had thrummed like it never had before. He was this tall, gorgeous guy with a chiseled face and this perfectly straight nose. Dark blue eyes, light brown hair parted on the side and swept up, away from his forehead—he was the perfect combination of class and sensuality. Designer jeans hugged his perfect butt and a pale gray button-down shirt couldn't hide the sinewy muscle covering his torso. The moment our eyes connected, I knew something was going to happen between us. It was seriously love at first sight for me. He took my breath away.

For two years, he'd owned me and I had willingly given him every beat of my heart.

Memories were making the ice cream taste sour. I placed my spoon in the bowl. "You finish it," I murmured.

Bryce smiled at me and scraped the bowl clean while my mind continued to race with the hellish year that followed our initial break-up. If I'd known why he'd ended it, I wouldn't have kept trying to win him back. If he'd only held his ground and stopped letting me back into his bed, I wouldn't have had my hopes rising and falling like the waves that make you seasick.

"Should we get going?" Bryce wiped his mouth on the white cloth napkin and smiled at me again. He'd been smiling at me a lot since we'd left the office, and with each hour that passed his gaze grew hungrier.

I nodded and stood, trying to decide how to play it.

I hadn't had sex in a while. It was almost tempting, but if I slipped my panties off for this guy, I was worried my brain would be massacred with reminders of Fletcher. I would never forget the way his tongue felt in my mouth and the power of his muscles as he lay on top of me, thrusting and panting. I missed the way he groaned into my ear when he came.

Heat pooled between my legs, but it quickly iced over as another memory flashed through my mind. My stomach knotted and my eyes started to sting. I couldn't go there. His words were permanent scars on my heart. It was the final blow that helped me walk away for good.

I rubbed the spot below my collarbone, wishing a whole heart sat inside my ribcage.

Bryce opened the restaurant door for me, his hand snaking around my back as we stepped into the cool night air. "Have you had a good evening?"

"Yes, thank you." I smiled up at him, admiring the lines of his face. The street lamps cast haunting shadows over his complexion. It gave him a sexy edge. Not that he needed one.

"How do you feel about making it longer?"

I kept my eyes on his face, taking in the curve of his lips and wondering what they'd feel like on my skin. Would they make me forget...or remember?

THIRTEEN

MARCUS

I slashed the sweat from my eyes and lay back down to do my final set of reps. Logan, the gym owner, was spotting for me while he waited for a new client to arrive. He'd started up Artisans Gym about a year ago on a shoestring budget. I was one of his first clients, and I loved the place. He opened at five in the morning, which meant I could get a workout in and still have plenty of time to get to the office early. The gym was small, and down an innocuous street that not many people knew about. That was just the way he'd wanted it.

"I'm not about big and flashy. I want clients that

are here to work out and stay healthy. Word of mouth is going to be my marketing strategy."

To my surprise, it had actually worked. The clientele had steadily increased and because it was all word of mouth, the atmosphere was low-key and friendly. Everyone was a friend of someone, and it made for a really non-pretentious environment.

"Come on, five more." He grinned at me.

I gave him a WTF look and he started laughing.

"You can do it, man. Come on, let's go."

I grunted and puffed, pushing the bar up and down five more times. My arms nearly gave out on the last, but Logan caught the bar and helped me lift it back onto the hooks.

Sitting up with a groan, I wiped my face while he patted me on the shoulder. "Good job, little man."

I punched the gorilla lightly in the thigh. He crossed his bulky arms and smiled down at me. I took it as a sign of respect that he hassled me so much. He'd never talk to a new client like that.

"So, did your girl end up starting those aerobics classes?" I stood and stretched my shoulders.

"You bet, man. They've been going strong for a couple of months now. It's all ladies at this stage, but you're welcome to join." He winked at me.

"Nah, I'm good. Think I'll just stick with the weights for now."

"Well, they're working. You're looking really good."

I smiled, casting my eyes around the various

machines that had slowly turned my muscles hard and sinewy. "I feel good. Thanks for the new program. I'm enjoying the switch."

"No problem. Make sure you check in with me at the end of February, we'll do a revision. Don't want those muscles getting too comfortable, right?"

I laughed and lifted my chin as Logan's new client walked in. He raised his hand at me before greeting the rotund man who was standing by the door looking reluctant. I grabbed my towel and headed for the showers.

I had ten minutes to get my ass out the door and on my way to the office. Rubbing the back of my neck, I let out a soft groan. I felt old. After Laser Strike with Chaos, who were freaking wild, I then slumped home to do some more work, but I hadn't been able to focus. All I could think about was Kelly out with frickin' Bryce Fisher. Images of her lying naked in his bed riled me so bad, I ended up pacing the house for half my evening. I finally fell into a fitful doze around midnight, only to be woken at three by Flash, who puked up a hairball next to my pillow. Worst wake-up ever!

Putting on a breezy smile was going to be a mission, but I refused to walk into work looking morose. I had to focus on the fact that Bryce would no doubt dump Kelly soon enough and I'd get my date. Well, hopefully—if she didn't renege on the deal. It was a bit of a juxtaposition in the sense I didn't want Kelly getting hurt by the dickwad, but I also really wanted my date.

I arrived at the office a couple of hours before

everyone else. The building was so quiet at six-thirty in the morning, and it gave me a decent chance to get stuff done. I cleared my inbox, spent a couple of minutes reading a few entertainment sites and was pleased to see the buzz around Chaos's upcoming tour.

I really loved those guys, and I wished them all the success they could get. My email dinged. I saw three new messages arrive. Dion Bonnet was coming into the studio that afternoon for a recording session. His Christmas album was selling steadily, and we were now working on his summer release. He wanted to do a collaboration album, so I'd been in touch with various singers who I thought would be a good fit. Three had already signed on to work with Dion, guaranteeing the album a few hit singles. It was going to be epic. A smile crossed my face as I made a note to ask Kelly to check that the studio was all set with Dion's preferred piano.

My office door was closed, but I could hear the muted sound of office traffic. Checking my watch, I figured Kelly and Marcia had probably arrived. Might as well give Kelly my message in person. It'd be a good chance to suss her out and see if all my late-night pacing had been necessary.

Going for a confident swagger, I ambled out to the front desk and spotted the girls sitting down with their morning coffees.

"Ladies," I greeted, leaning against the counter and flashing them a smile.

"Hey, Marcus. You're looking tired this

morning." Marcia grinned. "Rough night?"

I answered her with a chuckle then turned to Kelly. "How was your night?"

She glanced up, her blue eyes round and guarded. "Fine. Thank you."

"Where'd Bryce take you?" I shrugged like I wasn't interested…like I was just being polite.

Her look told me she was seeing right through my lie.

"You went out with Bryce?" Marcia made a face, but quickly pulled it into line before Kelly spotted her.

"He asked me out to dinner. I wasn't about to refuse." Kelly straightened her shoulders and almost looked relieved when the phone rang. She snatched it off the cradle before Marcia could reach for it. "Torrence Exec, Kelly speaking… Sure, one moment." She pushed a button then looked up at me. "Jimmy and Flick are here to see you."

"Really?" I glanced at my watch. They didn't usually surface this early in the morning. "Send 'em up."

I walked back to my office as Kelly finished the call. I'd gotten nothing from her, couldn't read her expressions, so I had to walk away just as frustrated as I'd been the night before. Stupid Bryce and his pretty-boy face. What was so great about being tall, anyway?

Slumping into my seat, I tapped my fingers on the desk while I waited for the boys to arrive. I left the door open and watched them saunter in with playful smirks on their faces. Jimmy raised his eyebrows in greeting before flopping onto the couch in the corner of my office while Flick ran a thumb over his smile and sat down.

"What's so funny?" I stood to join them.

Flick snickered. "Damn, that new chick is hot. She's like a freaking supermodel, man."

I rolled my eyes and grabbed a few Chaos posters and flyers off the side cabinet before joining them. Throwing two markers and the promo stuff onto the coffee table, I ignored their comments and asked, "Can you please sign these for Scarlett."

"Is that her name?" Flick snatched a marker. "Because I can sign her chest if she'd prefer."

Jimmy laughed and whacked his buddy on the back of his beanie. "Stop being a douche. That's Kelly, the new assistant Marcus is in love with."

"I am not." My denial was lame and transparent. "Just sign the posters already."

"Dude." Flick shook his head while scribbling his name below his image. "I am sorry, man, no offense, but that hottie is out of your league. She's not even in Jimmy's league. Hell, I don't even know if Jace could secure a hook-up."

Jimmy nudged him out of the way and scrawled a message to Scarlett before capping the pen and dropping it back onto the table. "She looks like she belongs on a Milan catwalk. You sure you want to break your heart over her?"

"She's owned my heart since high school, okay? It's not like I have much of a choice."

"No way." Jimmy leaned forward. "That's the girl? The troublemaker?"

I glanced over my shoulder with a restless sigh, running a thumb over my scar and whispering, "She only ever made trouble for me...enticing, tantalizing trouble."

Jimmy snickered and I turned back in time to see him press his phone and sing, "She's a troublemaker." He sang over Olly Murs's words, changing the lyrics from first person to second person and pointing his finger at me.

I could do nothing but shake my head with a red-faced chuckle as the guys danced on the couch, performing for me.

That song was damn perfect.

I wondered how Kelly would feel if I attached that to a morning email.

FOURTEEN

KELLY

Marcus had looked ragged when he showed up at my desk. I had no idea what he'd been up to, but his pale complexion and the dark circles under his eyes told me he'd had a restless night. But that still didn't mean he could ask me about my date with Bryce. That wasn't any of his business. Like he honestly wanted to hear what Bryce and I got up to.

I finished typing up the email Bryce had dictated in a voice memo and read it through before sending it to him for approval. Checking my list, I snatched the phone out of the cradle and called the studio to make sure it was ready for Dion. Marcus had popped by my desk as Jimmy and Flick were leaving to rattle off a list of things that needed doing. I was disappointed that I didn't have a chance to talk to the Chaos boys. I was going to ask them to sign a piece of paper for Scarlett. She would have loved that.

I spent the rest of the morning making phone calls to confirm that everything was set for Chaos's opening night. The concert was huge and the band members were nervous. They wanted everything triple-checked to make sure nothing could go wrong. Jimmy was particularly protective of Nessa, which was why he'd dragged his ass out of bed so early to swing by Marcus's office and go over every detail again in person.

"He doesn't want anything throwing her off. It's our responsibility to make sure tomorrow night is absolutely perfect." Marcus tapped the counter as he read notes off his iPad. "Oh, and make sure there's a spare drum kit backstage somewhere. Jimmy says Nessa plays when she's nervous. It helps to calm her. So let's make sure something is available for her if she needs to de-stress before going on stage."

By mid-afternoon, I was exhausted. My ear hurt from holding the phone against it, and I wasn't in the mood to talk to any more strangers. Marcus had left the office to hang out with Dion, and Marcia was packing up her stuff, ready to head to her daughter's dance recital.

"I'm so excited." She beamed. "Her first recital.

It's going to be adorable. Did you know her teacher is married to the guy from *Superstar*?"

"Which one?"

"Sean Jaxon. He plays the role of Harley. You know, the dance teacher?"

"Oh my gosh." My lips parted. "He's super hot."

"I know, right? Can't believe his wife teaches my daughter." Marcia giggled.

I grinned and waggled my eyebrows. "Maybe he'll pop by the concert this afternoon."

Marcia blushed and waved her hand in the air. "Oh stop it. My husband's going to be there!"

I laughed. It was cute the way Marcia's skin flushed pink when she got embarrassed. She tucked a curl behind her ear and lifted her bag onto her shoulder. "Thanks again for covering my station for the last hour. I really appreciate it."

"It's no problem, really."

Marcia squeezed my shoulder and was about to walk for the elevator when a harried-looking marketing exec appeared.

"Where are you going?" she snapped.

"Uh, to my daughter's recital. I emailed you about it last week. You all replied saying it was fine."

"Well, sorry. Change of plans. I need this stuff done now." She dumped an armful of files onto the desk. "This data has to be entered before you leave. Mr. Torrence wants it for an eleven o'clock meeting with London. I need you to make it into a PowerPoint presentation so he can use the data for his pitch."

"But I can't." Marcia shook her head. "I have to go to my daughter's recital."

The woman tipped her head with a frown. "Please tell me this recital isn't more important than your job. Get someone to record it for you." She tapped the stack. "Then get to work."

The woman walked away before Marcia even had a chance to argue. She stood opposite me with her mouth agape and tears quickly gathering on her lashes. I acted before I could think better of it.

Standing from my seat, I pulled the stack of files toward me and said, "Tell me what to do."

"Huh?" Marcia brushed a tear off her cheek.

"Tell me what to do and then get your ass out of here."

"But…"

"Just hurry up. I don't want you to be late."

Marcia's dimples appeared. "Are you sure?"

"By the look on your face, I am sure that your daughter's dance recital is more important than this job…and I really like working with you, so you're not allowed to get fired. Tell me what to do."

"It's going to take you well past five."

I shrugged. "I don't have any plans tonight, and as long as I'm done by eleven, we should be good, right?"

"You're the best," Marcia blubbered, sucking in a quick breath before rattling off what I had to do. Her explanation was hurried and I missed some of it, but I wasn't about to make her repeat anything.

She rushed for the elevator ten minutes later. As soon as the doors dinged shut, I dropped into my chair and tried not to let the daunting task overwhelm me. I scanned my own list and decided the last two things could wait until the morning then swallowed and made the dreaded call to my mother. She was offended that I couldn't make our weekly dinner, and I figured a work emergency would hardly win her over, so I lied and said I had a date. I turned Bryce into the son of a wealthy banker and exaggerated the facts I did know until my mother was tittering into the phone and telling me to have a good time.

Rolling my eyes, I hung up and moved into Marcia's space to get started.

The office cleared out an hour later. There was no way I'd be done fast. I'd only gotten through three of the twenty files, and although I was getting quicker, the stupid PowerPoint still awaited me once I'd finished the data entry.

Bryce stopped by my desk on his way to the elevator.

"You keen for a drink?" His smile was flirty and said too much.

"I've got a stack of work I have to get through before I leave tonight."

"Okay." He nodded. "No problem. I'll give you a call. Maybe we can hook up later."

Hook up later? His wording was so elegant. I nodded my goodbye and watched him leave...and then spent the next half hour trying not to be distracted by the whirr of the vacuum as the cleaning staff raced through. I was soon sitting in a very quiet, empty office.

The isolation was unnerving, but I managed to talk myself out of it...mostly. It didn't stop me from jumping out of my skin when Marcus closed his office door and strode into the main area. A dark leather satchel swung from his hand while he jiggled his keys in the other. He noticed me and stopped short with a quizzical look.

"What are you still doing here?"

I rubbed my stinging eyes and sighed. "Marcia got lumped with a bunch of work just before leaving for her daughter's dance recital. I said I'd do it for her."

A lopsided grin tugged at the corner of his mouth. "How's it going?"

I sighed. "It's taking a really long time. I've never used this program before. But I'm getting there."

Stepping to the counter, he peeked over the edge and spotted my pile of folders. "Do you need a hand?"

"No." I swallowed, flustered by his attentive tone and the smell of Sovereign wafting in the air between us.

"At least let me get you a coffee." He strode off before I could refuse him, returning five minutes later with a steaming cup of black liquid and a banana.

"Thank you." Part of me yearned to tell him he was sweet, but I didn't want to encourage him. My insides were rattling for some weird reason, and I needed him to go away so I could get the job done. "Have a good night." I nodded and turned back to the computer screen, but then noticed him heading away from the elevators. "Aren't you going home?"

He paused and turned with a smile. "I've got some extra work to get done myself. So, I might as well do it now."

I narrowed my eyes, fighting the grin that wanted to jump all over my lips. "Liar. Why are you staying?"

He looked to the floor, his cheeks heating with color before he gazed back up at me. "Maybe I don't like the idea of you walking out by yourself after dark. The underground parking gets kind of creepy at night."

My rattling insides stilled for a second, and all I could do was stare at him.

His grin grew to counter my surprised silence. "Mind if I put some music on?"

"Sure," I croaked and watched him walk away. A few minutes later, the soft strains of "Hey Soul Sister" came out of his office. I couldn't help a smile. I loved that song, and it definitely made working seem easier.

I ignored the fact that the song was hells romantic and pretended he wasn't playing it specifically for me. I told myself it was simply a song on one of his random playlists.

It was with a mixture of disappointment and relief that the tune ended and shifted to "Good Time" by Owl City and Carly Rae Jepsen. It was, however, another great song, and I bopped away while I worked, the file stack decreasing at a quicker rate than I expected.

At nine o'clock, I emailed Mr. Torrence a PowerPoint from Marcia's account. I even wrote the accompanying message from her so the bitch from marketing wouldn't try to accuse my coworker of skipping out early. The only giveaway would be the slightly amateur quality of the presentation. Marcia was far more adept at that kind of thing than I was.

With a weary sigh, I shut down the computers and collected my bag. I poked my head into Marcus's office and noticed him gazing at the screen. He looked so tired. The rectangular glasses he wore for reading had slipped down his nose. He pushed them up with his knuckle and sniffed, like he was trying to wake himself up. The small, black frames actually suited him. I'd never found the guy attractive, so it seemed really weird to be thinking the word *handsome* as I stared at him.

Was it possible for people to become more attractive over time?

I frowned and shook my head. No. Marcus wasn't... He didn't... Not my type!

"I'm done." I spoke softly, because it was all I could manage. My heart was trying to inch its way up my throat, making it hard to swallow.

Marcus jerked then gave me one of his bashful smiles. "Cool, okay. Let me grab my stuff."

I waited by the door while he packed up. Just before he left the office, he collected some shiny paper off the coffee table and handed it to me.

"What's this?" I took it from him and spotted Jimmy Baker's signature on the Chaos poster. And was that Scarlett's name?

"I got Jimmy and Flick to sign it for your friend." Marcus straightened his jacket collar while we walked to the elevator. "Sorry the others aren't on there. I can try to get them next time if you like."

I stopped walking and just looked at him.

I'd been doing that a lot tonight...just looking at him. He kept stealing my voice and I didn't know what to say.

"What?" He chuckled, stepping aside so I could enter the elevator first.

"Nothing." I shook my head. "I mean, thank you. Scarlett's going to love this."

"Tell her it was your idea." He winked, making everything worse.

I wasn't attracted to this guy at all, yet his sweetness was making my heart do these weird somersaults. I stood at the edge of the elevator, watching the side of his face as he slid his hand into his pocket and looked up at the descending numbers.

We reached the basement, and he once again stepped aside so I could exit first. He stayed close to me while I led him to my car. It made me feel safe. If anyone attacked us, I had a hunch my boss would kick some serious ass trying to defend me.

There was something so chivalrous and antiquated about his style. He wasn't like the men I was used to associating with. Most of them put on airs to impress anyone who might be watching. I got the impression Marcus did it because he actually wanted to take care of me.

"This is mine." I pointed at my car and slowed to a stop, spinning my heel into the concrete floor.

Marcus's eyes were glazed with tiredness, but his smile was still bright. "You know, what you did tonight was really sweet."

"Ditto." I grinned.

Marcus's broad smile turned into a yawn. He covered his mouth then gave me a sheepish grin.

"You should go home and get some sleep. You've got a big night tomorrow."

He opened his mouth to say something—I'm sure it was to invite me along—but then pressed his lips together and turned for his car.

"Good night, Kelly. Sleep well."

"Ditto," I squeaked. My voice was once again being cut off by my heart.

I unlocked my car and jumped in, waving to him before he turned and disappeared into the darkness. Starting up the engine, I let it idle for a moment as I tried to figure out what was wrong with my insides.

"Stop it, Kel," I muttered. "He's Marcus Chapman, the guy you went out of your way to avoid in high school. He's not your type, remember?"

The phone in my purse buzzed. I plugged it in then answered it on speaker while reversing out of my spot.

"Hey, Kelly. Bryce here. You done at work yet?

Thought you might like a drink."

I wanted to say no, but I blurted out a yes. Bryce would help dampen my confusion over Marcus. He was my kind of people. Marcus wasn't.

Our worlds would never collide, and I couldn't let that guy with his sweet smile and hazel gaze rattle me again. It wasn't fair on him or me.

FIFTEEN

MARCUS

"Yes, Garrett. I get it. Caris is a pain in the ass. But Mr. Torrence wants us to hold on to her, so just lump her complaints and make it work." I rubbed my eyes and ran a hand through my hair. I felt like I'd never left work. Staying late for Kelly had been worth it, but I'd ended up skipping dinner and falling into a coma the second I walked in the door. My alarm went off at four-thirty, so I'd dragged my ass to the gym and then came straight to the office. My breakfast had been McDonald's drive-thru, which now sat in my gut—an oily, abusive mistake that would punish me for the rest of the day.

Garrett, the sound tech, groaned. "We can't run through a song twenty frickin' times when it was perfect the first time we recorded it. You're always going on about the cost of studio time. She's taking twice as much as everyone else! And don't even get me started on that fucking candle."

I pinched the bridge of my nose. "I know, I know. We just need to give the girl a little leeway."

Garrett swore again then hung up before I could say any more. Dropping my phone, I leaned my head back against my chair and prepped myself for another irritating call with the young pop star. She'd flounced up to the office earlier that morning to piss me off with a series of demands including twelve bottles of Evian water that had to be at seventy degrees Fahrenheit and a lotus incense candle, which had to be burning the entire time she recorded.

Kelly was nice enough to spend an hour on the phone for me, tracking down building and safety codes to make sure we were allowed that particular candle in the recording studio.

Caris made everything difficult, and it pissed me off that the staff had to put up with her bullshit, as well. I wanted to tell Mr. Torrence she wasn't worth it, but I couldn't do it. He needed me to make it work, and I needed to prove to him that I was capable of doing the job well.

A figure appeared in my frosted glass door and knocked once before entering. Kelly looked tired and a little unsettled as she walked toward my desk with some paperwork.

"These all need signing before you leave for the arena. I've booked you a car for three, and Chaos is being picked up in an hour or so. They'll be in hair and makeup by the time you get there. As far as I can tell, everything should go smoothly."

Her lips twitched at the corners but didn't rise into a smile. This surprised me after all the effort she'd put in. I was expecting pride, but all I captured was a weary restlessness. I understood the feeling all too well.

"Are you okay?"

"Yeah." She rubbed her forehead and wouldn't look me in the eye.

"Liar," I murmured, trying to make her grin.

She scowled at me and crossed her arms. "I'm just tired. I had a late night."

"Really? I was home by like nine forty-five. Where do you live?"

She blanched, a tendon in her neck pinging tight.

"Oh, I see." I swallowed. "You went out after work."

"With Bryce." She nodded, crossing her arms and looking a little tortured.

My insides jerked with a protective angst that had me gripping the pen in my hand. It dug into my thumb until a round indent formed. "Did he do something that you didn't want him to?"

Her gaze shot to my face, her bright eyes lighting with a look I couldn't quite understand. Her lips flashed with a smile, and she shook her head. "No. I'm not hurt, I'm just tired."

She was still lying, but I couldn't push her further because my phone rang and she darted out of the room before I could stop her.

"Hello," I barked into the receiver.

"Is that really the way you want to greet your star performer?"

I cringed at Caris's acidic tone before squeezing the bridge of my nose and forcing a cheer I was far from feeling. "Hey, beautiful. Listen, I'll call you back. I have something urgent I need to deal with and then you'll have my full attention, okay?"

"Well, I was just ringing to tell you that my recording session was perfect, except for the sound man who was quite rude to me as Mom and I were leaving. I'd like you to have him fired."

I clenched my jaw and swallowed down the string of swear words resting on my tongue.

"I don't actually have the authority to do that."

"Well, find out who does and arrange it for me, because I will not be recording any more songs if he is in the booth."

"Yeah." I nodded, having absolutely no intention of firing one of the best sound techs in the business. "I'll work something out."

"I'm trusting you, Marcus. It'd be so sad for Torrence to lose me to another recording company. I have offers coming in all the time and I keep saying I have the world's best manager. Let's not make a liar out of me." Her words would have had so much more impact if they hadn't been said in such an irritating little-girl voice.

I cleared my throat and hitched my pants as I

walk to the door.

"Don't worry, Caris. I won't let you down."

She giggled and said goodbye, sounding like a five-year-old princess. I could picture her pink tutu and plastic tiara as I stormed toward Bryce's office. I knocked once then thundered through the door.

"What did you do to Kelly last night?"

"Nothing that she didn't want me to." Bryce winked, making me want to hurl my phone at his face.

"Did you hurt her?"

"No." Bryce glared me. "Not that it's any of your business."

I gritted my teeth. "Did you dump her?"

"Not yet. That girl's quality, and you don't throw that away after only one quick lay."

"You're such an asshole," I whispered.

Bryce heard me anyway and let out a hearty laugh. "Don't be jealous."

"Of you?" I scoffed. "I wouldn't waste my energy." The twinkle in his eyes set off alarm bells in my head. "You don't even like her that much, you're just doing this to piss me off!"

"She's pretty enough."

"She's fucking gorgeous! And deserves a hell of a lot more than you!"

Bryce sniggered, sliding his hands into his pockets and looking at me. "I'm trying to teach you your place, little man. I saw you make a pass at her. Save yourself the humiliation. She's out of your league. Women like her don't date losers like you."

He turned away from me, pulling open his filing

cabinet and making me feel like the dregs at the bottom of a coffee cup.

I clenched my fists and swiveled out of the room. I had to find Kelly and tell her to dump Bryce before he did anything else to her. I didn't even care about our deal anymore. Nothing would be sweeter than the satisfaction of knowing she'd bested that asshole. I'd forfeit a date with Kelly if it saved her from another interlude with Bryce Fisher.

SIXTEEN

KELLY

I gazed down at the photocopier display screen, watching the numbers tick down as I copied another pile of pages for Bryce. I'd been feeling low ever since I woke up. I'd even skipped the gym. Instead, I stood in the shower, staring at the white tiles and feeling dirty right down to my core.

Sleeping with Bryce had been a drunken error that I couldn't erase from my history. He'd been all hands and tongue—squeezing and prodding until he'd thrust inside me. I'd tried to pretend I was into it but quickly gave up. He wasn't paying attention anyway. I'd stared through the dim light at his sex-face while he ground into me, feeling nothing but a hollow emptiness. He hadn't reminded me of Fletcher in the end, yet I'd still thought about my ex while I lay on my bed, wishing for his company.

Thankfully, Bryce left about five minutes after he was done. It was way awkward, and I'd escaped to the bathroom to clean up, calling through the door that I'd catch him tomorrow.

Avoiding him had been my main priority for the day, but I was finding it hard to face Marcus, as well. I didn't want him to know that I'd let Bryce stumble into my apartment and do me on my crisp, white duvet.

Hanging out with him had achieved nothing that I'd wanted it to. It'd only made me feel worse, but I was worried that if I dumped him he'd make work difficult, and I didn't trust him not to spread some sordid rumors about me around the office. The humiliation of having that happen to me in high school still burned bright. I didn't think I'd ever get over it. Nearly losing my virginity to the guy who decked Marcus was one of the biggest mistakes I'd ever made. The way his eyes had roved my naked body while I nervously took off my clothes freaked me out. He'd been like the hungry wolf and I'd been an innocent sheep. Much to his dismay and annoyance, I'd pulled my clothes on and ran.

People had been eyeing me up and down my whole life. I'd seen every expression from admiration to jealousy, hungry lust to unimpressed scrutiny. I put on a show because my parents made me, but that didn't mean I liked the vulnerability of someone leering at me behind closed doors. It was probably one of the reasons I never had sex with the lights on. I liked to be hidden away beneath a body and a sheet.

I winced, shaking my head against a different memory.

Maybe sticking with Bryce wasn't all bad. He was too self-centered to notice my prudish quirks in bed, and I *was* attracted to him. Besides, it definitely took the heat off with Mom. She'd called me on my way to work to ask about my date. I'd spun a story that appeased her. Her approval had given me a warm buzz that was slightly addictive. I hardly ever got it, so when I did, it was like an unexpected present.

Bryce and I did look good together, and as for the sex thing, well, I could put up with it. Sex wasn't meant to be enjoyed. It was a power play...at least that's what my mother always said. I'd never thought to doubt her on it, until Fletcher happened and I found out about my dad. So far, Mom's power play theory was a complete crock.

So, why the hell had I let Bryce have me the night before?

Because you were drunk! I scowled. *And rattled.*

Two large hands landed on my hips, making me jump. I looked over my shoulder and blushed as Bryce's breath tickled my earlobes. He nibbled the edge of my ear.

"Hey, sexy," he murmured while his hands slid between my thighs.

"Bryce," I whispered, trying to push his hands away. "Not at work."

He chuckled, gliding me away from the copier and down into the unlit area of the filing room. His lips cut off any form of argument, pressing against mine with hungry force. Once again, his hands were everywhere, squeezing my breasts and my ass while his tongue tried to choke me.

I pushed at his shoulders, forcing some space between us.

"Seriously, Bryce. Not at work." I tried to smile and make light of his hungry antics, but he just frowned at me.

"Really?" He almost whined. "No one can see us down here. We'll be quick."

I know we will.

I kept my derogatory thoughts to myself and forced a smile. "Come on, show a little class."

"I don't care about class." Bryce's hands slid up my thighs, cupping my ass. His erection rubbed against me and he groaned. "Come on, baby. Let me have you."

He spun me around, grinding into me while he cupped my breasts and kissed the back of my neck. I wriggled out of his grasp and shoved him away from me.

"I said no, and if you think you're going to take me from behind you've got another think coming." I straightened my blouse and lifted my chin imperiously. "I'm not a dog."

Bryce's mouth curled before dipping into a disappointed frown. "You never do it from behind, huh?"

"We're not animals." I scoffed, trying to hide the fact I'd only ever had sex missionary style. It was the only way I felt comfortable—any other position would have made me feel too exposed and vulnerable. "Now, stop acting like a hungry beast and be patient. Why don't you take me out to dinner, and then we can spend the night at your place." I shrugged, not loving the idea, but I was trying to make the best of things.

"The night?" Bryce hissed. "Yeah, feels like that's rushing things a bit."

My right eyebrow arched. "But you're ready to screw me in the back of a filing room?"

"You really don't find that sexy?" He looked so surprised.

I pressed my lips together and shook my head.

"Geez, sorry to say this so early on, but I don't think we should see each other anymore."

"What?" I placed my hands on my hips. "You're dumping me?"

"Look, you're pretty and everything. I did enjoy your company, but I like my girls a little more adventurous. I just don't see this going anywhere."

A black acid burned inside me as he stepped forward and patted my shoulder. "Thanks for a good night, though. You are one gorgeous woman, Kelly."

He swanned out of the room, even having the audacity to whistle. I stayed where I was in the dark, staring straight ahead. The rows of files and the light over the photocopier disappeared and were replaced with the image of Fletcher as he strode away from me. He hadn't waltzed with the same arrogant swagger as Bryce. He'd known how much he was hurting me and he hated himself for that, but it didn't change the fact that I just wasn't the girl for him.

"You're gorgeous, Kelly, and I'll always love you. But I just don't see us having a future." His words would haunt me forever. The 'I'll always love you' part had teased me back to his side over and over again.

The number of times I'd tried.

"You said you'd always love me."

"I do," he'd whisper before pulling me against him.

Our make-up sex would be hot and frenzied. He'd move on top of me, moaning *oh, yes, Kelly, yes* into my ear...and then he'd date me for a while, strutting around campus with the gorgeous DeMarco girl on his arm.

But then the high would end, we'd come crashing back to earth, and a few weeks later, Fletcher would start having doubts. I'd spent months trying to lure an engagement ring out of him, but in the end I hadn't been enough.

My nails dug into the palm of my hand as I curled my fingers into a tight fist and tried to dodge my final memory of Fletcher. Sucking in a trembling breath, I blinked against the stinging tears and made a beeline for my bag. I was done.

SEVENTEEN

MARCUS

Kelly wasn't at the front desk when I rushed past. I glanced into the photocopier room, but she wasn't standing by the machine. Paper was spitting out of it, which meant she must have started a run and ducked away to get something. I looked in the lunchroom and breezed through every department but didn't spot her anywhere.

By the time I'd gone full circuit, I was feeling harried and irate.

"Where's Kelly?" I barked at Marcia.

Her eyebrows slowly rose, and she gave me the kind of look my mother would have given me before telling me off for being rude.

"Sorry," I muttered then forced a lighter tone. "You seen Kelly around?"

Marcia eyed me carefully before brushing a finger under her nose and saying, "She's left for the day. She wasn't feeling well."

"Did she look okay?" I leaned against the counter.

Marcia sighed. "I don't know exactly what's going on, but I saw Bryce come out of the photocopier room, and then ten minutes later Kelly appeared with tears in her eyes saying she had to leave."

"Shit." I yanked the phone from my pocket, dialing her number and walking back to my office. It went to voice mail, so I called again. The second time around, it cut off after only three rings, which meant she wasn't in the mood to talk.

I wanted to barge back into Bryce's office and find out exactly what the fool did, but my alarm started beeping.

"Dammit." I ran a hand through my hair and snatched my satchel off the floor, storming to the elevator and my waiting car.

Chaos needed me on form tonight, not worrying about a girl I'd spent most of my teenage life adoring. I was going to be hard-pressed to do it. I didn't know what the hell Bryce said to her, but I hoped it wasn't enough to scare her away from Torrence.

"Leaving in tears," I mumbled as the driver pulled into LA traffic.

I wanted to throttle Bryce.

Sure, he may have given me the chance I'd been looking for. If he'd dumped Kelly then our deal was on.

But he'd made her cry.

He'd fucking made her cry.

My guts were a curdling mess as we drove to the arena. All I wanted to do was find Kelly and make sure she was okay, but I had to play the role of band manager. Chaos needed me, so Kelly would have to wait.

EIGHTEEN

KELLY

I spent Friday night and most of Saturday in bed. It was torture. No amount of music or television could stop the replay of Fletcher's parting words. The entire event ran through my head on repeat. The sound of his grunts and Evangeline's pitchy moans as he buried himself inside her. I'd stepped into his room with a confused frown and stuttered to a stop in the doorway.

She'd been on her knees, fisting the sheet while he stood behind her, pounding back and forth, his fingers digging into her ass cheeks. They were both caught in a state of pure ecstasy. I'd clutched my keys. The metal dug into my palm, hurting me, but I kept squeezing.

Evangeline's eyes had opened first. She'd looked up at me and squeaked, jerking away from Fletcher and covering herself with the sheet. Fletcher stood there fully exposed, his dick still firm and pointing at me.

"Kelly, I'm sorry," Evangeline whispered.

Her words tore me out of my shocked stupor, and I raced from the room.

"Kelly!" Fletcher followed me down the stairs of his house, stopping me before I'd reached the door. He'd flung his boxers on, and I wished he'd gone for a shirt, as well. His chest was so chiseled and perfect.

"I'm sorry. I should have told you."

I wrenched my arm out of his grasp. "She's my roommate! I grew up with her! How could you do this to me?"

"She's... We didn't mean... It just kind of happened."

"Kind of happened? How long has this been going on?"

Fletcher looked to the floor, running a hand through his hair. "About a year."

The air punched out of my lungs. "Is this why you broke up with me in the first place?"

He shrugged. "One of the reasons."

"But you kept taking me back!"

"Evangeline understood. She knew how hard it was for you. She was willing to compromise while I made my decision."

A rock plummeted into my gut, cold and hard. "Made your decision?"

"Marriage is a big step. I need to be sure."

"We're not lab rats!" I smacked him on the chest. "I wanted to be your wife."

Fletcher's face crested with sorrow. "I wanted that too, but…Evangeline is just so…" He gazed up the stairs, a look I didn't recognize cresting over his face. "She's willing to try things, you know. She's not…" He turned back to me with a sad smile, wincing as he whispered, "Like an ice queen."

I stumbled back from him, feeling like he'd punched me in the stomach…and then he made it a million times worse.

"I think I love her, Kelly. Maybe she's the girl I should be marrying."

My throat was so swollen I couldn't even speak.

"It doesn't mean I won't stop loving you. I'm just not sure what to do. I don't want to hurt you."

"Too late." I glared at him.

His smile was weak, somehow beseeching me not to hate him. "Kelly, please. I think you and I are a great match, but…" He looked up the stairs again. "Maybe we could figure out some kind of arrange—"

"No. We're finished. You go be with her…and don't ever speak to me again."

I stormed out of the house and didn't look back. Six weeks later, Mom informed me that Evangeline and Fletcher Winslow were engaged. I quit college that day.

Slashing the tears from my eyes, I sniffed and tried to swallow. "Stitches" started playing on my stereo. I let the words cover me until I was drowning in them. Fletcher had torn me wide open, and I'd let Bryce taste the damaged goods, like some slut who didn't know any better. What the hell was wrong with me?

Why was I always attracted to these gorgeous assholes?

My people, right?

"My people suck!" I shouted, snatching my pillow and hurling it at the family photo on my dresser. My dad's handsome face disappeared behind the furniture, sliding down the wall and getting stuck.

When I'd returned home a blubbering mess, my mother had shown me no sympathy, telling me I was a fool to talk to Fletcher that way.

"Of course men like him have mistresses. Grow up. But you should be the one on his arm in public. You're far prettier and more sophisticated than Evangeline. Everybody knows that. You're Jacqueline Kennedy, she's simply Marilyn Monroe."

I'd made a face then run to the bathroom and thrown up.

The phone beside my pillow lit up. I'd muted the sound hours ago but was still tempted to check the screen every time it vibrated.

MARCUS - work flashed on my screen. He'd been calling relentlessly since Friday afternoon. I dropped the phone and rolled away from it, bunching the pillow beneath my cheek. I didn't have anything to say to him. Bryce had dumped me, which meant the deal was on. Although I had a suspicion he wasn't calling me to gloat or make any demands…which was why I couldn't answer the phone.

*****

I spent the weekend in solitude. I felt like a nun and was ready to start banging my head against a brick wall by the time Monday rolled around. In spite of that, I was tempted to call in sick. I didn't want to bump into Bryce and his imperious smirk. Why I hadn't kneed him in the balls still bothered me.

"Can't believe you let that ass dump you." I cringed, burying my face further into the pillow.

My phone buzzed, and I flipped it the bird.

"Not interested, Marcus!" I yelled. "Maybe I should call in sick." I reached for the phone, practicing my croak voice and answering without even looking at the screen. "Hello," I answered feebly.

"Are you sick, too?" Isla's snuffed-up voice made me jerk. I pulled the phone away from my ear to check the screen and make sure it was my friend. "Are you okay?"

"No," she whined. "I've got the world's worst cold, I've been sick all weekend."

"Oh no." I sat up and wrapped my arm around my knees. "I'm so sorry."

"It's okay." She sounded like a pouty little kid. "Logan's been looking after me. But I was just wondering if you could cover my six-thirty class at the gym. You'll be there anyway, right? So could you just run it for me?"

"Run it for you? I can't... I'm not..."

"You helped me choreograph the set. Just get your butt in there and do this for me, please. Logan's stressing."

I sighed, resting my head against my knees. "Okay, fine."

"Thank you." She sucked in a breath then sneezed. "Dammit, I am so unsexy right now."

"You're gorgeous, baby," Logan murmured in the background then kissed her. "I'll come back and check on you at lunchtime, okay?"

"Love you," she whispered.

I rubbed the aching spot beneath my collarbone, wondering if my soul would ever fully recover. I hated that I still loved Fletcher and that I wished for his morning kisses before he left for work. That he could still make me pine for him after what he'd done was sinful, but I did.

"Thanks for your help, Kels. You're the best."

"Get better. I'll call you later, okay?"

She hung up and I dragged my sorry butt out of bed. Pulling on my gym clothes, I decided to leave my work stuff behind. I wasn't even sure if I wanted to go anyway. I'd come home and make my decision after showering. Being a little late for work wouldn't be the end of the world. Marcia could cover for me...or I could still call in sick.

NINETEEN

MARCUS

I missed my alarm—didn't even hear it buzzing. The fact it was under my bed thanks to Pumpkin getting curious in the night didn't help. When I opened my drowsy eyes and spotted the time, I nearly had a heart attack.

I fell out of bed, whacking my elbow on the side cabinet and bellowing a curse before scrambling off the floor. It'd been an intense weekend. Chaos had performed both Friday and Saturday night. Both concerts couldn't have gone better. The crowd went wild over Nessa singing lead, and everyone had been chanting her name by the end of the first set.

Jace became the star of the second set with a drum solo that rocked the entire stadium. The roar of approval had been deafening, and by the end of the show, "We want more! We want more!" was the passionate anthem of the audience.

Chaos was a hit.

I checked the Top 100 playlist as I threw my work clothes into a bag.

"Yes!" I pumped my arm in the air. As predicted, Chaos had moved up the charts. "Agility" was sitting at #1 with their other two hits on #28 and #51.

I laughed as I yanked on my gym clothes. Mr. Torrence would be stoked, which meant I could afford to be a little late to work. It was still only six, so I had time to fit in a workout before heading into the office. I couldn't start a workday without some exercise; my mind would be a fuzzy mess if I drove straight in.

I jumped into my shoes and hustled to the kitchen.

"Good morning, my little terrors." They meowed at my feet and rubbed my arms as I poured them some milk and biscuits.

"I'll see you guys later." I petted their heads and raced out the door.

The gym parking lot was more crowded than usual and I had to find a spot down the road. I guessed I was ninety minutes later than normal. I figured I'd be waiting for equipment, which would put me even later for work than I intended. I'd just have to do a short cardio and get right into it.

I opened the door, and a thumping music greeted me. "Work This Body" by Walk the Moon pounded out of the side room. I'd usually left before the aerobics classes started. Curiosity pulled me past the equipment toward the archway.

I glimpsed inside and my heart stopped working.

Kelly stood on the stage, a broad smile on her face as she bopped and moved.

"Good job, girls!" she shouted. "Work that body, you hot things!"

Some fumbling ladies in the back giggled while they tried to keep up with her. She stepped forward then back, her arms pumping as she went.

"And to the side!" She jumped across the stage, looking so damn hot in her gym gear that saliva pooled beneath my tongue. The knee-length leggings wrapped around her thighs showed off how strong and fit she was. Her dark hair was bunched in a high ponytail, a few loose tendrils framing her sweaty face. Exertion made her skin glow, but the thing that captured me the most was the sparkle in her eyes. She looked caught up in the moment, like nothing else existed but the music and the moves.

"Four more, let's go!" She grinned.

It was a rare glimpse of unguarded Kelly.

Damn, it was beautiful.

TWENTY

KELLY

The set finished with a flourish, and I stood on stage panting while the tired women collected their stuff. Two of them came up to thank me on their way out the door.

"My pleasure." I grinned.

It really had been. Dancing like that was a rush. I loved the music, the beat pulsing through me. The aerobic steps Isla, Scarlett, and I came up with made me feel strong and confident, like I could do anything.

The last gym member disappeared through the archway, and I jumped off the stage. The instant I hit the floor, the weight of my weekend and pending workday settled on my shoulders. Slumping down with a sigh, I wiped my face with a towel and checked my watch. Marcus would be at work already. If I headed home, I could still call in sick then maybe pop over to spend the day with Isla.

I made a face, not loving the idea of catching her germs and *actually* being sick. My other option was to wallow in bed all day.

"Or you could stop feeling sorry for yourself and go to work," I muttered.

Exercise always gave me a more positive outlook. As soon as I'd come home from college, I'd joined Logan's gym and worked my body to skin and bone. I was up to going twice a day and living on protein shakes before Logan told me to quit it before I made myself sick. That was when Isla had moved out of her dorm room and in with me. She'd set me up on a proper diet and exercise plan, mothering me until I finally saw where she was coming from.

"How's it going, gym bunny?" Logan leaned against the archway frame and grinned at me.

I smiled back. "It was a good session."

"Thank you so much for covering. You looked like you were having fun up there."

I stood and hitched the bag onto my shoulder. "I was."

"Well, you should do some more. Isla's having a hard time fitting in all her senior classes as well as doing this. How'd you feel about covering for her every now and then?"

"As long as it doesn't interfere with work." I shrugged, confused by why I'd said that. I wasn't even sure I wanted to go back to work, ever.

I stopped next to him in the archway and was about to ask him what sessions Isla needed me to cover when I spotted something delicious on the other side of the room. The guy was working the shoulder press, his taut arms strong and muscular. He had a towel draped over his head, so I couldn't see his face properly, but my breath hitched with desire. The guy was in a loose tank top that gave my eyes full access to his muscular arms. He wasn't bulky like a body builder but had these tight, shapely arms that I imagined lifting me off the floor. My lips parted as I watched his biceps round and flex with movement.

Holy crap, he was hot.

I inwardly cringed, annoyed with myself for finding anyone attractive. I should have been swearing off guys for good, not ogling them.

Logan noticed my gaping stare and followed my line of sight. He placed his finger under my chin and, with a little chuckle, closed my mouth for me. "You know Marcus?"

"Marcus?" My head snapped in his direction, and then I spotted Mr. Muscles pull the towel off his head and wipe his face dry.

My stomach jerked then started rattling while my eyes bugged out big-time. It was Marcus. Oh, shit. I had just been drooling over Marcus Chapman.

I squeezed my eyes shut and turned to face the wall.

Logan gave me a quizzical frown then looked back at Marcus. "How do you know him?"

"He's um…he's my…boss."

A smile lit Logan's face. "Oh, of course, Torrence, yeah. Cool. He must be a nice guy to work for."

I glanced up at my friend and had to nod. "He is."

"Well, he's a good man. He's in here every weekday morning. Doesn't miss a beat." He glanced at his watch. "Although he's later than usual this morning."

Logan's easy tone helped me relax. I turned back and pressed my shoulder against the wall, flicking a glance at Marcus. He'd started his second set, grimacing as he lifted the heavy weights. "He had the Chaos concerts this weekend. He's probably exhausted." I didn't miss the whiff of admiration in my tone.

"I guess you'll have to be extra nice to him at work today." Logan winked at me then moved away to correct someone's position on the chest press.

Marcus set the weights down and looked up at me. He caught my eye and a big grin spread across his face, but then it faltered, settling on a look of concern. I wasn't sure whether to approach him or not. I was dripping with sweat and stank like a pigsty. My skin was probably blotchy and red—it always did that when I worked out. I stared down at the industrial carpet beneath my sneakers, trying to make a decision.

Marcus's worn shoes came into my line of sight, and I looked up with surprise.

"Hi." I caught a running drip of sweat with my hand towel then pressed it against my upper lip.

"I didn't know you came here. Isn't it a little out of the way for…you?" I knew what he was implying. Why did a snobby rich chick like me attend an out-of-the-way gym like this?

"For your information, I like working out here. My best friend's fiancé owns this place."

"Wait, Isla. From school? No way." He chuckled. "I never put two and two together. He talks about her all the time, but she's never here at the same time as me. That's cool." His grin was getting kind of adorable.

I jerked my eyes away from it.

"You looked like you were having fun doing the class."

My cheeks flushed, and I wiped a bead of sweat off my forehead. "I was just filling in. Isla's sick, so…" I cleared my throat.

"Are you okay?" His voice was tender and sweet, making my insides rattle again.

"I've been sick this weekend," I lied.

"Glad you're feeling better. I called you a couple of times just to check on you, but…"

He let the sentence hang, and I didn't correct his lie. A couple of times? The guy had been stressing for me, and I'd let him sweat it out. Man, I could be such a bitch sometimes.

I swallowed. "Bryce dumped me."

Marcus's nostrils flared. "Idiot."

My lips rose with a smile before I could pull them into line. I liked the way his eyes flashed when he got indignant. The flecks of green kind of sparkled.

"Anyway, I'm not really looking forward to work today."

"Well, you're in luck. The guy's away this week. Renegade's playing in New York, and he wanted to be there to support them." Marcus shrugged. "It was a late decision. He texted me last night."

"Right." I nodded. "So, I guess I can't use him to get out of work today…and you know I'm not sick, so I'm basically screwed."

Marcus laughed, crossing his arms and making his biceps pop. "Come on, it'll be a quiet day at the office. If you like, we can even skip out early to go on our date." He winked.

Shit! The deal.

My eyes bulged. "Um, are you still serious about that, because I don't know if I'm in the mood to…"

"Kelly." He stepped into my space. With us both in sneakers, he was only a touch taller than me and I could look straight into his eyes. "I'm not going to force you to do anything you don't want to do. You *did* shake my hand." He grinned. "But I'm not an asshole." His nose wrinkled, a pleading smile flashing across his face. "One date. Just one little, itsy-bitsy date. I'll even have you home before your glass slippers fall off, I promise."

There was that charm again.

I opened and closed the cap on my water bottle as I tried to think of a plausible reason to turn him down. I had a dozen, but they were all lame and couldn't outshout the quiet voice in my head that wanted me to go.

"Tonight," I whispered. "And then you'll never ask me out again?"

He nodded. "Not unless you want me to."

I pressed my lips together, my heart skipping softly. "Okay, fine."

"Excellent." Marcus flashed me his goofy grin, and a flurry of doubts scuttled through me. "Make sure you wear something comfortable. We'll leave straight from work."

"Comfortable?" My head jerked back. "Where are you taking me?"

"It's a surprise." He winked.

I narrowed my eyes and pointed at him. "It better not be embarrassing."

His laughter was rich. "Trust me, you're going to love it."

"I'm highly doubting you right now."

"Don't make that mistake. I'm not going to let you down, Kel."

His words clung to me as I raced home to get ready for work.

I had no idea what he meant by comfortable clothing, but I chose a charcoal pantsuit and married it with a fitted, ruby-red shirt. I went to wear a pair of stilettos but changed my mind last minute and slipped on a pair of black flats. They were my most comfortable shoes and I usually reserved them for casual meals with my friends, but Marcus had said comfortable.

I rolled my eyes, white-hot uncertainty doing a number on my brain as I walked out the door to work. A date with Marcus Chapman. I was out of my freaking mind.

TWENTY-ONE

MARCUS

"She what?" I snapped.

Justin stood in front of my desk, looking apologetic. I couldn't take it out on him. The poor guy had only been working with Torrence for half a year. He'd arrived fresh out of college and wasn't even a qualified lawyer yet. I didn't envy him, but he was in my line of fire and I didn't have anyone else to yell at.

"You have *got* to be joking."

"I-I'm not. Um, I-I'm s-sorry."

I sighed, feeling bad for making his stutter worse. Stress makes it even more noticeable than usual.

"I didn't mean to yell. Sorry, man."

He shook his head with a kind smile before scratching his black curls.

"You know, I'm not usually a violent man," my voice shook, "but I want to maim that freaking princess right now."

Justin laughed, then swallowed. "Understandably, but unfortunately that st-still won't change the fact that T-Torrence is being sued."

"Okay." I pinched the bridge of my nose. "Does the big guy know yet?"

"You're the first person I've told."

"So, there's still a chance we could make this work. How much damage did she do to that hotel room?"

"It's tr-trashed."

"Of course it is," I muttered, reaching out for the legal notice in Justin's hand. He passed the pages over and talked me through the jargon. The hotel wanted compensation for damages and emotional stress to the cleaning staff. "That's pushing it a little." I made a face.

"They're going t-to try and milk this, of course. To-Torrence Records is a big company and they know it."

I slumped back in my seat. "Is there any way around this? How can we get them to drop the suit?"

Justin worried his lip. "Well, w-we could try striking some kind of free advertising deal. Chaos is touring the country for the next few months. Maybe w-we could get this hotel chain some ex-exp-exposure."

I nodded, liking that idea. But I couldn't approve it without Everett Torrence's say-so. I looked sideways at Justin, wondering if I could send him into the lion's den for me. After all, he was the guy's son-in-law. I couldn't do it to him, though. Justin was a stress bucket, and I didn't have it in me to pile on any more pressure.

"All right, if you could just double-check with legal that we're allowed to do this, then I'll run it past Mr. Torrence as the best solution."

"Do you think he'll drop Caris?"

"Let's hope so." I sighed.

Justin made a face. "Don't tell him I-I said this, but mules have nothing on his st-stubborn ass."

I laughed and nodded. "Thanks."

Justin shrugged and walked for the door, leaving me the photos of Caris's handiwork. Empty bottles of booze were scattered across the bed and carpet; yellow stains marked the bedding. She'd even drawn on the walls with lipstick. What was she? Five?

I tossed the photos off my desk and watched them scatter across the floor. My light mood from earlier was turning into a black cloud. Pitching this to the CEO was going to suck. He wouldn't congratulate me on my smooth solution. If anything, I'd get another firm word about how important keeping her was for the company, and that I'd just have to work a little harder to control her.

Control her?

Impossible.

What she needed was a short stint in juvie. I rolled my eyes. That princess probably didn't even know what the word *discipline* meant. It pissed me off. I was supposed to be taking Kelly out on a date, showing her a good time and making her laugh. How the hell was I supposed to do that when I was up to my eyeballs in Caris bullshit?

My only real choice was to cancel on her. She'd probably be relieved. She was only going out with me because we'd made a deal, and even though I'd given her an out, she was too nice to take it.

Pushing away from my desk, I headed out of my office to look for Kelly.

"She's just getting a coffee." Marcia pointed down the hallway.

I shuffled in that direction, reluctant to bail on my one chance. As I neared the lunchroom, I could hear someone humming. I popped my head in the door and spotted Kelly at the counter. She was singing "Downtown Girl" and jiggling her hips. Lifting the teaspoon out of the mug, she held it up to her mouth and sang, "Her lips are red…"

I ducked back into the hall before she could see me. Leaning against the wall, I listened to her sweet voice and grinned. Like hell I was canceling. Caris could stick it. This entire job could stick it!

I was taking Kelly DeMarco on a date!

The heavy blackness evaporated, and I loped back to my office with a goofy grin.

TWENTY-TWO

KELLY

I glanced at my clock. It was nearly four pm. Marcus said we'd leave for the date early, but he'd been in meetings most of the day, and I had a suspicion he was going to cancel on me last-minute. I was kind of relieved. I wasn't a huge fan of surprises, and Marcus no doubt had something wacky planned. It was probably best that we didn't pursue this. After Bryce, I was crazy to even consider dating someone else from the office.

So, why had I been in such a good mood all day?

And why did the idea of going home alone

make me feel sad?

Relief, Kelly. You feel relief.

My firm reminders weren't working.

"So, it's one minute to four." Marcia spun in her chair to face me, a playful smile on her lips.

"Ugh." I dipped my head. "I wish I hadn't told you."

She giggled. "I'm glad you did. This is fun."

"For who?"

"Me." She shrugged and laughed. "Come on, stop being so antsy. It's Marcus. He's a nice guy. No matter what you do, it'll be lovely."

"I know," I whined. "I guess I'm just worried it'll be embarrassing. The guy has no shame."

My inbox dinged with a new message, and I moved to clear it. It was from Marcus, marked urgent and important. I bit the corner of my mouth and clicked on it.

The opening guitar riff for "Live While We're Young" came out of my speakers. I made a face and reached for the volume, but Marcia grabbed my wrist.

"Don't you dare." She grinned, pointing to the corridor behind me.

I spun in time to see Marcus walking into the room, lip-syncing the words. He moved his hips and started dancing toward the front desk. I groaned and covered my face with my hand while Marcia laughed beside me. The chorus kicked in and I glanced up. Marcus was going for it, swinging his arms and shuffling across the floor like a cowboy before pulling a few robot moves then going old school with the running man.

A smile was aching to spread across my face. My cheeks burned trying to hold it steady, and eventually I lost the battle. He looked hilarious. His tie kept flicking him in the face as he worked his hips.

Surprisingly, he had pretty good rhythm, but he was too busy being a goofball to let that fact shine.

People from bordering offices poked their heads out to watch him, some cheering. I cringed and leaned down to grab my handbag.

"I'm going to regret this," I muttered to Marcia.

"Or you're gonna love every second." She was near giddy with excitement for me then started singing the words to the second verse. "Hey girl, it's now…"

I stood on shaky legs and moved away from my desk. As I rounded the counter, Marcus spun toward me and grabbed my hand. Raising it to his lips, he kissed my knuckles then winked at me.

"Just…let's go." I pointed for the elevator and he danced across to it, doing another spin before punching the button. Another cheer went up as we stepped in. I pinched my lips together, trying to be unaffected by his playful grin.

I cleared my throat and trained my eyes on the control panel. "So, where are we going?"

"You want me to ruin the surprise?"

"Just please tell me you're not going to throw another *Saturday Night Fever* in my face."

He tutted. "I can't. I'm not wearing the right pants."

I giggled as he tried to pull a few John Travolta moves then pointed at his crotch. "See, not tight enough, right?"

"Or white enough." I laughed.

He chuckled with me, stepping aside to let me out first. I followed him to his car. He opened the door for me and I slipped inside. The vehicle was pretty old and didn't have that new leather smell I was used to, but it was immaculate. I settled the bag at my feet and prepared myself for whatever came next.

*****

"Disneyland? Really?"

We walked toward the ticket booth, and I couldn't hide my uncertainty.

He pulled out his wallet and looked at me like *I* was the weird one. "It's a first date. I had to do something special."

"But we're not kids." I smiled awkwardly at the ticket lady while Marcus paid for one evening pass then flashed his annual passport at her.

Seriously? How often did the guy come?

"You don't have to be a kid to enjoy Disneyland. This is way better than some fancy-schmancy restaurant."

I tipped my head with an unimpressed frown. "Please. A three-course meal, nice wine, candlelight. *That* is romantic. This is…" I waved my hand at the entrance gates, unsure what to say.

"The happiest place on earth. It's the perfect

location for a first date. I'm telling you." He walked toward the large floral display of Mickey's head and beckoned me over.

"I'm not really a Disney girl." I wrinkled my nose as we stopped to admire the display. Even so, a small, childish buzz of excitement sparked inside of me.

"Wait a second." Marcus turned to face me. "Have you never been to Disneyland?"

I shook my head then shrugged at his horrified gasp. "My family doesn't do this kind of thing."

"Even when you were a kid?"

"We grew up in different worlds, Marcus." I gave him an "I told you this wouldn't work" look, but he just smiled and shook his head. Turning for a brick archway, he placed his hand on my back and gently propelled me forward.

"Well, let me introduce you to mine."

TWENTY-THREE

MARCUS

I led her through the archway, keeping a close eye on her face as we walked down Main Street. Her lips twitched and her eyes kept darting from one store to the other. I couldn't tell if she was impressed or not. I had to wonder if she was forcing herself to think it was dumb and immature. My stomach knotted. Maybe bringing her to one of my favorite places was a stupid idea. I so desperately wanted us to work and fit together, but Kelly had a point. Our upbringings had been miles apart. Was this just some foolish dream I couldn't get out of my head?

My heart and soul rebelled against my questioning. I couldn't ignore the fact that after all this time, she'd walked back into my life. That had to mean something, and I refused to waste the opportunity.

We started with the Indiana Jones ride. The wait time was around forty minutes. I thought about doing the fast pass but decided against a frantic race around the rides like my sister and I always did. Standing in line would give me more time to chat with Kelly. That suited me just fine.

My hot assistant gave me a droll look as I led her under the swinging sign and up the walkway that had been staged to look like a jungle.

I grinned. "You have to trust me on this. It's going to be worth it."

She made a face and crossed her arms as we stepped onto the winding path. People around us were buzzing—raucous teens, a cute couple gazing at each other, a large family of tourists. I studied them all as we inched our way closer to the ride. I loved this place. The variety, the people-watching. The lines never bothered me.

Kelly checked her watch and sighed.

"Okay, let's play a game." I nudged her elbow with mine.

"Excuse me?"

I ignored her frown and pointed at her. "Would you rather…"

She rolled her eyes. "We're not in high school anymore, Marcus."

"Come on, Kelly. Play with me." I winked.

"It's silly." She winced and pressed her lips together.

Doubts charged through me as I looked away from her. She was so different from Allison. My college girlfriend loved my games. I could always win her over with a wink and smile...which was why she'd become more like a sister than a lover. Hanging out with her had been so easy. Kelly made everything hard work, yet I wanted her more than anything. I must have been completely insane. What guy in his right mind would relentlessly chase after a woman who wasn't interested? Was it honestly just her beauty that captured me?

No, I refused to believe that. Kelly had been love at first sight for me, but the feelings had only grown the more I'd spied her unguarded smiles and quiet intelligence. She was a loyal friend and had a strength and dignity that was compelling. There was so much beneath the protective layers she'd wrapped around herself, and I wanted to discover it all.

Running a hand through my hair, I turned to look her straight in the eye. "Okay, here it is."

Her thin, dark eyebrows shot up. "Here what is?"

"The truth." I swallowed. "See the thing is, ever since the first time I saw you, you've been on my bucket list."

She leaned away from me, bumping into the rope behind her. "What?"

The confused look on her face made me grin. "Making you laugh has been on my bucket list for…" I flicked my hands upward. "For forever. You're locked up so tight sometimes, you know?"

She stiffened, and I was worried I'd said too much.

I went to brush my hand down her arm—a friendly, reassuring gesture—but her posture was so guarded I thought it'd be safer to stick with words alone. "I want to make you smile. I just…when you smile, the whole world lights up. My whole world…" I looked to the ground and scuffed my shoe on the rough path. "Seeing you happy makes me happy, so please, just open your mind to the idea that this could be fun. You don't know anyone around here." I spread my arms and pointed to the crowd. "No one's watching you or judging you. Just let loose and help a dying guy out."

Her eyes bulged, her pallor dropping to a translucent white. "You're not dying."

I chuckled, a little chagrined. Her shock of fear both surprised and delighted me. I scratched my forehead. "I will one day, so do me a favor and enjoy this." I winked.

She slapped my arm for scaring her then looked away with a shake of her head. A small smile teased her lips, but she brought it into line by pressing her lips together.

We shuffled forward, and I decided to keep my mouth shut. My speech hadn't worked, and it could potentially be the worst date in the history of mankind.

She cleared her throat and murmured, "Would

you rather go to a family wedding dressed in drag or perform the chicken dance on stage at a Chaos concert?"

I tipped back my head, a loud laugh booming out of me. She flushed, slapping her hand over my mouth as those around us all turned to see what was so funny. She gave them a demure smile then bulged her eyes at me with a clear "don't embarrass me" look. I stifled my laughter, delicately removing her long fingers from around my mouth and running my thumb along the palm of her hand.

Her smile was fleeting and chased away by a nervous titter as she withdrew her hand and tucked it into her jacket pocket.

I scratched my top lip. "I think I'd have to go for the chicken dance, although dressing in drag could be pretty funny. I'm just worried I'd snap an ankle in a pair of heels."

She snickered then dipped her head, a thick waterfall of dark hair hiding her face from me. I wanted to tuck it behind her ear but forced the thought away by rubbing my hands together.

"Okay, my turn. Would you rather eat a bowl of snails or a fried tarantula?"

"Ew!" She made a face, poking out her pink tongue.

Even pulling a disgusted face she looked pretty.

"You have to answer it." I pointed at her.

"You're disgusting." She said it like she meant it, but her eyes were twinkling.

I chuckled. "Hey, you started this game."

"You start—" Her indignant reply was cut short by my playful grin. Her lips rose into a knock-out smile. "Tarantula. It'd be over quicker, and I could maybe fool myself into thinking it was something else. Snails are just all slime."

"Not a fan of the ol' escargot, huh?"

"That would be my dad." She pulled another face, which made me laugh, and we moved another few paces up the line.

The game carried us through until we got inside. When it came to theme parks, Disneyland was the best of the best. They even made the wait for a ride interesting, and once we got inside Kelly was completely enraptured with our surroundings. She couldn't hide her awe, and I couldn't help my chest puffing with just the teensiest bit of pride. Maybe this hadn't been the world's biggest mistake.

I told her about some of my previous Disney experiences and how my family came here at least once a year as a fivesome. Sixsome now that Griff had gotten married. Kelly seemed impressed and mystified at the same time. I still couldn't believe her parents had never brought her to a place like this, even when she was a kid! My parents broke the bank getting us here when we were younger. Once Mom started working again, we were able to afford annual passports, and we'd never looked back.

Our turn arrived and as we were put into the final line, I noticed how quiet Kelly had become. I studied her out of the corner of my eye. The delicate dimple in her chin kept appearing as she clenched her jaw. When the 1930s-style car lurched to a stop in front of us and we were told to board, her nostrils flared.

As we slid into place, I reached for her hand and gave it a light squeeze. "Trust me."

Her eyes glimmered with a smile and then we were off. I kept a close eye on her and grinned as her expression morphed from terror to wonder to screaming and finally (triumphantly) unadulterated laughter. We got off the ride and she leaned against me, giggling like an excited kid. As we stepped back out into the late afternoon light, she became aware of the people around us and pulled herself together.

I nudged her arm and tipped my head. "This way. Let's go do the Pirates of the Caribbean."

We spent the next four hours on some of my favorite rides. The lines were made short by playing "Would you rather..." and, without realizing it, Kelly told me a lot about herself. I'd already guessed some of it, but I'd garnered insights into her favorite foods, music, and movies all by asking the right questions. She asked about my college experience and how I got the job at Torrence. I told her everything; after all, Mom always said honesty was for the best. Kelly stayed pretty tight-lipped about her college experience, and every time I felt her tense up beside me, I steered the conversation toward another game. By the time we were lining up for the nighttime performance and fireworks display, we were playing the Alphabet Game and laughing as we tried to think of a famous actress whose name started with X.

The crowds were getting thick as we shuffled onto the platforms surrounding the lake. I threw caution to the wind and pulled Kelly close to me before she could get bumped or knocked over by somebody. I really didn't want to scare her off or push her away, but like hell I was going to see her get hurt. Every time I drew her close, I'd immediately drop my hand away. By the time the fireworks were lighting up the sky, her back was pressed against my side and I could smell the blueberry shampoo in her hair. I wanted to dip my nose into her luscious locks and inhale. It was damn hard resisting the temptation, but I managed to stay strong and not screw up what had ended up being a pretty successful evening.

After the light show, we were heading for the exit when I managed to coax the truth out of my date and she admitted she wanted to stay 'til closing and do a few more rides. It took everything in me not to jump in the air and whoop.

The date lasted for seven hours. Yes, seven! I'd never had so much fun in my life. I drove her back to the Torrence parking lot so she could collect her car. As much as I wanted to kiss her, I didn't. I'd promised myself that if I ever wanted a shot at date number two, I couldn't make the experience about my attraction for her. She was stunning and used to guys fawning all over her body, but I wanted to prove that I wasn't like the rest. I kept my distance and walked her to her car, even sliding my hands into my pockets so I wouldn't be tempted to renege on my resolve.

"Well, thank you for giving me the date I always wanted. I hope it wasn't as terrible as you imagined it would be."

She grinned as she dug the keys out of her bag. "You did good. I had fun, but you still need a lesson in how to take a girl out."

"Oh really?" I tipped back on my heels, adoring the playful way she was smiling at me. "Why don't you show me then." My voice nearly broke as I attempted to make light of my thundering heart. Was I seriously trying for a second date?

"Excuse me?" Kelly's eyes narrowed, and I forced a nonchalant shrug.

"If you think you can do better, why don't you take me out and show me how it should be done?"

She pursed her lips, playing her usual fight-the-smile game. She lost...again, then bit her lips together before finally nodding. "Okay, fine. I'll show you what a date is *supposed* to look like. We'll leave after work on Friday."

"Yes, ma'am." I gave her a double-finger salute.

She snickered and turned to unlock her car. I stood by until she was safely inside and waited until she was driving away before leaping into the air and pumping my fist.

"Yes!" I stumbled over to my car with a heady laugh.

Kelly DeMarco just asked me out on a date! Holy freaking crap! In that moment, reality couldn't have been sweeter.

TWENTY-FOUR

KELLY

"Torrence Exec, you're speaking with Kelly. How can I help you?" My voice had been chipper throughout the week. I couldn't figure out why.

"Well, you're obviously feeling better." Mom's terse voice soaked the inner dance party that had been happening in my belly since Monday night.

I was blaming Disneyland—the fireworks, the rides...*nothing* else. Most certainly not the fact Marcus was there.

Clearing my throat, I shifted in my seat and forced a breezy smile that would hopefully soak into my voice. "Yes, I am. Thank you. Sorry about missing dinner last night."

My "I'm sick" call had been totally fake. I just hadn't wanted to go over there and somehow spill that I'd spent a really fun evening at Disneyland with a guy who I had no intention of making my boyfriend. My mother would give me a brusque look that told me I was wasting my time having fun when I should be out husband-hunting. Her views were so archaic it made me want to scream, but I didn't want to upset her.

Never awaken the beast.

The thought made me smirk, and I had to press my lips together to stop myself from giggling. She was rabbiting on about Abelie making me a special meal that I missed out on. My inbox dinged. I had a new email from Marcus. It was labeled important, which meant it was the morning song. I pulled my earphones out of the drawer in preparation.

"However." Mom ended her rant before killing my happy buzz with a non-negotiable invitation. "You can make it up to us tomorrow night. We're having a dinner party, and I expect you to be there. Bring that man along, the one you've been dating. I looked him up on the Torrence website. He's quite the looker. I'm surprised he's working in such a low-class job considering he's the son of a banker, but anyway."

At first I was confused. She thought Marcus was a looker?

Then it dawned on me. She was talking about Bryce.

I cringed. "Uh, actually. I don't—That's not…"

179

"Kelly, stop stumbling over your words. It makes you sound inept."

I swallowed and licked my lips. "Bryce and I are no longer dating. He didn't want to take things further."

"What's wrong with him?" Mom snapped.

I shrugged. *Where do I start?*

"Is there someone else you can bring?"

Marcus popped into my mind, but I shook my head. There was no way I could bring his happy, scruffy face to a DeMarco party. They'd derail him before he reached the dinner table. No, Marcus could not be exposed to that side of my life.

The minions inside me all sank with a united sigh of dismay. So, what the hell was I doing encouraging Marcus with another date?

"Well, that is a shame. Fletcher's parents are going to be there, and you know what they'll be thinking. Poor little DeMarco girl, still single. It's embarrassing, Kelly. You far outclass Evangeline, and she's the one marrying the most eligible man in California. You can't even find yourself a simple boyfriend."

I rolled my eyes.

She sighed. "Just make sure you wear something jaw-dropping. I want them to know what their fool of a son is missing out on. Actually, let me send you something. I'll arrange to have Franco bring you a dress. Have him do your hair and makeup while he's there."

"Sounds great." My voice and words didn't match, but she didn't seem to notice and hung up with a cheery goodbye, no doubt swanning off to the Echelon offices to meet with one of the designers and procure me the perfect dress.

I shouldn't really complain. The outfit would be stunning. My mother knew how to dress me, and Franco would make me look the best version of myself. I usually got a kick out of dressing up, but as I hung the phone back in the cradle, I felt weighed down by the impending dinner party. It would be an evening of false smiles and small talk where people spent more time judging each other than actually enjoying their company.

I couldn't imagine any of them playing "Would you rather…"

A grin wanted to pull my mouth wide, but I caught it. I shouldn't be smiling. I should be walking into Marcus's office and canceling our date. It was a waste of time hanging out with him when I knew we couldn't go out again.

The email in my inbox caught my eye and I grabbed my earphones. Slipping them in, I double-clicked the message. A strong dance beat had my head bobbing in two seconds flat and then the words came in. The smile I'd been trying to control broke free, and I nearly laughed aloud as I listened to "Epic" by We Are Leo. Marcus had sent the message to his usual email group, but he'd been thinking of me when he chose it.

My little minions leaped up and started dancing again. I slapped my hand over my stomach then quickly yanked the plugs from my ears. No, I couldn't get excited. I had to control myself. This date with Marcus was nothing more than a little friendly banter. I was going to show him what a real date should look like so the next time he asked a girl out, he could woo her properly. It wasn't for me. It was for him. And that would be the end of it.

I couldn't get involved with a guy who, one, wasn't my type, and two, my mother would never approve of. How could I ever let him into my world? It was crazy.

Rolling the earphone plug around my hand, I threw them into my drawer and slapped it shut. Marcus sauntered past with a wink and an easy smile. I turned away from it, pressing my lips together and focusing on the task I had to complete for Bryce. Marcia was home, looking after her sick daughter, and I agreed to cover her phone and any urgent work for the day. It made things busy, which was great because it was going so fast. It also made me nervous, because it was going so fast!

My date with Marcus loomed ever closer, and I needed to figure out how to play it.

A shuffling behind my back made me jump, and I spun to see Marcus place a steaming cup of coffee next to my phone.

"Th-thanks," I stammered, surprised by his sweet gesture.

"No problem." He grinned. "You sure you're okay covering the front desk on your own?"

"Yeah, it's going to be fine."

"Good. Let me know if you need anything." He turned to leave and I was grateful. I'd really appreciated the fact that, in spite of his grand musical number leading up to our Disney date, he'd been very subdued since, keeping things professional in front of all our colleagues. Maybe he knew I would have cancelled the date in a flash if he'd tried to behave any other way.

"One more thing." He came back and placed his coffee mug down. Leaning over the counter, he whispered, "What should I wear tonight? I'm okay like this, right?"

I rose up in my seat and looked at him. He stepped back, spreading his arms wide and doing a circle. Damn, he was cute…his ass wasn't bad, either.

I flinched at the thought and had to force my face into a bland expression. This was insane. I had to put this guy off before he totally won me over.

"Of course not." I wrinkled my nose. "I'm expecting a little class. We're going to a top restaurant, not some hot dog stand."

"Got it." He nodded, taking his coffee back to his office and looking thoughtful.

I grimaced. The whole second-date thing was a mistake.

He was so sweet, and I didn't want to hurt him the way I had in high school. He'd been so shameless and humiliating back then, but now he was just a nice guy trying to show me how much he liked me. What he didn't understand was that we couldn't work. The idea of being with him presented so many uphill battles I didn't even want to go there.

I had to make him see that we couldn't be more

than colleagues…and tonight was my chance to do that.

TWENTY-FIVE

MARCUS

Kelly was the kind of girl you went out of your way to impress, so that's exactly what I did. I shot home during my lunch break and pulled out my black suit, the one reserved for only the most important engagements.

This was one of them.

At five, I snuck out of my office and went to use the shower in the exec bathrooms. I took the time to do my hair, taming it into a style I'd spotted in a men's magazine a few weeks back. The suit had been custom-made, a college graduation present from my parents, and I looked pretty damn good.

Sure, it was uncomfortable and I'd have much rather been in a pair of faded jeans and a baggy tee, but Kelly was worth the effort.

My shiny black shoes, which pinched my toes, squeaked on the glossy bathroom floor as I left. By the time I strode down the corridor, the office was pretty much empty. Kelly was no longer at reception, so I dumped my stuff in my office then headed back to wait for her.

She appeared less than a minute later, looking so damn sexy my mouth actually fell open.

"Holy shit," I breathed.

Her hips swayed as she approached me. They were kind of mesmerizing and hard to take my eyes off. She was dressed in a simple, black number that hugged her perfect curves and ended just above the knee. The neckline was low and scooped with sparkly thingies lining the edge. Her diamond drop earrings matched a small clip in her hair, which was knotted loosely at the side of her head. Long tendrils kind of framed her face. She looked like a freaking movie star.

It was a battle not to feel like a scruffy hobbit next to her. The heels she was wearing gave her at least four inches on me. I didn't know how the hell she walked in those things, but they made her legs a mile long.

I cleared my throat as she stopped in front of me. "You look…" I gazed into her eyes and smiled. "Beautiful."

"Thank you." She was used to hearing that. I could tell by her glazed expression and the polite way she tipped her head.

"So." I clicked my fingers and smacked my hands together. "Should we get going?"

"Of course." Her smile was demure and checked.

I followed her to the elevator, studying her out of the corner of my eye. Her shoulders were tense. There was something holding her back, like she was trying to keep it together. I wanted to chip away at her irritating affectations, bring her around to the giggling, carefree girl on our Disneyland date, but I had a sinking feeling it was going to take a little more effort. I was entering her world, and the terrain would no doubt be harder to navigate.

We caught a taxi to the restaurant. I couldn't figure out why we hadn't taken one of our cars but chose not to question it. Maybe she didn't want someone on her side of town recognizing her car, or maybe she planned on getting us both drunk.

The host led us through a flashy restaurant—all white, starched tablecloths and wine glasses the size of fruit bowls. I counted six pieces of cutlery as I took my seat and knew I was in trouble. How the heck was I supposed to impress this girl when I felt like a poor mouse in a room full of jewel-clad felines?

Kelly gave me an assessing look before she opened her narrow menu. There were like eight things on it and no prices. A place with no prices on the menu meant the food cost a bazillion dollars. I sweated it out as I made my choice. The gentleman in me would offer to pay when we left.

The mortgage owner in me was slashing at dollar signs.

I adjusted my tie as I scanned the choices.

What the hell was champagne citrus beurre blanc?

"Is there…um, anything you'd recommend?" Trying to sound like I knew what I was doing would have been a joke.

Kelly smirked. "It's probably safest if you stick with the steak."

"Okay." I had to push the word out of my mouth. What I really wanted to say was, "How much do you think that will cost? One mortgage payment? Or maybe just this month's electrical bill."

Kelly took her sweet time deliberating while I fiddled with my forks, lining them up precisely along the bottom edges.

The waiter appeared with a bright smile. His white shirt and black pants were spotless, and he stood with his hands behind his back, ready to take our order. I went for the steak, and Kelly chose some fish thing that sounded awful. She also picked a bottle of red wine. I didn't recognize the name or brand but put on a suitably impressed face when it was served and I tasted it.

Kelly's tongue skimmed her lower lip as she gently placed her wineglass down. I scanned the patrons, wondering what they were talking about.

Leaning across the table, I tried to start up a game of "What do you think those people do for a living," but my elbow caught on the cutlery and I ended up knocking my spoons to the floor. They clattered on the polished wood, drawing all eyes to the table. My cheeks flamed and I ducked down to collect everything, rubbing the spoons with my napkin before lining them up again. The waiter appeared with a bemused smile, offering me a full set of clean cutlery and removing the offending pieces.

"I guess the five-second rule doesn't apply here, huh?" He didn't even pop a half-grin at my jest. I made a face at Kelly. Her lips fought a smile, but she pulled them into line. Classical music floated around us, a soft aria that was quite pleasant.

"So..." I smoothed down my tie. "How was work?"

It was a lame-ass question and we both knew it. Even so, Kelly answered it, and we ended up talking shop for a while. Chaos was currently in San Francisco performing to a big crowd.

I checked my watch. "They'll be starting their first set any minute now."

It'd been tempting to go up and be with them, but exec had told me to stay in LA until the band went out of state. I would be allowed to accompany them to Las Vegas and get them set up once they were officially on the road and traveling by bus. I was still on call while they were up in San Fran, but so far, they hadn't needed me. It was more important that I remained in LA to deal with Caris anyway.

"How's that going?" Kelly asked. "I haven't been fielding any Caris calls lately."

I shook my head. "She's been kind of quiet this week, after the hotel incident. But she'll be in studio on Tuesday and I haven't fired Garrett like she asked me to, so there'll no doubt be hell to pay when that happens."

"Caris." Kelly shook her head and flashed me a sympathetic smile.

I nodded. "Caris, sweet Caris. I'd like to send her to Paris with a no-return label on her ass."

Kelly snorted then slapped a hand over her mouth, ducking her head so no one could see her laughing. Her shoulders shook, and I grinned as I watched her try to compose herself. The waiter appeared with our food. It smelled expensive, which only added to my triumph of making Kelly snort with laughter.

She sat up and gave him a demure smile before collecting her cutlery and acting as though she'd never even cracked a grin at my rhyme.

I narrowed my eyes as I watched her. She sat like a true lady, cutting her meal into minuscule bites and using all the etiquette of a highbrow woman. She sipped her wine and we talked some more, about mundane things that had no depth or flavor. By the end of the meal, she was bored out of her wits. I could see it in her masked sighs and the way her eyes lost focus when she was telling me about Milan fashion week.

I reached across the table and touched her hand. "What are you doing?"

"Excuse me?" She leaned away from me, tucking her hands beneath the table.

With a sigh, I took the napkin off my knee and wiped my mouth. "You told me that you were going to take me out and show me what a real date should look like."

"Which is what I'm doing." Her swan-like neck extended as she raised her chin at me.

"So, you mean to tell me that this is how to win a girl over? You take her to some restaurant where everyone around you is hyper-aware of what everyone around them is doing? It's so quiet in here, you can barely crack a smile without someone hearing your lips move."

Her nostrils flared. "Are you saying my date's not good enough for you?"

"No, I'm saying it's not good enough for you. You're bored out of your brain." I liked the way her skin blanched when I called her on her bullshit. "You can't possibly tell me that you are having more fun now than you did at Disneyland."

Her lips pursed into a slight duck face, and she looked away from me.

"Frankly, Kelly, I'm a little disappointed. You talked a big game, and I was expecting a little more than some hobnob dinner where we talked about work and things that don't interest you."

Her eyebrow arched in time with the curl of her lips.

Encouraged by the twinkle in her eye, I leaned forward and whispered, "Come on, admit it. This isn't your ideal date. Now, if it's not the happiest place on earth, where is it? Show me what the perfect date looks like to Kelly. Not the daughter of

Enrique DeMarco, but the friend of crazy Isla and Scarlett. Show me what that girl does for fun."

She stayed statue-still for three long beats then her face started fighting another grin. Her nose twitched, and her teeth brushed over her bottom lip. I would have loved to know what was going through her brain in that moment. It was like she was fighting some inner voice. I watched the battle rage over her expression before she finally let out a huff and grinned.

"Fine. Let's get out of here." She picked the napkin off her knee and plonked it on the table. Tinkling her fingers in the air, she summoned the waiter and bobbed her knee while we waited for the check.

"I can get that." I reached for the padded folder when it arrived, but Kelly snatched it from my hand as soon as the waiter left. "I thought I was taking you out tonight." She winked and my heart tripped over itself.

Half an hour later, Kelly tugged me out of the taxi and we entered a thumping club with flashing lights and a dance floor filled with gyrating bodies.

"Scarlett's boyfriend mixes here some nights." She pointed to a stage stuffed with electronic equipment. A guy with a teased-out afro was jamming in front of the sound board, swiveling his fingers on the record discs and amping up the crowd. "Oh, and she loved the Chaos posters, by the way. I lost hearing in my ears for about thirty minutes after her excited screaming. Thanks for that." She squeezed my forearm and winked at me.

My heart tried to bust right out of my chest. I'm sure it showed when I smiled at her.

She dipped her head and moved away from me. I followed her, and we wove through the tables to find a spot near the dance floor before shedding our jackets. Kelly was beaming. An intoxicating glow emanated from her as she gazed at the dancers. Beautiful didn't cut it. There was no word invented to describe how amazing she looked.

I leaned toward her and shouted, "Do you want a drink?"

She shook her head and slipped off her heels. "I just want to dance." Her expression gave away the fact I'd just discovered her guilty pleasure.

As if the music gods heard her, "Shut Up and Dance" exploded out of the sound system. She turned to me and mouthed the opening line. I pointed at her and mouthed the response. Her smile was electrifying as she tipped her head to the dance floor and sang, "Shut up and dance with me."

I followed her swaying hips onto the floor and nearly melted when she lifted her arms and spun to face me. Her lithe body was hypnotizing and her eyes were alive, a sparkling ocean on a crystal-clear morning. I stepped into her space and started dancing with her, laughing as she threw her head back and whooped. The chorus kicked back in, and she rested her arms on my shoulders and mouthed the words again. I joined her and we laughed our way through the song. The beat pulsed through us, an electrifying narcotic that made me dizzy. I took her hand and spun her around. Her hair fanned out like a glossy satin sheet in the wind, and then she was in front of me again. The music dropped away to a light beat, and I pulled her against me. The look in her eyes shifted. She gazed at me like she was noticing something she never had before. Her breath teased my skin while her long fingers played with the back of my hair. All I could do was watch the way her lips moved as she mouthed the first line of the chorus. I responded, saying, "You're holding back," and then she pressed her lips to mine.

They were warm and enticing, a sensation explosion that took over my entire body. I ran my hands around her waist, palming her lower back as she tipped her head and deepened the kiss. She tasted like the mints we'd eaten on the way out of the restaurant. The heat from her tongue as it brushed against mine made the world spin away. I closed my eyes, entranced, and lost myself to everything but the feel of the girl I'd always wanted in my arms and making out with me.

The song came to a pulsing end but flowed straight into "Better When I'm Dancin'" by Meghan Trainor. We didn't even notice. The crowd surged around us and we stayed put, exploring each other's tongues while the music pulsed and swayed. Kelly's hips started moving beneath my arms, and I could feel her smiling as she started dancing and kissing me. I chuckled into her mouth and joined her, molding my body against hers. We moved to the beat together, smiling and kissing the night away.

Things didn't fall apart until we got back to Torrence Records and I made a move I thought I'd be proud of. But it left me feeling like a world-class fool.

TWENTY-SIX

KELLY

My cheeks burned with humiliation as I drove up my parents' driveway. I lightly rubbed them, willing the color to ebb from my skin. I was infuriated with myself. I shouldn't have been sparing Marcus Chapman a second thought, but I couldn't get our stupid date out of my head.

Every aspect of it taunted me through my sleepless night and plagued me all the next day. I pulled the car to a stop and gripped the wheel, forcing air in through my nostrils.

He'd rejected me. The guy who had hounded me in high school, bugged me at work until I'd finally relented, had fucking turned me away!

I slapped the wheel and jolted back against the leather.

Tears scorched my eyes as I fought for composure. My mother would see right through me if I didn't pull it together. She couldn't know the story. She'd be absolutely mortified by my behavior. A lady did not take a man out to dinner and then pay. She most certainly did not dance in a nightclub, let alone barefoot, and then spend half the time making out with her boss...a guy she wasn't attracted to.

"Oh, would you shut up!" I snapped at myself.

Memories of his tongue in my mouth completely erased my non-attracted lie. Marcus's hands on my body had been freaking hot, which was why I'd suggested we take things back to his place.

He'd chuckled between my hungry kisses, easing away to look into my eyes. I must have flashed him a nervous grin or something because when I tried to dive back into another kiss, he wouldn't let me. He held me at arm's length and gave me a sweet smile.

"We don't have to do this tonight."

"Yes, we do." I pushed against him, trying to close the gap. "Come on, let's make it a night to remember."

"It has been a night to remember." He grinned. "And I don't want to take things further unless you really want that, too."

"I wouldn't be kissing you if I didn't!" Shouting

that line at him was probably another giveaway.

He stepped right back from me then, running his hands through his hair and giving me a sad smile. "Kelly, I want this, but not if it's a one-night stand. I don't want you having any regrets in the morning."

I'd had no response. I couldn't reply with, "Of course I won't," because it wasn't the truth. The nightclub had made me drunk with its music and pulsing beat, then Marcus's chivalry had brought me crashing back to earth.

He'd tried to rectify his subtle rejection by stepping back into my space, but I wouldn't let him touch me again. Instead, I shouldered past him and stormed to my car, ignoring his feeble apology. I screamed out of that parking garage like I was fleeing a crime scene.

What the hell had possessed me to kiss him in the first place? And why hadn't once been enough?

A tapping on my window made me gasp. I jerked to look out the glass and saw Stuart, our house butler, trying to get my attention. I unlocked my car and gave him a tight smile.

He opened the door for me. "Everything all right, miss?"

"Yes, fine, thank you." I handed him my keys and brushed past him, my ankle nearly rolling in the strappy heels my mother had sent over with Franco.

"The guests should be arriving in half an hour," Stuart called to me.

I raised my hand to acknowledge I'd heard him,

but kept on walking. I didn't have time for chit-chat. I had to prepare myself for a torturous evening of hanging out with people who were hyper-aware of what others were thinking of them.

My lips toyed with a smile as I remembered Marcus's insightful observation. My heart twisted painfully in my chest.

"Oh, darling, you're here." Mom stopped to assess me as I walked through the door, critically taking in her selection. "Your father was right," she muttered. "That color does make your eyes pop." Her smile was proud as she gave me a kiss then stepped back and nodded again. "Very nice. Enrique, your daughter's here!"

Dad came tapping into the room and wrapped me in a delicate hug that wouldn't mar my dress or makeup. His lips kissed the air rather than my skin.

"You look beautiful." He stood back to admire me. "This was designed by one of my new girls." There was a sweet admiration in his deep voice that made my mother flinch. He caught the back end of her toxic expression and chuckled. "She is a newlywed, my dear. Fresh out of college and all talent."

My eyes darted between the two.

"I'm sure she's very beautiful, as well."

An elephant lumbered into the room and I started fiddling with my drop earring.

"Hmm." My father responded with a noncommittal smile and clipped out of the room.

Mom's jaw clenched, but then she caught my stare and gave me a sunny smile. "Let's talk strategy for when Fletcher's parents arrive, shall we?"

I didn't want a strategy. I didn't even want to be there!

What I wanted was to be back in a nightclub making out with Marcus Chapman. The idea made me jolt to a stop.

"Kelly, darling, what's the matter?"

Mom's manicured brows dipped together, and I quickly pictured myself spilling the beans. *"There's this guy at work and he's so not our style, but he's sweet and funny and knows how to make me laugh. He's different from any guy I've ever dated, and fuck me, does he know how to kiss!"*

The idea of what he'd be like in bed made me flush.

"Why are you blushing?" Mom snapped.

I sniffed and pulled my shoulders back. "Nothing, I just…"

Mom sighed, giving me a glum smile before squeezing my arm. "Look, I know you miss Fletcher and it's too late to rectify your mistake, but we will find you someone who will blow him out of the water. He'll be so handsome and rich, Fletcher will be green with jealousy." Her eyes flashed, reminding me of Snow White's stepmother. I could see the shiny, red apple in her hand as she cackled.

I cleared my throat and stepped out of her grasp. "I don't need to make him jealous. It's not like I'll ever be seeing him again."

"Of course you will. He's doing a spring

semester in town for his father's law firm. They arrive next week. Plus, we just received an invite to the wedding."

I blanched. "You're not expecting me to go to that."

"Well, obviously you are. Echelon is designing Evangeline's dress. Everyone who's anyone is going to be there." She spun and started walking to the dining room, her heels sounding like gunshots on the tiles.

"What!" I chased after her.

"Kelly, don't raise your voice like that, it makes you sound immature." Mom tipped her head as she assessed the arrangements on the table.

"I'm not going to that wedding."

"Yes, you are. You're not humiliating this family, or yourself, by being a no-show. You are going to turn up to that wedding looking like a goddess, and Fletcher is going to spend the entire ceremony wishing you were standing in Evangeline's place."

"Mom—"

"I'm not going to argue with you!" she snapped, her eyes nailing me with a look that told me I would lose. "You will walk into that cathedral with your head held high."

I had no rebuttal against her tone or stance. Fighting with my mother was always a waste of breath. It was just easier to sneak out and do my own thing. That's why she never knew about the dancing and why she'd only met Scarlett and Isla briefly at my high school graduation. If she'd known how much time I was spending with those girls, she probably would have pulled me out and shoved me in some snooty private school.

I'd gotten away with it for so long, secretly living out my guilty pleasures behind her back. But it only worked if I did what she wanted, and I had no freaking idea how I would ever wrangle my way out of attending Fletcher's wedding.

The doorbell rang and I backed out of the room, figuring I'd set up position on the far side of the party room until my mother shot me her evil eye and I was forced to circulate.

Mom bustled for the entrance while I shimmied through the opposite archway.

"Hey, Aunt Imogen." A perky voice that always made me grin greeted my mother. Then came the loud kiss. I could picture my mother's face scrunching as her least-favorite niece gave her a kiss on the cheek.

"Hello, Charlene." My mother's reply was demure and polite.

I giggled on the inside, my eyes sparkling as I spotted my favorite cousin loping through the dining room. She glanced at the finger food, and her tongue peeked out the side of her mouth as she stole an appetizer off the tray. She popped it into her mouth then made a face, spitting it into her hand before hiding it in one of the potted plants.

I made a mental note to retrieve it later.

My cousin noticed me laughing at her and flushed, creeping into the spacious room with a giggle. "Hey, sexy thing."

"Hey, Charlie." I wrapped my arms around her and kissed the top of her head.

She stood back and looked me up and down. "Well, you're looking particularly hot tonight."

"Thank you." I dipped my hip and put on a show.

Like Scarlett and Isla did, Charlie had the ability to bring out my crazy. That girl knew how to party. Luckily for her, she was actually allowed to. My mother and her sister were like Egyptian cotton versus hessian. I'm sure Mom wanted to pretend her older sibling didn't exist, but that would only make her look cold and heartless. The media would be all over a headline like that, so whenever it came to a large function, Mom always scribbled down her sister's name at the end of the list. She sent the invite last-minute and crossed her fingers. Bummer for her that her sister lived a far quieter lifestyle and was always available to attend.

"So, how's it going?" I tugged Charlie's straight brown pigtail. She got away with the cute look considering she was eighteen. She'd dressed up for the occasion...well, Charlie dressed-up. She wore a denim miniskirt and black, knee-high boots. Beneath her leather jacket was a fitted, pale pink shirt with sparkling writing on it. Her glossy pink lips matched perfectly, and she was even wearing mascara. It made her big blue eyes look even bigger, making me think of Rapunzel from *Tangled*.

"Yeah, not bad." She brushed the bangs out of her eyes. "Less than six months of high school to go. If I can survive the dreaded SATs, I may come out with my brain still intact." She grimaced and poked out her tongue.

I chuckled. "You'll survive…and then you have all of summer to look forward to, right?"

"Totally." Her eyes lit up. "Nix and I are going camping in Yosemite. I'm hoping to get some really decent shots up there."

Charlie was an amazing photographer. She'd always been fascinated by light and colors. I was surprised she wasn't born with a camera in her hands. I spotted the bag over her shoulder and guessed she had her favored Canon EOS 600D in there. That was the only reason Mom tolerated her at these things. She spent most of the time behind a lens, taking flattering photos Mom could post online, giving her *world's best hostess* status.

I nudged her with my elbow. "So, is he your boyfriend yet?"

Charlie rolled her eyes and looked away from me, but I didn't miss the red tinge on her cheeks. "We're just friends. I mean, he's cute and everything, but I don't want to complicate what we've got. Nixon's the guy you hang out with, not the one you make out with. You know what I mean?"

She didn't believe a word she was saying, and for the first time in my life I understood exactly how she felt.

My brows dipped together. "Well, I guess you better get clicking. I'm going to go grab a drink."

"Coolio." She slid the bag off her shoulder and crouched down to get her camera ready.

My legs felt like driftwood as I walked into the dining area. Waitstaff were wandering the room with drinks, and I snatched a flute off the tray. It was tempting to gulp the lot, but I sipped the champagne the way my mother taught me while I watched high-class people wander the room, smiling plastic smiles at each other and talking nonsense.

My mother's face was radiant as she lavished the attention. My father stood beside her, his hand on her lower back as they played the role of loving couple. I remembered Marcus's hand on my lower back as he led me into Disneyland, trying to introduce me to his world.

I'd loved it.

I couldn't imagine him feeling the same way about mine.

He didn't belong beside me, so why did I want him there?

TWENTY-SEVEN

MARCUS

I couldn't stop thinking about Kelly. She'd felt so damn good in my arms—the way her body moved against mine as she danced, the sound of her laughter as I spun her, the wet heat of her tongue…

"Marcus, it's your turn." My kid sister, Felicity, slapped me on the back of the head. She was five years younger than me, but we became close when Griffin moved to Seattle. I stayed at home while I was studying at USC, and we hung out a lot.

"Fliss," Mom warned. "Stop beating on your brother."

"He can handle it." She winked at me. "I'm just trying to knock those fairies out of his head."

I gave her a dry glare, which she giggled at. The sound reminded me of Kelly. I wrinkled my nose and reached for the dice.

"You are pretty distracted today." Dad smirked. "You're not in love or anything, are you?"

My whole family leaned forward to study me. Thank God Griffin wasn't there. I snatched the Coke-bottle playing piece and thumped it around the board. I landed on Spotify.

"Oh, that's me." Fliss jumped in her seat. She always got excited when we played Monopoly Empire, because she always frickin' won. "That'll be five hundred thousand, please." Her smile was toothy, and if I didn't love her so much, I'd find it damn irritating.

I handed over the money and slumped back in my seat.

"Drinks break." Dad slapped the table with both his hands and stood. "Scruff, can you help me, please?"

I stood from the table and followed him into the well-lit kitchen. Sun sparkled off the stainless steel sink. I squinted and looked to my dad as he opened the fridge and pulled out the pineapple juice. I collected four glasses from the cupboard above the counter.

"So, what's got you so quiet today?"

"Nothing." I shrugged, placing the glasses down beside my dad.

He snickered. "Liar."

I rested my butt on the edge of the counter and crossed my arms with a sigh. "Do you remember Kelly DeMarco?"

Dad stopped pouring to look at me. "She's a hard girl to forget. Particularly for you."

"Yeah." I winced and rubbed my eyes. "She works for me now."

The juice carton wobbled in Dad's hand, and he ended up spilling a great blob over the edge of the glass. It pooled on the counter and started dribbling down to the floor. I snatched a cloth and wiped it up.

"Since when?" Dad stared down at me as I crouched on the floor and cleaned.

"Since…November."

"That's nearly three months, why didn't you tell us?"

I stood and rinsed out the cloth, refusing to make eye contact. "I don't like to talk work when I'm hanging out here."

"Excuses, excuses," Dad muttered. "The way you were gone for her, I thought you'd be tripping over yourself to tell us."

"I didn't want to pin my hopes on anything."

Dad's smile was sad when I turned to face him. "Probably for the best, I suppose. She wasn't really into you in high school."

"Thanks for the honesty," I scoffed and crossed my arms again.

"I love you, Scruff. Of course I'm going to be honest with you." He patted my shoulder. "Now, you be honest with me."

I swallowed. "I took her out on a date...to Disneyland."

Dad's face lit like a Christmas tree. "Smart move." He held up his fist and I pounded it. "She must have loved that."

"She did...eventually." I grinned. "Thing is, I think she might like me, but..."

"Who wouldn't?" Dad shrugged.

I rolled my eyes. My parents were proof that love was blind.

"She kissed me last night and it was..." I shook my head, feeling the heat rise as I remembered it.

Dad laughed and waggled his eyebrows.

"I screwed it up." I cringed. "I just...I want more. I want...real, and when she asked to come back to my place, I felt like it was too good to be true. And then I started thinking that maybe she didn't mean it, so I told her I wasn't after a one-night stand."

"I take it from the look on your face that it didn't go down too well."

I pinched the bridge of my nose. "I'm such a freaking idiot."

"You know what?" Dad's hand landed on my shoulder, and he gave it a firm squeeze. "I'm proud of you."

"You're always proud of me," I muttered.

"No, listen. You really care about this girl, and you showed her by not taking advantage. Not many guys would do that."

"You didn't see her face, Dad. I totally humiliated her and then gave her the perfect chance to show me just how unserious she is about me. She doesn't want more! I was a night out, that's it!"

"You have to tell her the truth."

I let out a breathy laugh. "I did, and then missed out on taking her to bed."

Dad tipped his head and pierced me with a stern glare. "If you'd had sex with her and then she'd scurried out of your house all shame-faced, how do you think you'd be feeling right now?"

I opened my mouth, but he pointed at me and cut off my reply.

"Don't you dare say satisfied, because you know that's a lie. She's more than just a body to you, she always has been. Have you ever told her that?"

"I..." I tutted and sighed. "I tried and I scared her off. I just have to let her go."

"No, you need to trust yourself and call her on her bullshit. You took her to freaking Disneyland and she enjoyed it. The girl is obviously in denial."

"She's not..."

Dad pointed at me. "Don't you wimp out on this. You think you would have gotten the job at Torrence Records if you hadn't walked in there with a confident swagger and shown them what you're really capable of? You are the man, and you have proved yourself time and time again. Nothing beats you, Marcus. Don't shy away from this Kelly thing. Go for it. Be strong. Be courageous." Dad put on his macho voice and started flexing his muscles.

"Okay." I patted his shoulder.

He bared his teeth and growled.

I winced. "You can stop doing that now."

In true Grant Chapman style, he kept going, making it impossible not to crack a smile. I did my best to ignore him and carried the drinks back to the family room, but he followed me in there, chanting, "You da man. You da man."

Mom beamed and laughed at her silly husband while Fliss and I bulged our eyes at each other. Yes, Dad was embarrassing, but when I took my seat and spotted the look on Mom's face, I got why he did it. He was right—making your lady laugh was a beautiful thing.

I'd made Kelly laugh by being honest, and I wanted to make her do it again…and again…and again. I just needed to figure out how to get her to trust me.

TWENTY-EIGHT

KELLY

Monday morning came way too quickly. I shuffled into the elevator and rode to the exec floor, praying Marcus would be out of the office for the day.

He wasn't.

I spotted him as I walked to my desk. He caught my eye, and I couldn't look away from his soft smile. I responded with an icy glare that I hoped would put him off.

It didn't.

He called me into his office five seconds after I placed my bag on the floor. Snatching the iPad out of my drawer, I strutted into his office and was all business.

"What do you need?" I tapped the screen and pulled up my notes page. My gaze was glued to the device in my hand, and I wasn't budging it. I didn't want to notice the way his mussed hair looked particularly cute or the way his hazel gaze caressed my face like a soft kiss.

"I just want to go through our week. I'm heading out with Chaos next Thursday and I'll be gone for a week, maybe a little longer, so I want to make sure you have everything you need to handle Caris and Dion while I'm away. We also have some last-minute tour plans to finalize. I need the schedule for Vegas locked down before we leave. We've got eight working days to make this perfect."

"Okay." I nodded, doing that head-bobbing thing I do when I'm nervous. I kept it up the entire time he was talking, taking notes and bob-bob-bobbing.

"And, I think that's pretty much it."

"Okay." I spun on my heel and made for the door, but his soft call stopped me. "Kelly." He sighed my name like it smelled sweet and tasted delicious.

I was tempted to keep walking, but my body had other ideas, spinning toward the sound, hungry for another taste of it.

Our gazes locked across the room, and I couldn't tear my eyes from his sweet expression.

"I'm sorry," he murmured. "I didn't mean to

embarrass you…or hurt you the other night. I just…" He smiled. "You're so amazing, you know? You, on the dance floor and your smile and just…when you let yourself go, you shine. I can't even explain how intoxicating you are. There are no words sufficient in the English language to describe the effect you have on me."

I swallowed, my heart doing this weird thrumming thing.

"We have fun together. We make each other laugh, and being with you when you're not trying to impress anybody is the best thing ever. I love it. I love spending time with you. And kissing you was like…whoa, and then you offer me this chance and damn, I wanted to take it. I wanted you so bad on Friday night." His voice became soft and croaky, his brows dipping with remorse, regret maybe, but the look faded and was replaced with this confident beam that was, well, sexy.

"Thing is, Kel, as much as I wanted you, I want an *us* more. I don't want one night, I want every night and then every morning."

I scoffed and looked away from him, trying to hide the glistening tears in my eyes. "You're talking like you're in love with me."

"Maybe I am."

"You're not!" I snapped, terrified by the very idea. "I'm not right for you. I don't want to be in love with you," I whispered the last three words. "It's too hard and complicated and it wouldn't work. Don't waste your time, Marcus. You did the right thing the other night, okay? I'm…I'm grateful." I shot out of the door before he could say anything else to me. I didn't want him to see how rattled I was.

In love with Marcus Chapman. Honestly! That could never happen.

I'd been in love once, and I didn't fancy going through that again. Besides, it was absurd. Marcus wasn't my type.

I thumped into my chair and yanked it into position.

"Good morning." Marcia gave me a puzzled grin.

I nodded at her, turning on my computer and waiting for it to come to life. I opened my mail and clicked on my new messages without even thinking. "She's Not Afraid" by One Direction blasted out of my speakers. I secretly loved the band and recognized the song before the lyrics even kicked in.

I scrambled for the speakers and knocked my coffee mug over. I hadn't seen Marcia bring me a fresh cup.

"Damn it!" I pulled tissues free of the box and began mopping it up while the music played loudly through the reception area. Marcia started giggling, which didn't help because all I could hear was the song.

Marcus's morning selection was abundantly clear, and I wasn't about to let him get away with it. Standing tall, I slammed my finger on the space bar to shut the song up before straightening my skirt and storming back into Marcus's office.

TWENTY-NINE

MARCUS

Kelly barreled through the door, not even bothering to knock. Her flushed cheeks and wild eyes made my crotch stir. She looked ready to tear shreds off me, and I couldn't help a nervous chuckle.

"You think this is funny?" She stopped at my desk, her chest heaving. "If you're going to send me shit like that, then I'm not going to open any more of your emails."

"Kelly," I chided. "It was just the morning song."

She bristled, her nostrils flaring slightly. "May I

suggest you be a little more thoughtful with your selection next time."

The way she clipped her words when she talked was kinda cute. I snickered. "I just chose upbeat, cheerful—"

"Oh, please! I know what you're trying to imply. You think I'm that kind of girl," she snapped. "Afraid of falling in love."

I took a slow breath and looked at her. "Well, you are."

Her mouth fell open with an incredulous frown. "You're not supposed to tell me that. Honestly, no wonder Allison dumped you. You don't know anything about women."

It was a low blow, and a big fat lie. Allison hadn't dumped me, just like I hadn't dumped her. The split had been mutual and amicable, something I guessed Kelly knew nothing about. She'd been wounded. Her expression screamed pain, and the only thing to dampen that look was a brief flash of remorse. She pulled her expression into line and swallowed, pressing her lips against the apology she owed me.

I wasn't about to call her on it. Instead, I picked up my pen and tapped it on my desk.

"I know I'm not the suave, sophisticated guy you're used to, but I do know a thing or two about women. For instance, I *know* they need to be treated with respect, and respect without honesty is worthless. So yeah, I am going to call you on your bullshit. You are afraid. You're petrified of falling in love. Now, you might not be ready to tell me why, but I want to prove to you that love doesn't have to be treacherous. Love is supposed to make you happy, make you smile and laugh...make you feel safe."

My words were doing something to her. She went really quiet as I spoke, her arms dropping to her sides as she backed away from my desk. Her head was shaking like she didn't want to buy into what I was saying.

Her finger trembled when she raised it at me. "You don't want to say that to me."

"Yeah, I'm pretty sure I do."

"No. You don't know me, Marcus! You don't know what I'm really like. I was horrible to you in high school. I'm a mean cow!"

I could see what she was trying to do...just like she had on Friday night, finding some way to put me off. It wasn't going to work.

I smiled. "Beef's my favorite kind of meat."

The corners of her mouth curled up, but she bit her lips together to stop the smile forming. Blinking rapidly, she looked to the floor and tried again. "I yell. I curse like a sailor when I'm really mad."

"One of my best friends in college had Tourette's, so I think I'll be okay."

She frowned, her perfect features wrinkling. "I...I'm cold, like an ice queen." Her eyelids fluttered when she said the words, like they were somehow painful.

I spun the pen in my hand and cocked my head to the side. "I don't think that's actually true, but I'll wear my winter jacket...just in case." A slow, hopeful smile spread over my lips.

The scowl she was wearing deepened, the look in her eyes more desperate. Finally, she let out a loud huff and rattled off a string of mumbled curses before placing her hands on her hips and barking, "Dammit, are you free tonight?"

A smile bloomed across my face, making it hard to say anything.

I nodded.

Her lips twitched and she looked to the ceiling. "Okay, well, maybe we could do a movie or something."

"Sounds good." The triumph pulsing through me was hard to hide, so I didn't bother. I let out a giddy chortle.

"Shut up." She snickered. "What time are you going to pick me up?"

"Hey, you invited me out. I think it's only fair that you collect me."

Her nose wrinkled. "You know, for a gentleman, you're really not that sophisticated."

"Maybe that's one of the reasons why you like me so much." I shrugged. Her eyes flashed with chagrin, and her lips formed a thoughtful pout like she was once again battling it out on the inside. I started worrying I'd put my foot in it again and quickly spoke before she could renege on her offer. "Seven works for me." I ripped off the corner of my daily planner page and scribbled down my address.

She tentatively retraced her steps and snatched the paper from my hand. "Seven it is then."

"What should I wear?" I tipped my head with a playful smirk.

She rolled her eyes and headed for the door. "Wear whatever the hell you want."

I laughed as the door flicked open and she disappeared through it. My heart was skipping a beat as I leaned back in my chair and grinned up at the ceiling.

A third date with the girl of my dreams.

I had no idea what it held. All I knew was that the hours couldn't tick by fast enough.

THIRTY

KELLY

Sweating fingers.

It was my best indicator that I was stupidly nervous walking up Marcus's front path. My nude pumps clicked on the concrete as I edged toward the front door. Marcia had told me he owned the little bungalow. It was cute and simple—a Spanish-style box with slate roofing and flax bushes lining the edge. I walked through the rounded archway and held my breath as I rang the doorbell.

I didn't know why I'd agreed to another date. It was insanity. But Marcus had been so incredibly adorable with his argument that I found myself arranging the date before I even knew what I was doing.

He'd wear his winter coat.

I shook my head with a soft chuckle before running a hand down my navy skinny jeans. They were rolled at the bottom to show off my skinny ankles, and I'd matched them with a sleeveless, purple top that hugged my middle. It was cool enough to need a jacket, so I wore my brown fitted leather and finished off the ensemble with dangly, round earrings that had an Aztec look about them.

I left the apartment feeling sexy and confident. I arrived at Marcus's door with sweaty fingers and rattling innards. What the hell was my problem?

"Maybe it's because this is the worst idea ever," I muttered.

The door opened to reveal Marcus decked out in full clown suit—red and white stripy pants, a bright yellow vest, and rainbow wig. He was even wearing a red nose that I'm sure if I squeezed would make a loud, honking sound.

I placed my hands on my hips and narrowed my eyes at him.

He smiled. "You ready to go?"

He made a move to step out the door, but I stopped him with a hand to his chest. "What are you wearing?"

"You told me to wear whatever the hell I wanted." He grinned.

"No." I shook my head.

His clown nose drooped as he pulled his lips into a sad pout. "No?"

"No, you look ridiculous." I started to laugh but cut the sound short with a frown. "You are not leaving the house like that. Or should I say, we will not be seen in public together if you leave the house like that."

"Aw, come on. It's funny. People will laugh."

"I'm not interested in making people laugh." My voice started to tremble as giggles got the better of me. I dipped my head and covered my mouth, determined not to snort like I had in the restaurant.

Marcus started to chuckle—a deep, sexy sound that I felt in my core.

"Oh, all right. Come in, I'll go change."

"Thank you." I followed him inside, letting the laughter break free as he did a few dance moves then bopped out of the room. "Such a clown," I murmured, my cheeks still blazing.

Placing my Fendi handbag on the side table, I scanned the living room. It was a simple, neat space filled with a mishmash of what looked to be secondhand furniture. The coffee table had a chip in the corner and the tartan couch was covered with a burnt-orange throw rug. The carpet looked new. I dug the point of my shoes into it then jumped when I spotted a flash of movement. It scurried past me then darted under the sofa.

"What the…"

A scratch from the doorway made me yelp, and that was when I spotted another little creature—a ginger cat with curious blue eyes. I pointed at the sofa.

"Were you just…?" My question was answered

when a tabby cat darted into view, jumping up and playfully knocking into the ginger cat.

"Flash!" Marcus clicked his fingers. "Leave your sister alone."

The cat ignored the command and bumped into the ginger cat again, until she squawked and swiped at his face. She knocked him down, and they started a quick tussle that I shied away from.

"Pumpkin, stop." Marcus appeared in the doorway. He was wearing faded blue jeans and a checkered shirt that still needed buttoning. I glanced away from his firm chest as he pried the two cats away from each other. "They've been play-fighting a lot lately." He shook his head then turned back to his cats. "Which is all well and good until someone gets hurt, right?"

He lifted them into his arms and walked toward me, brushing his nose through the top of Pumpkin's head. She purred.

"So, these are my kids." He grinned. "Pumpkin has just turned six months old, and Flash will be seven months next week."

I tinkled my fingers at them. "Hey, guys." Then Marcus freaked me out by passing me the orange one. "Uh."

"It's okay, she's the calm one." He winked.

I took her in my arms, and she squirmed for only a moment then settled in with what sounded like a happy cat sigh. I tentatively stroked her head as I walked to the couch and perched on the edge.

Marcus snickered. "You nervous?"

I glanced away from his assessing gaze.

"I just…" I shrugged. "I'm not used to animals. My mom, she…" I shook my head, not wanting to bring her into Marcus's house. "I didn't figure you for a pet man."

"Yeah, me, neither." Marcus dropped a wriggling Flash to the floor. He darted off. "My sister volunteers at an animal shelter on the weekends. I went to pick her up one time and these two little guys were there. They needed a home, and I couldn't resist."

The gooey look in his eyes gave away what a softie he was.

"They're good company, and they've become little buddies. I like having them around." He started buttoning his shirt and I glanced down at Pumpkin. She was purring in my lap, making a rhythmic, soothing sound.

"So, what movie do you want to go to?"

I glanced up. His shirt was buttoned, and he looked pretty damn good in the casual ensemble. I gazed back down at the cat on my knee and then shrugged. "Do you just want to stay here? We could order takeout or something."

"Okay." He grinned. "I'll grab the phone. Can I get you a drink while I'm in the kitchen? I've got beer or pineapple juice."

"Just water will be fine, thanks." I didn't feel like drinking, which was weird for me, but I wanted to keep my wits about me. The idea of a relaxed, casual night with Marcus and two cats for company was oddly appealing, and that freaked me out. I kicked off my heels and gently shrugged out of my jacket, laying it neatly on the spare chair before snuggling onto the sofa.

I tucked my feet beneath me and resettled Pumpkin on my lap. She purred as I ran my fingers through her soft fur. Her rhythmic vibrations made me smile.

Marcus's place was so different from my apartment. It was cozy and sweet. Mine was meticulous and...cold. I studied the photos on the walls and the framed family shots cluttering up the bookshelf. There was a messy order to the place...so Marcus.

He set a water bottle on the coffee table then ran his thumb over the phone. "You like sushi?"

"I love sushi." My eyes popped wide. "You eat sushi?"

He punched in some numbers and lifted the phone to his ear, throwing me a confused frown. "Why wouldn't I eat sushi?"

I shrugged, unsure why I'd made that judgment. I'd always pictured him as a pizza and soda kind of guy. That was what he'd eaten at Disneyland.

He placed the order, rattling off a list of goodies that all sounded divine, before placing the phone on the bookshelf and switching on some music.

"Troublemaker" by Olly Murs started playing.

I grinned. "I love this song."

Marcus flopped onto the couch beside me and rested his foot on the coffee table. "Yeah? It always makes me think of you."

I scowled at him and he just laughed. "You must know how hard I've been trying. We're talking years of pining here. Even though I dated Allison right through college, you were always in the back of my mind. Always."

My throat was thick and gummy when I tried to swallow. "I don't understand it. I've never given you reason to like me."

"You didn't need to. One look and I was gone." His expression was so sweet I wanted to kiss him again.

I pulled away from the idea and wrinkled my nose at him. "Yeah, I get it. I'm pretty."

"No, it's more than that." He shuffled to face me. "I didn't know you that well in high school, but I used to watch you all the time."

"Stalker," I murmured then winked at him.

He groaned. "Oh man, probably! I swear I never came to your house, though, okay?"

I laughed.

"But we have something, Kel. I can feel it." He took a swig of beer and nestled into the sofa cushions. "We like the same kind of music. There's a good start."

"How do you know what music I like?"

"Oh please, you are always singing and dancing to the songs I send you each morning." I pointed at her. "Admit it, you love poppy dance music."

I flushed and dipped my head with a rueful grin.

"See." He nudged me with his elbow. "We're a match made in Heaven."

I rolled my eyes at his cheesy line but didn't refute it. Being with him, in the little bungalow in

Culver City, felt so easy and comfortable.

Marcus started chatting about work for a few minutes, but it quickly progressed into other things. Takeout arrived in a flash, and we laughed our way through the sushi dinner, playing a game of "What would you do if..." Some of Marcus's scenarios were hilarious. I'd giggle and he'd go on to elaborate with stories from his childhood. The antics he'd gotten up to with his brother had me in stitches. My stomach was actually hurting by the end of the meal.

I laid my plate on the coffee table and giggled again. Uncontrollable twitches kept assaulting my belly, and a fresh wave of laughter would start. It was so embarrassing, but it also felt damn good. Scarlett and Isla were the only ones who'd ever made me laugh that way before, and we hadn't had a chance to get that silly since high school. College had hardly been a hotbed of humor.

Thoughts of Fletcher's withering look and my mother's disapproving scowl sobered me up. I cleared my throat and leaned back into the cushions, dabbing my lips with a paper napkin.

"You okay?" Marcus washed down his food with the last of his beer.

I nodded. "This is...nice."

"Nice?" He handed me the glass of pineapple juice I'd asked for mid-meal. "Come on, you can do better than that, can't ya?"

I took the glass and had a few sips before placing it down and gazing across the room at Pumpkin and Flash. They were snuggled up in their little bed, oblivious to the world. They looked so happy and content. How was it possible to envy cats?

"It's different," I whispered. "It's light, it's fun, it's…"

"What happened to you in college?"

His soft question caught me off guard. I flinched in his direction, my eyes large, my breaths punchy. I gripped my hands together and swallowed, wondering how quickly I could grab my jacket and bolt from the room.

"Hey, it's okay." Marcus brushed the backs of his fingers down my arm. "You're not ready. That's all right."

I flashed him a glance and felt the effects of his sweet smile.

He tipped his head to look at me. "Do you miss business studies?"

"No." I answered way too fast.

His eyebrows rose, and he gave me a curious smile.

My chest deflated with a sigh. "I was only taking it because my father wanted me to. I'm the heiress to the Echelon Fashion empire, and I need to be able to run the business. My mother determined for me to marry someone who can help expand the company. I need to understand enough so that we can work together and make the empire even bigger." I flicked my hand in the air and let out a cynical laugh. "Because you think small and insignificant when you say the word *empire*, right?"

Marcus didn't respond to the way I spat out my

question. His gaze was kind and truth-inducing, so I foolishly kept going.

"The thing is, it doesn't matter what I learn. At the end of the day, I'm there for show. When I'm forced to take over, there'll be a room full of business-savvy executives who will do all the work for me. My only role is to make the company look good. That's it." I shrugged. "That's all I'm ever good for. I'm an ornament." I didn't realize I was snapping out the words so harshly until the following silence engulfed me.

Marcus's compassionate stare drilled into me and tears smarted. I blinked and looked away from him.

"That's why I never got serious with anyone in high school, because I thought they only wanted me for my body and my money. I was right, too. They…" I shook my head. "I was popular because of who I represented, not who I really was."

Marcus didn't say anything, just keep looking at me like he already understood and I was the one who was late to catch up with the news. It compelled me to keep talking. The words tumbled out in a shaky torrent of realization.

"In college, I found the perfect guy. I was a freshman and he was a junior and…he was smart and handsome. He came from a wealthy family, so I knew he wasn't after my money. He seemed to really like me, you know? And my mother approved, of course. She was already picking out wedding dresses." Brittle laughter shot out of me. It was a hard, ugly sound that I quickly gulped back.

"I tried to be everything they both wanted me to be, but..." I shrugged. "I wasn't enough. He chose someone else. A girl who could give him more than just a pretty face. I look good on someone's arm, but that's it. I don't know how to be more than an ornament."

Tears crept out the corner of my eyes. I slashed them away, mortified that I was crying. Fletcher didn't deserve my tears, and I sure as hell didn't want Marcus to see them.

The cushions beneath me dipped as he scrambled to my side. His arm rested against the back of the sofa while he lightly took my face, making me look at him.

He drank me in, searching my gaze like he was pleading for me to believe him.

"You are so much more than that. You always have been."

I let out a watery breath then pressed my trembling lips together.

"I see you, Kelly...and I love you."

I couldn't breathe. The world stopped moving, and all I could see was Marcus's face. His eyes shone with a look only he had ever given me. It had a lot more impact up close.

The piano riff for "Beneath Your Beautiful" started softly in the background. Marcus grinned, no doubt thanking the music gods for their perfect timing. I closed my eyes and listened to the words, imagining Marcus singing them to me. Tears trickled down my cheeks. He gently brushed them away, and I opened my eyes and looked at him.

Gripping the front of his shirt, I closed the space between us. His lips were pliant, moving softly against mine until he opened his mouth. I responded in kind, relishing the way his tongue curled around mine, feeling safe and warm. Our hot breaths swirled together and the rattling inside of me shifted to a mounting desire that scared me.

I pulled back, out of breath and hyper-aware of the intense electricity sparking between us.

"You have to trust me," Marcus whispered. "I'm not going to hurt you. All I want to do is love you...and make you happy."

My heart started thrumming the way it had in his office that morning. That look was in his eyes again. It wasn't hungry or leering, or wanting anything from me. It was an open invitation that awakened a yearning. Brushing my teeth over my lower lip, I leaned away from him and lifted the bottom of my shirt, slowly raising it over my head before laying it down next to my jacket.

Marcus hadn't expected the move and sat back with wide eyes. His lips parted as he gazed at me with a stunned look of awe.

He tried to say something but couldn't form any words. His eyes kept drifting from my face and down to my lacy bra and naked torso. His gaze was once again like a soft kiss, making me feel warm and safe. I wanted to wrap him around me like a cozy blanket.

The music continued to flow, inspiring me to reach for his hand and lift it to cup my breast. A short puff shot out of him as he squeezed and rubbed his thumb over the lacy fabric. My nipple hardened beneath his touch, my body and brain battling it out as I tried to ignore my nerves and let Marcus see beneath the surface.

I never liked to be visibly naked in front of Fletcher. I felt like if he spotted a blemish, he somehow wouldn't want me anymore. We always had sex in the dark, with the curtains drawn and the lights off. I didn't even like candles.

But it felt different with Marcus. I wanted him to see me. I wanted that sparkle in his eye caressing me and making me feel beautiful.

His fingers trailed up my body and caressed my bare shoulder, before gliding along my collarbone. He leaned forward and licked my skin then pressed his mouth against the base of my neck, lightly sucking while my senses spiraled into new territory. His firm hand wove around my back, running up my spine before expertly unclasping my bra.

I gasped as it popped open and fell off my body.

"You have to trust me," Marcus whispered again.

"I do," I squeaked.

He leaned back and smiled. It was a knowing one that told me he could see through my trepidation.

"We don't have to do this."

"Yes, we do," I whispered, lurching forward and taking his mouth like a hungry lioness. He met my force, countering my urgent need to control the situation. His deft tongue teased and tempted mine before pulling back and skimming my lower lip.

Desire, hunger, fear battled for top position as he held me back, taking in my expression with a tender smile.

"Should we take this to the bedroom?" My voice was a shaky mess.

Marcus's lips rose in a half-smile. Running his fingers up my arm, he unhooked my hands from around his neck and threaded his fingers through mine.

He pulled me off the couch and lifted me into his arms, carrying me like a princess down the short corridor to a dimly lit bedroom. A Japanese-style queen bed dominated the center of the room, illuminated by the soft glow of a box lamp on the bedside table.

He set me down on the edge of the bed and I stood, leaning toward the lamp, ready to snap it off and get things started. But Marcus stopped me. His firm fingers trailed down my arm and wrapped around my wrist, pulling my hand away from the switch.

"I want to see you," he murmured in my ear.

A puff of nervous energy shot out of my mouth. During sex? He wanted to watch me? I hadn't minded him looking before, but when things really got down to business, I...

I swallowed and, for some weird reason, almost felt like crying. I was a wreck. I hadn't even felt this scared doing it with Fletcher the first time. It was like I was losing my virginity all over again...and maybe I was.

Fletcher had taken my body, but I'd never given anyone my soul.

I had a feeling Marcus would know just how to claim it.

THIRTY-ONE

MARCUS

I slid my hand back up Kelly's arm, intrigued by the tense set of her muscles. I probably should have let her switch the light off, but I needed to see her eyes, to know how far she really wanted me to go.

"It's okay," I whispered against her skin before gliding my fingers up her quivering stomach and cupping her breasts. They fit into my hands perfectly—like they'd been made just for me.

I rubbed her nipples and she leaned her head back against my shoulder. I kissed the base of her neck, massaging her breasts until she let out a soft whimper. Heat was rushing to my crotch at lightning speed. My dick strained against my pants, yelling at me to get on with it. But I wasn't in a hurry. It was Kelly DeMarco. You didn't rush with a girl like that—you savored every freaking second of it.

Kelly pushed back against me and felt my erection. She stiffened and leaned away from me, spinning around to face me. She hid her nerves behind a seductive smile, sitting on the edge of the bed and brushing her lower lip with her teeth.

I stepped between her legs, holding her face and kissing her slowly. She tasted like sweet pineapple juice. I ran my tongue along her lips before dipping in for another taste. She gripped my shirt and started tugging on it. I stepped back with a chuckle and she helped me unbutton it, slipping it off my shoulders and running her hands over my torso before grazing the tuft of hair on my chest. Goosebumps rippled over my skin, and her lips quirked with a smile.

She skimmed her manicured nail over my belly then tucked it into my boxers. My dick strained to reach her, desperate for a little play. Kelly did him a favor and unbuttoned my fly, pulling the denim wide so I could have a little breathing space. With her teeth still nibbling her lip, she pulled my pants south until I stood before her stark naked. Her eyes drank me in, studying the contours of my body. Her fingers traced the V-shaped line running down from my hips before finally reaching my gaze.

I tipped my lips at her and she smiled, leaning back on the bed and slowly unbuttoning her own pants. I helped her wriggle out of them, running my hands up her smooth thighs and kissing her belly once her jeans were heaped on the floor.

I dug my nose into her belly button and she giggled, but it was a nervous, short sound.

"Relax," I murmured, gliding my tongue up her body and between her breasts.

She lightly tugged the back of my hair so I'd be forced to look at her.

"Do you have protection?" she whispered, her cheeks flushing pink.

"Of course I do." I smiled. "But why the hurry?"

Her eyes flashed with uncertainty as I skimmed my fingers up her inner thigh and explored the exquisite mystery between her legs.

She gasped. "What are you doing?" Her question came out breathy and panicked yet was tempered with an underlying desire that I didn't miss.

"I'm touching you." I rotated my fingers then kissed the dimple on her chin.

Her soft, sweet pants were broken by an unchecked moan. I rose up on my elbow to look her in the eye but didn't stop stroking her.

Her hooded gaze shimmered with wonderment.

"Have you never been touched like this before?"

She shook her head, tipping it back with another moan as I teased her sweet spot. A smile lit my lips. I pressed it against her neck then trailed my tongue down to her nipple, sucking it lightly until she started moaning again.

"What are you doing to me?" She fisted my hair

and writhed, her stiff legs giving way as I switched position and pushed my fingers inside her. She was a hot, slippery mess, her inner walls vibrating as I dove a little deeper.

Her moaning shifted to gasps of pleasure, her chest heaving with short, high pants.

"Marcus," she cried out my name. "Oh, my…" A groan of desire rocketed out of her mouth as an orgasm rippled through her body. She arched her back, her heels digging into the mattress as she gripped the covers. I kept going, fondling her delicate center until I was sure she was completely sated.

My desire was in the red as I watched her sink back to the mattress. I throbbed for her, aching to get inside and feel that silky sweetness encase me.

Her chest still heaved like she'd run a marathon, and she dug her fingers into my arm. "What are you waiting for?"

"I just wanted to make sure you were ready."

Her eyes rounded. "I'm ready," she puffed. "I'm…that was…"

I rested my hand on her belly to quiet her. "It's only a taste of what you deserve, Kelly."

Her gaze met mine, a fine sheen turning it to a glossy, powder-blue sky. "I want you to show me more."

I smiled and ran my knuckles down her torso before sitting up and reaching for a condom. I quickly wrapped myself and nestled between her legs. My tip touched the hot edge of her sweetness, and it was like trying to hold back a charging stallion. I'd wanted this for so long, but this first time wasn't about me. I had to show Kelly what it could be like, what it was *supposed* to be like.

Running my hand down her leg, I lifted her under the knee and slowly sank into her. Damn, she felt good. Her core clamped around me, drawing me in and begging me to start thrusting. Kelly's hot breath skimmed my cheek as she hooked her leg over my butt and whimpered, "You better start moving."

I pressed my nose into her shoulder and snickered. "I just want to savor it."

"It's like some kind of sweet torture." She wriggled beneath me, but I shifted my hips and pinned her to the bed.

It was taking every ounce of control I had not to start charging.

She scowled at me, her perfect nose wrinkling as she slapped my ass. I flinched from the sting, and she tipped her head back and groaned. With a deep laugh, I captured her wrists and held them above her head. A slight flash of uncertainty flickered across her face again. I smiled at her, mouthing the words "trust me" before giving in and surrendering control to my pulsing desire.

I started moving, creating a tantalizing rhythm that only grew faster as she lifted her other leg and wrapped it around my waist. I shifted my weight, digging my elbows into the mattress but not relinquishing my hold on her arms. Her sweet groans only grew louder as I penetrated harder...faster, galloping to the edge of sanity as the only thing to become real was the feel of Kelly wrapped around me.

I shifted even deeper, thrusting until she cried out, and I exploded inside her. I groaned and let go of her wrists, pushing myself up and thrusting into her one last time. I held myself there, puffing and vibrating until my eyes regained the ability to see.

My arms gave out and I slumped on top of her, brushing my lips across her cheek as she heaved beneath me. I pressed my nose into the side of her face, my lashes tickling her skin when I blinked.

She snickered and shuffled out from beneath me, rolling onto her side and giving me a dreamy smile.

"Thank you," I whispered, tucking a lock of hair behind her ear before drawing circles around her earrings.

"For what?" She smiled. "I didn't do anything."

I grinned and dragged her across the bed so as much of our skin was touching as possible. "You did everything." I kissed her nose. "You trusted me."

THIRTY-TWO

KELLY

Okay, so orgasms are freaking amazing.

A grin curved my lips. I couldn't believe I'd gone so long without one. My mother had always told me that proper ladies didn't touch themselves. She'd made it sound like the dirtiest thing on the planet, so I'd never experimented with it. Scarlett and Isla had sometimes joked and shared stories about their experiences with their lovers, but I'd just laughed along with them, too embarrassed to admit I had no idea what they were talking about.

Fletcher had never touched me the way Marcus had. He'd kissed my breasts sometimes, but only briefly. As soon as my legs were spread, he was in there getting things done. Sex with him had been short and sweet. We undressed then I would lay on the bed and let him have his way. He'd tried to coax me into rolling over or sitting on top of him, but I'd always shied away from it. The idea of it made me feel too open and exposed. I liked him covering me, hiding me from the world. It was probably why he'd given up on us and started banging Evangeline. She did it from behind. I'd seen proof.

A beautiful song wafted through to the bedroom from the living area. We'd never turned off the music, and I liked hearing it. "This Is What It Takes" floated in the air like a lullaby, filling me with all kinds of emotions I wasn't prepared for. I gazed at Marcus through the darkness. It had been a few hours since our interlude, and my body was only just starting to simmer down. I thought I'd never stop buzzing. That had been unreal. Marcus didn't know it, but I'd been looking right at him when he came inside me. His muscles had been taut and sexy as he held himself above me, filling me with a pulsing pressure that had sizzled every nerve in my body.

He'd stroked me and teased me until I'd fallen apart, shouting his name like I was on some movie set filming a love scene. It was ridiculous. I'd never even whimpered during sex before. I was the silent partner, there to pleasure, not...

I traced the curves of Marcus's face as he slept beside me, running a finger along a faint scar beneath his eye. How was it possible that a man who wasn't even my type was turning into the most perfect human I'd ever met?

He'd unlocked something within me, made me feel like I was all that mattered. I didn't have to prove myself to him or do anything to win his affection. He saw me, and he loved me.

The thought made my insides spasm and I flinched away from him, wondering if I should sneak home. I could leave him a note, thanking him for a great evening.

I could...

Marcus's hand clamped onto my hip, pulling me back toward him. "Where you going?" he mumbled.

"Just thinking I should head home," I whispered.

His eyes popped open. I could see them twinkling in the soft moonlight. I ran my thumb across his lips and he whispered, "Stay."

"I shouldn't."

"Why?"

"Because you're not my boyfriend."

"I could be." He grinned, his white teeth flashing in the darkness. "Please, let me be."

My heart wriggled in my chest, squeezing tight before taking off like a sprinter. "You're not like the guys I'm used to."

"Perfect." He smiled. "The guys before me have all been dicks. I'll treat you right, Kelly. I won't hurt you. I'll respect you and love you any way you want me to." He cupped the side of my face, caressing my cheekbone. "I'd choose you every time. You're the only girl I've ever wanted."

Tears built on my lashes without my say-so. I blinked and they spilled down my face. Marcus shifted onto his back, pulling my arm until I was nestled against his chest. He brushed my hair back and kissed my forehead, murmuring, "Stay. Be my girl."

I closed my eyes and cried against his chest—slow, soft tears that felt like comfort rather than pain. Marcus's arm wrapped around my back, and he held me tight until my soft sniffles changed to even breaths of sleep.

THIRTY-THREE

MARCUS

I didn't want to leave.

It was Thursday afternoon, and I was hitting the road with Chaos in less than an hour. A month ago, I would have been pumped to get the out-of-state tour started. But things had changed.

I grinned...again. The smile on my face came quick and easy these days. I'd had the best week and a half of my life. Kelly stayed. She stayed!

We woke up next to each other on Tuesday morning and headed to the gym together. I did my workout while Kelly attended Isla's aerobics class. She disappeared after that, and the next time I saw her, she'd been at work, looking edible and giving me coy smiles that did embarrassing things to my body.

I made excuses to take her out for a "business" lunch, and we ended up back at my place, rolling in the sheets and forgetting there was such a thing as "the world outside." We'd returned flushed and giggling. I swear if I was Peter Pan, I would have been flying. I didn't need happy thoughts—I was *living* them.

Kelly had spent seven nights in my bed, including most of the weekend. I didn't want to leave her. When I woke that morning, she'd already been up and feeding the cats. She'd been really quiet, and I had to assume she was feeling the same way as me. A nine-day honeymoon period was way too short.

"You okay?"

I heard Marcia's voice before I saw her. I had three coffees in my hand, two for the ladies and one for me. I was hoping to quickly down my cup before rushing out the door to the airport.

"Yeah, I'm fine. Why?" Kelly's reply was short, giving away her "I'm fine" lie.

"You seem a little quiet today. You've been so bright and happy this week."

I peeked my head around the corner and spotted Marcia's sly grin. Her dimples and wriggling eyebrows made me smile.

"Oh, stop it." Kelly swiveled in her chair and focused on her computer screen.

"Come on, tell me. Did you and Marcus hook

up?"

My insides sizzled.

"No." Kelly frowned. "Of course not."

My insides deflated.

"Really?" Marcia's voice pitched with surprise. "But you guys went on that date, though, right? And then I...well, I didn't want to pry, but I just assumed you guys had."

"Nope. It was just the one date because we had a deal. Nothing ever came from it." Kelly spun back around to face Marcia, her tone almost forceful. "Marcus isn't my type. I was just being nice with that one date thing. He's never going to be my boyfriend."

I frowned while my mind raged from anger to disappointment, flashing past understanding before landing right back on a big, whiny *Awww!* I wanted her to claim me, not keep me a secret. It was hard not to feel a little offended. Why was she hiding us?

Clearing my throat, I made my presence known, hoping they didn't realize I'd been eavesdropping.

"Afternoon, ladies." I smiled, placing the mugs down beside them and avoiding Kelly's eye.

"Thanks." Marcia smiled in return then looked between Kelly and me before turning back to her computer.

"Thank you." Kelly checked over her shoulder to make sure Marcia wasn't watching before giving me a playful wink.

I narrowed my eyes at her and flicked my head toward my office. "Can I see you for a minute? I just have a few things to go over before I leave."

Her smile faltered. "Sure."

Collecting her iPad, she left her coffee and trailed me into my office. As soon as the door clicked shut, she snickered. "Thank you. I was hoping for a goodbye kiss."

I spun around to see her place the iPad down and walk toward me. I held up my hand to stop her.

"Are you sure you want one? I thought I wasn't your type."

"What?" Her face wrinkled with confusion.

I raised my eyebrows and tipped my head until a light flicked on in her eyes. She huffed then looked to the ceiling.

"Please don't be all precious about this. I don't want anyone to know."

"Why?" My suit jacket pulled tight across my shoulders as I crossed my arms.

"Because! I…" She huffed again and flicked her arms wide. "Gossip. Office rumors and…I just… I would prefer to keep this on the down low. I…" Her shoulders sagged and she looked to the floor. "Please, can we keep this quiet for a little longer? I'm not ready to announce what we have to the world. I haven't even told Scarlett and Isla. I just…" She stepped across to me, running her hand from my chest to my shoulder. Her whisper was soft and sweet against my skin. "I like the bubble, and I'm not ready for it to pop. I just want you and me and no one else." Her lips brushed against my cheek, undoing any kind of resolve I may have had.

My arm encircled her waist, and I pulled her against me. "I'm proud to be in love with you."

She smiled at me but didn't say anything. It unsettled me a little. Would she ever tell me she loved me? Would she ever claim me as her man?

Her sweet lips and warm tongue forced me to store the questions away until after I got back. I guessed the bubble was kinda nice. Her long fingers dove into my hair, mussing up the back as she deepened the kiss and we lost all track of time.

A knock on my door startled us both, and she jumped away from me, straightening her dress and giving me a fleeting smile before snatching her iPad and walking for the door.

"I'll get those things done while you're away," she said over her shoulder and opened the door to the legal assistant. "Hey, Justin."

"H-hi." He raised his hand in greeting and moved aside so she could disappear.

I watched her tight ass sway out of sight before smoothing down my tie and giving Justin a friendly smile. I was going to miss her. All I could hope was that our week apart would make her pine for me so bad that when I got back she'd be writing *Kelly and Marcus 4eva* in her diary.

THIRTY-FOUR

KELLY

Marcus left a few hours later, giving me a simple wave before disappearing behind the elevator doors. Marcia kept checking on me out of the corner of her eye, but I kept my lips sealed. I wasn't about to announce our love affair to the world. I wasn't ready. I didn't know if I ever would be. Marcus made me feel things that were foreign and terrifying. I was so giddy and happy, but it was tempered by an undeniable reality. Marcus Chapman did not belong in my world. I had no idea how to make him fit, so it was just easier to pretend he didn't exist.

I spent the weekend fielding curious questions from Isla and Scarlett. It was unlike me not to share the goods. They knew most of the details to do with Fletcher and Evangeline. I'd sobbed my way through the retell, downing wine and tubs of ice cream. It was so cliché it made me cringe, but it'd been what I needed at the time.

But I couldn't bring myself to tell them that, thanks to Marcus Chapman—the weedy little senior from Beverly Hills High—I'd experienced my first orgasm and plenty more after that. He'd even gone down on me, which I thought would be so awkward and disgusting, but…

My soft spot tingled and I crossed my legs at the sizzling memory. Marcus had this way about him that made me feel so comfortable and safe, yet at the same time, the idea of claiming him was terrifying. I could only imagine what my mother and friends would think.

I picked up my coffee cup and raised it to my lips. The cup was trembling a little, and I didn't want to figure out why. Quickly taking a sip, I placed it down and adjusted the shades on my nose. The midday sunlight was soaking my lunch table—a flawless winter day. Marcus would have loved it. My thoughts fled to him like they'd been doing constantly. He'd called me twice and texted numerous times. Our thread was pretty funny, and when I missed him the most, I'd pull it out and reread his funny observations. It was obvious how much he loved Chaos.

Pulling out my phone, I unlocked the screen and

reread our banter from the previous night. Marcus had such a quirky way of looking at things. It always made me smile.

I'd spent the weekend missing him. Arriving to work on Monday had been a real drag. His office sat empty and cold, and I'd spent most of my day dealing with Bryce. By the time lunch came around, I'd had to get out of there. I wanted to pop over to Marcus's place and say hi to Flash and Pumpkin. He wouldn't have minded, but it felt a little too familiar. Besides, his siseter was taking care of them, so it's not like I needed to go over there. I'd only be reminded of what we'd done on previous lunch breaks and how I still had to wait nearly a week before I could do that again.

I placed my phone down with a pitiful sigh and picked at the remainder of my chicken salad. I wasn't hungry, not for food anyway. My lips quirked with a grin as I pictured Marcus's return. A giddy titter bubbled inside me until I looked up and spotted the last two people on earth I ever wanted to see.

Fletcher and Evangeline.

Damn it, I'd forgotten they were coming to town. Why did they have to eat here?

And why the hell did Fletcher still have to look so damn amazing!

His large hand skimmed down his fiancée's back as he guided her into a seat. His charming smile was in play as he smoothed down his tie and took a seat opposite her. He had yet to notice me. He was too enamored with the strawberry cupcake sitting across from him.

"Can I clear that for you, miss?" The waiter captured my attention, and I gave him a stiff nod, leaning back so he could take my plate and dirty cutlery. He left my coffee and I snatched it, drilling the couple with a righteous glare as I sipped the tepid brew.

Evangeline tucked a lock of short hair behind her ear. Her bob cut with the straight bangs really suited her, dammit. She had a sharp, pixie-like face and the cut made her look far more sophisticated than she actually was. Honestly, Fletcher was way out of her league. Even the wealthy weren't created equal.

I tried my best not to look at them, but my eyes kept tracking back to Fletcher no matter how hard I tried. His face was so beautiful. He looked like a model. That was what had first attracted me to him. His chiseled, perfect face and that confident glint in his eye. The man oozed charisma, plus he could pull off an Armani suit like no other. He was the perfect man to take over his father's textile business. I was sure he could sell wool to a flock of sheep.

We would have made the perfect pair.

I swallowed and glanced down at my phone. Marcus's thread was still up, and I reread his parting words to me. It was a song he'd sent me as I was getting into bed. I'd held the phone to my ear and laughed as "Kiss You" by One Direction played. I still thought it was hilarious that a grown man liked tweeny pop music, but he did...and he didn't mind admitting it, either.

I played the song three times before finally setting my phone down with a goofy grin. It'd taken me forever to drift off. I couldn't get replays of our interludes out of my head. He was one hot lover. He wasn't the type you swooned over, but what he could do with his hands, lips and…

My eyebrows rose as a hot flush skimmed down my body.

I glanced back at Fletcher, his eyes still fixated on Evangeline. I wondered what their sex life was like. The part I'd walked in on had been pretty steamy. Was that why he'd gone for her over me? Because I was the uncertain ice queen and she was the adventurous slut?

A spurt of anger made my stomach gurgle. I wished for Marcus. He would have known exactly what to say to make me feel better, some derogatory quip that would get me laughing. Snatching my phone, I thought about texting him, but then remembered he was in a media conference with the band.

With a huff, I stared at my phone screen then felt a spark of inspiration and opened Spotify. If Marcus was in my position, he'd be emailing his douchebag ex a song. Something strong and sassy—the proverbial finger, so to speak.

My eyes hit a song in my "Home Dancing" playlist that fit the bill nicely. Selecting "Gives You Hell," I turned up the volume and placed the phone on the table, angling it toward the traitorous couple.

The song drew a few eyes around me, but I trained my scowl straight at Fletcher and his lady-love. He looked up and flinched, his lips parting when he spotted me. I raised my shades and added extra heat to my glare, crossing my arms and nailing him with a look that hid nothing of my anger. Hurt lurked behind it, fighting to show through as I gazed into Fletcher's eyes. I felt myself breaking, wooed by the power he'd always had over me.

Evangeline glanced over her shoulder and spotted me. She tried to smile, that sickening apologetic one she always wore. It tipped me that much closer to the breaking point, so before I could lose my cool, I stood and snatched my phone off the table. Sliding my shades back down, I wafted past them like I didn't even know who they were. The song came to a finish as I stepped onto the sidewalk and headed back to work.

I arrived at the office a shaky mess. Playing that song and drawing Fletcher's attention had been a mistake. I thought it'd make me feel good, confident...but it only reminded me of what he'd done, and how he'd chosen her over me.

Much to my relief, Marcia wasn't in her seat. I didn't need her curious gaze trying to suss me out. Thumping into my chair, I brought the screen to life and noticed an email from Marcus.

To: Kelly DeMarco
Subject: Put your headphones in for this one - it's just for you.

At first, I didn't want to open it. I don't know why. I was still reeling from seeing Fletcher, and I didn't want to confuse myself even more by getting mushy over something sweet Marcus was trying to do.

But I couldn't help myself.

I settled the plugs into my ears and opened the message.

I know it's old school, but I heard it playing on the radio and thought of you.

I double-clicked the track and "Uptown Girl" started. I bit my lips together, but it didn't work. My smile grew so broad it almost hurt.

I rested my chin in my hands and listened to the words, my expression turning dreamy as a little Marcus magic erased the lunch break from my mind.

THIRTY-FIVE

MARCUS

"So, you liked the song?" I had to ask. I wasn't sure how she'd take it with me sending it to her at work.

"Yeah, I liked it." There was a smile in her voice, and I immediately relaxed.

Resting my arm beneath my head, I nestled into the hotel pillows and felt like a lovesick teen, talking to my mega crush on the phone.

I chuckled. That was exactly what it was, minus the teen part.

"You didn't mind me sending it to you at work?" I winced.

She snickered. "Luckily for you, it was perfect timing."

"Oh yeah?"

"I saw Fletcher and his fiancée today." She sighed.

My guts twisted and I sat up, insecurities racing through me, knocked aside by a crashing wave of protectiveness. "Are you okay?"

"Yeah. Yeah, I am. It's the first time I've seen them since I left Stanford, and it threw me a little...but then I got back to the office and heard the song...it made it all better."

I grinned. "I'm glad I sent it then."

She paused, and I could picture her scratching the side of her nose or running a finger over her eyebrow. "Yeah, you should probably be careful with that. Sometimes Marcia jumps onto my computer."

"Is it really so bad if she finds out?"

"Marcus, please don't," she whispered. "I like the status quo."

My lip curled. I was grateful we weren't on FaceTime. As much as I wanted to see her pretty face, she didn't need to see how much her denial of us riled me. I couldn't push her, though. I'd finally scored the girl I'd always wanted. I couldn't risk losing her.

Forcing my lips into line, I cleared my throat and lay back down on the pillows.

"So, Chaos was awesome last night. I don't even know what I'm doing here. It's not like they need me."

"Maybe you should offer to do the chicken dance." Kelly giggled. "You know, add a little extra to the show."

I guffawed. "I'm sure they'd love it."

"It'd be a Vegas sensation."

"And then Everett Torrence would fire my ass."

She laughed. "He's lucky to have you. You're an amazing manager."

The sweet way she said the compliment made my insides warm. I glanced across to the window, wishing she was with me so we could stare out at the Vegas lights together.

"Chaos is lucky you're there to look after them."

"They make it easy on me. They're pros with the media stuff. They're such a tight unit that the press can't find any scandal or juicy tidbits on them. They protect each other like family. And Nessa is a dream come true on stage. Everybody loves her. I wish all my artists were that uncomplicated." I thought about Caris and the impending bullshit that awaited me. Justin's visit before I left the office was hardly stellar. The lawsuit was still in contention unless Caris was willing to give a formal apology, which, last time I spoke to her, she wasn't.

I ran a hand through my hair, annoyed that the impetuous princess was putting a dampener on my return to LA. I couldn't wait to see, touch, taste Kelly again, but I wasn't too happy about returning to work. I'd been fielding calls all weekend. It got to the point I actually had to turn off my phone to avoid Caris and her wretched mother.

My phone beeped, alerting me to an incoming call.

TORRENCE flashed on the screen. I pulled it back to my ear and groaned.

"Sorry, beautiful, I gotta go. Work calls."

"Okay." Kelly's voice was gentle and sad.

It made my heart hitch then jiggle. She didn't want me to go. I smiled slowly. "Do you want me to call you after I'm done?"

"No, I'm going to jump in the shower then head to bed."

"Wish I could join you." My smile grew even wider.

She paused again, and this time I couldn't picture what she was doing with her hands. Was she surprised, awkward, swooning?

A soft sigh later and she eased my fears with two murmured words. "Miss you."

"Miss you, too." I smiled. "See you in a few days."

I hung up before I could lose Everett's call and get lectured for not making him my top priority. I caught it in the nick of time and had to force Kelly out of my mind as Everett boomed at me. "How hard is it to ask someone to apologize? I thought you'd dealt with this, Marcus. The hotel is milking this for all it's worth, and Torrence is going to look bad if we can't wrap this up quick smart."

"I'm trying my best, sir, but Caris is a difficult person to deal with."

"She's also a pot of gold."

I pinched the bridge of my nose, recognizing the

looming discourse before it even started.

"You need to make this work. I want you back early to clean up this mess and get Caris back on track. I notice she's behind on her recording schedule, what's that about?"

"She had a run-in with one of the sound guys." I swallowed while Everett huffed.

"Marcus." The man cleared his throat. How anyone could make a throat tickle sound ominous was beyond me, but he did. "I knew Caris would be a challenging gig. It's why I picked you. Did I make a mistake?"

I lurched off the bed and shuffled to the window. "No, of course you haven't. But if you could give me a little more breathing room...an opportunity to put Caris in her place, I think we might have more luck."

"I will not risk losing her to another company. We have to find that balance of giving her what she wants so that she'll make us the money we deserve."

I closed my eyes and rested my head against the cool glass.

"That's your job, and I'm trusting you to do it. Now, get Chaos safely to their next venue then head back to LA. I don't care what you have to do, but make sure Caris has apologized to that leeching bastard by the end of the week."

I hung up and stared out at the twinkling lights with a frown, which ever so slowly morphed into a smile.

As much as I didn't want to have to face the

Caris fiasco, I was getting back to LA early. Spinning on my heel, I raced for my laptop and plopped down on the bed. It didn't take me long to find the song I wanted. I quickly attached it to Kelly's personal email then smiled as it whooshed out of my heart and into her inbox.

THIRTY-SIX

KELLY

"Back For You" by One Direction blasted through the house. Marcus had sent it to me the night before, and I'd been listening to it all day. He was returning early. He didn't say why, but I couldn't help the zing that kept buzzing through my chest every time I thought about seeing him again.

I'd given him my address so he could come around as soon as he returned. I felt a little edgy about that fact. I didn't share my address with many people, and my mother would have a conniption if she knew I was inviting random men over. Marcus wasn't random, but as far as my mother was concerned, he'd be a no-go, which was why she could never find out about him.

I danced around the kitchen, pouring myself a drink and singing the words I knew. Marcus hadn't texted all day, and I wasn't sure what time he'd arrive. I did know he was traveling a lot with Chaos, and he'd most likely catch the red-eye to LA. Would he come straight over and see me?

Probably not. Knowing Marcus, he'd be too polite to wake me.

A smile brushed my lips as I headed for my phone, set on texting him so he'd know I'd get up in the middle of the night to let him in. The doorbell stopped me. I glanced at the clock, surprised that he'd made it so soon. Turning down the volume, I skipped to the door and flicked it back with a grin that immediately disappeared.

"Fletcher? What are you doing here?"

My ex stood in the doorway, tall and enigmatic in his charcoal suit with a crisp white shirt. He was tie-less and the top button was undone, giving me a glimpse of his collarbone. I always loved how strong and angular it was. I used to run my finger along the hard edge then trace the line between his pecs.

"Hi, Kelly." His deep voice was smooth yet husky, a spine-tingling sound that still got to me.

I gripped the door and gazed up at him. "What are you doing here?"

"Can I come in?"

"Um." I pinched the crook of my neck.

"I just want to talk for a minute."

Pressing my lips together, I stood aside to let him walk past me. He smelled good. I couldn't place the scent, but it wafted up my nose and tickled my taste buds.

Fletcher glanced around my minimal apartment, sliding his hands into his pockets and turning to give me an appreciative smile. "This is nice."

"Thank you." I crossed my arms. I was wearing sweatpants and a fitted tee. It didn't matter that they were both designer. Next to Fletcher, I looked like a frumpy slouch.

In spite of my self-conscious qualms, Fletcher gazed at me with a sweet warmth. It reminded me of my freshman year at Stanford and how I had lived for that look every day of the week. It had melted my insides every time. I glanced away from it.

"Sorry to turn up like this, but after seeing you yesterday, I just…" His soft snicker was abashed. "I can't stop thinking about you."

I gripped my arms and shifted uncomfortably, hating the effect his words had on me.

He doesn't mean it, Kelly! Remember!

I raised my chin and glared at him. "How are the wedding plans going?"

"I don't know what I'm doing." Fletcher closed his eyes with a heavy sigh.

Was he talking about being at my apartment or the wedding?

"Evangeline is a sweetheart, she really is, but…" Fletcher's jacket rustled as he shrugged.

I made the mistake of looking at him. His gaze caught me and locked me in place. I couldn't move as he stepped forward, stopping close enough that I could feel his words on my skin. "She's not you."

It was hard to breathe. "You chose her."

"No, you left me, and I had no other choice."

I stepped away from him, bumping into the side table and rattling the keys in the bowl. "You're marrying her."

"That doesn't mean I'll stop loving you."

His words twisted my stomach into a tangled knot of confusion.

He reached for me, cupping my cheek and brushing his thumb beneath my eye. "We were a good match, Kelly. You always looked better on my arm than she did."

"So, what are you saying? You want to call off the wedding and marry me instead? You can just keep Evangeline around for hot sex when I'm too frigid for you, is that it?"

Fletcher grimaced and dropped his hand. "I didn't mean to make you feel that way. I was confused and I wasn't sure what I wanted...or needed. When you left, I thought it was so easy, decision made, but you're always in the background of my mind, taunting me, reminding me of what we had."

"You dumped me first, remember?"

"Yeah, a mistake I'll always regret." His expression crumpled with remorse.

I snapped my eyes shut, trying to sever our connection.

"You remember the times we had. We looked so good together."

Fletcher was smiling. I could hear it in his voice, but I didn't want to look. My heart was thumping so loud I could feel it in my head. What the hell was he trying to do to me?

An old, desperate part of my heart wanted me to open my eyes and run into his arms. But the girl I was slowly becoming opened her eyes and managed to throw him a hot glare.

"You're engaged to another woman. And you're standing in my apartment telling me all this stuff? How do you think Evangeline would feel if I told her?"

He gave me a chastened grin. Dammit! Even his half-smile was charming. "Maybe you're right. I probably shouldn't be here, but I just can't help wondering if letting you go was the biggest mistake I ever made."

I smashed my teeth together. Hot tears were building beneath the surface. It would have been so easy to take that route. My mother would love it. I could go back to striving for the life I'd mapped out—the perfect wedding, the perfect man. Fletcher was right about one thing—we looked good together.

But something inside me couldn't go back.

I didn't recognize what it was at the time. All I knew is that a silent force within me had the strength to utter, "You may have made the wrong decision, but I didn't. I can't trust you, and that means we can't be together."

"Kelly…" He reached for me again, but I slapped his hand away.

"I want you to leave."

He stepped back, his nostrils flaring slightly as he gazed down at me. I kept my eyes on his shiny, black shoes and opened the door for him. I wanted to say something snarky but couldn't think of anything clever. So, I silently stood by the door, forcing air through my nose and trying not to cave in as once again I let my first love go.

I slammed the door behind him and slid to the floor. I'd done the right thing. So why did I feel so bad?

I couldn't figure it out. Fletcher would only hurt me again. Being with Marcus was safe and secure…yet it wasn't. He made me feel things that terrified me. He opened me up to a life I'd never experienced before, and as tantalizing as that was, could I honestly make it long-term? How would that even work?

There was no way my mother would accept him. I could just imagine him at our dinner table trying to strike up a game of "Would you rather…" She'd peer over her crystal glass and say everything with one demeaning glare. I didn't want to expose him to that. He deserved better. Appearance was everything to my family, and Marcus could never fit the mold. He was too homegrown and sweet for their tastes.

Tears burned my eyes as I stopped and forced myself to really think it through. No wonder I'd wanted to keep things quiet at work. I didn't want to have to admit who I really was and what my future held.

What I had with Marcus could never have been more than a reckless fling.

I slashed a tear off my cheek and sniffed. "Time to pop the bubble, Kelly." I dipped my head with a whimper and, for reasons I couldn't understand, my stomach started jerking with uncontrollable sobs.

THIRTY-SEVEN

MARCUS

"Caris, you know I love you," I lied, "but we can't move forward with this lawsuit hanging over us. You have got to find it within your gracious self to apologize to the hotel."

Her skinny legs were crossed, and she swung her booted foot up and down with a childish pout. "They're being ridiculous! I *did* apologize."

I cringed and tipped my head. "I don't think five words scribbled on the back of a Burger King receipt is really what they're looking for."

"Oh, come on!" She slapped the table. "You know they're only doing this for publicity. You are feeding into their hands by agreeing to advertise for them."

"Why'd you have to trash the room?" I rubbed my forehead, wondering if I was leaving red marks behind.

"I was drunk. I didn't know what I was doing."

"How'd you even get the alcohol!"

She smirked—a playful, flirty one that I simply glared at.

"Don't look at me that way." She frowned. "You're my manager. You're supposed to be taking care of me. I could choose any record label—"

"Yeah, I know." I raised my hand to stop her, squinting across the street. We were sitting outside at the Quirky Corner Cafe. I took all my artists there. It was private and out of the way so we could have uninterrupted conversations. I thought back to the chat I'd had with Jimmy all those months ago. Man, he'd come a long way, and so had I.

I started to grin, remembering how I'd told him about Kelly. She was mine now. Damn, it was unbelievable.

"What are you smiling about?"

I glanced down at Caris's swinging boot, rubbing a hand over my grin. Like hell I was telling her about my love life.

"Okay." I tapped the table and checked my watch. It was nearly five. I hadn't seen Kelly since I got back and was desperate to get around to her place before she left for dinner at her parents' house. I was hoping to convince her to come back to mine after she'd eaten with them. What I really wanted was to join her, but I couldn't see her agreeing to that in a hurry.

"Caris, honey, I need you to help us all out and tell the hotel that you are gravely sorry for damaging their property."

Her sharp face bunched into a tight scowl, accentuating her high cheekbones. "I'm not doing it in front of a camera. The press will go to town on me."

"No, we'll keep it out of the press. We'll just quietly drive down there tomorrow and you can say a formal apology. If the press gets wind of it, it'll reflect well on you. Shows your humility."

She huffed and rolled her eyes, flicking a thick curl over her shoulder. "Oh fine, then. I'll say sorry, then sign some shit for his kids or something."

"And, maybe sing at his daughter's fifteenth birthday party?" I mumbled.

"What!" Her petite face scrunched into an ugly scowl.

"Come on, it'll be one hour out of your evening. I had to pull something big to appease this guy."

"He's an asshole!" Caris's hoop earrings swung as she jerked her head.

"You and your friends caused thousands of dollars' worth of damage." I tapped the table to emphasis my words. "They had to refurbish two entire rooms."

"They can afford it."

"You can't." I leaned toward her. "Do you get that?"

Her eyes sparkled as she eyed me up. "Torrence is *not* going to drop me." She smirked. "I'm a gold mine. Anyone with half a brain knows that."

I looked away from her triumphant snigger and cleared my throat. Adjusting my tie, I stood from the table and threw a couple of bills down. "I'm late for a meeting. Do me a favor and don't get into any more trouble."

Her tongue skimmed the side of her mouth when she winked at me. I turned away to hide my disgusted frown. The only thing stopping my mood from turning completely black was the thought that I'd soon be holding Kelly and giving her a hello kiss to remember.

*****

The door eased open to reveal my stunning girl. She was still in her work clothes, but her blouse was untucked and her feet were bare. She looked like she was about to get changed for dinner.

"Hey." Her smile was soft as she looked at me and leaned her head against the door.

"Hello, beautiful."

Her gaze shifted to the floor, and she stood back to let me in. I wandered past her, checking out the apartment as I shrugged off my jacket. It was nice, although completely different from mine. Hers was all muted tones and straight lines. There was one feature wall painted grape purple and showing off an abstract oil painting that probably cost more than my car. The living area was spacious, squared off by two black couches with thick, rectangular cushions on them.

Kelly hadn't said anything as I admired her open-plan house. The kitchen was off to the side, and I could see a stack of subscription magazines and flyers on the counter that had yet to be sorted. She must have only just gotten in.

"How was work?" I spun to watch her move to the stereo and flick it on. "One Step Closer" by Shane Harper filled the room. I grinned. Man, I loved her taste in music. Her smile was stiff when she turned back to face me. "It was okay." She shrugged. "Nothing exciting to report."

My brow dipped as I moved across to her. Gathering up her hand, I pressed her knuckles against my mouth and whispered, "What's the matter?"

She shook her head and stared at the floor. Her fingers felt a little hot and sweaty. I gave them a squeeze before dropping her hand—I could sense her wanting to step back from me.

I clenched my jaw, sliding my hands into my pockets and trying to appear casual as my insides started quaking.

"I, um…" She licked her lip. "I need to get ready to go out."

My smile was forced. It was impossible to hide my disappointment. "You're not happy to see me."

Her brow crinkled and she glanced away from me, blinking rapidly. "It's not that." She sucked in a shaky breath. "I just…I'm not sure what we're doing."

I narrowed my gaze. "I think it's called dating."

A fleeting smile brushed her lips, but as usual, she bit it into submission.

"Kelly, where's this coming from?"

I made a move toward her, but she swiveled out of my reach and stepped into the lounge, creating a distance that was trying to cut off my air supply.

"Do you honestly think this could work?" She pointed her finger between us.

"Yes." I nodded, stepping after her. "I love you, and I know you feel something, too. You're not ready to admit it, but you like us."

"This bubble is going to pop." Her voice shook. "And then all we'll be left with is two broken hearts. We should get out now before that happens."

"What, so we'll only be left with one broken heart then?"

Her expression crumpled at my sharp tone. I swallowed back my angst, scouring my mind for a way out of the soul-destroying conversation. We'd been together less than two weeks and she was already putting the brakes on. This couldn't be happening.

"Kelly—"

"I think you should go." She was a trembling mess. Her voice was all over the place, and her fingers were shaking as she tucked her hair behind her ear.

"I'm not leaving."

She closed her eyes. "Marcus, please. I can't give you what you want."

"I just want you." Emotion was making my voice thick. "And you can give me that, Kel. It doesn't have to be complicated. You and me. It's that simple."

Her lips wobbled as she brushed a tear off her cheek.

I couldn't stand it anymore. I closed the gap between us, wrapping my arms around her and skimming kisses up the side of her face. She held me tight, her nails digging into my shoulders as I met her lips with a kiss neither of us could pull away from.

The music shifted to "Marvin Gaye," and we started swaying to the beat. I clung to her with all I could, pouring every emotion I felt into the kiss. I wanted it to be enough. I *needed* it to be enough, but I couldn't shake the feeling that maybe it wasn't.

THIRTY-EIGHT

KELLY

"Marvin Gaye" by Charlie Puth was playing.

Marcus's arms were around me. He smelled like Sovereign cologne, and his tongue was in my mouth, electrifying my core...making it impossible to pull away. I wanted him. I wanted to feel every inch of him and stay wrapped around him like there was no place but a little bubble containing two people who loved each other.

My insides shuddered.

I didn't love him. I couldn't.

Pushing out of his embrace, I tried to step away, but he tugged me back, spinning me around so my spine was pressed against his muscular torso. His chin rested on my shoulder while his hands danced across my belly.

The song, Marcus, my need all combined to take control, and before I knew what I was doing my thrumming body took over.

"Touch me," I whispered.

Grabbing his hand, I guided it down between my legs. He lifted my skirt and cupped my panties. I tipped my head back, resting it on his shoulder with a soft whimper. We were still swaying to the beat, my bare feet brushing across the carpet. Marcus's lips skimmed my neck, his tongue drawing a fire trail up to my earlobe. While his tongue got busy, he unbuttoned my shirt. I leaned forward and dropped my arms so the fabric could slide away. I then listened to the zipper of my skirt coming down, and I was soon dancing against him in nothing but my soul. He pulled me back, crushing any space between us, and his deft fingers found my sweet spot, sending me up to that cloud he'd helped me discover only two weeks ago.

I lifted my arm and gripped the back of his neck, panting against the side of his face. His touch was making my limbs slack, but his firm body behind mine was like a strong pillar, holding me steady. His arm gripped me to him, massaging my breast while his fingers kept working me.

The song was still playing, making my pleasure ride that much greater and faster. I came with a gasp—a sweet explosion that soared through my body, making me shake and quiver. It was only then I became aware of Marcus's erection. It was digging into my butt; another turn-on I couldn't pull away from.

A thought skirted through my mind—terrifying and tantalizing at the same time. I never thought I'd do it, but I squeezed his hips and shuffled us toward the couch. We stayed locked together, connected by some invisible super glue. My heart was thundering, ready to explode in my chest in the two steps it took to reach the sofa. I could barely breathe as I rested my knees on the edge and bent forward.

Marcus's hands caressed my hips, his thumbs brushing over my butt cheeks.

"Are you sure?" he whispered.

"Yes." My reply was barely audible, and I nearly changed my mind twice as I listened to him unzip his trousers. I glanced over my shoulder in time to see him wrap himself. He caught my eye and gave me a gentle smile as he slid off his shirt. I gazed at his bare chest with that fine tuft of hair before tracing back up to his face.

The calm sparkle in his eye settled my racing nerves a little. His soft fingers skimmed my back until they reached my shoulders. He replaced that sweet caress with his lips. My jaw shook as he moved down my body, kissing and teasing. He felt so damn good I didn't know how much more I could stand. I was still sizzling from my orgasm, and I wanted him inside me.

I thrust back impatiently and he chuckled. His lips left me, his fingers digging lightly into my hips before sliding down my thighs. With a gentle nudge, he parted my legs then stood behind me, his fingers brushing my hyper sweet spot as he pierced me. He slid in slowly at first. The sensation was new somehow, the angle slightly different, and we both moaned in unison, like a rich sigh we'd been holding in since seeing each other. He placed his hands on my lower back and started thrusting. He was being careful and tentative, obviously not wanting to hurt me. It was like tickling my hungry taste buds, but not feeding me.

I nudged back against him.

"Tell me what you want, Kel," he gasped out the words.

"Harder," I whispered, burying my face in the cushions.

He gripped my hips and did as he was told, sending a shock wave of pleasure coursing through me. My toes curled as I lifted my head and panted, "Faster."

His pace quickened and I clutched the cushions, crying out as a force made up of rapture and stardust shot down my legs. My belly quaked as he thrust into me, our skin slapping together in a rhythmic beat. I'd never felt anything so reality-defying before.

Marcus groaned, thrusting into me one final time and holding himself there. I pushed myself up, still gripping the cushions, because that's all I could do.

"That was amazing." I puffed, my bare chest heaving.

Marcus's strong, sure hands came around me. He cupped my breasts and kissed my shoulder. "That's because you're amazing."

I smiled. Only Marcus would say something that sweet. Only Marcus would make me feel this secure after what I'd just done.

Only Marcus.

*****

My clothes felt tight and restrictive as I sat at my parents' dinner table. I'd left Marcus over an hour ago and my body was still pulsing. As I drove away, what we'd done started to sink in. My bubble shimmied and popped as I moved out of his reach and back into the Kelly DeMarco world I'd grown up in.

He'd taken me from behind, something my mother had sworn only porn stars did. She'd never told me how amazing it would feel. I'd always imagined it to be so degrading. The few times Fletcher had suggested it, a thick wave of vulnerability had frozen me solid, but I'd wanted to with Marcus.

"So how was your day, darling? Get up to anything interesting?" Mom's simple question made me choke on my wine.

I covered my mouth, coughing and spluttering while my eyes watered.

My mother gave me an incredulous look until I pulled myself together and I was able to breathe without gurgling.

My head finally gave a stiff shake. "No, Mom, nothing out of the ordinary."

"No gentleman callers?" Her thin lips edged up into a knowing smirk.

How the hell did she know?

"Are you… Who…?"

She chuckled. "Oh, stop playing coy with me and tell me about the visit."

My mouth dried up like the salt flats, and all I could do was stare at her. My heart was beating so hard and fast, I thought it might travel up to my brain and explode.

Her eyes rolled and she shook her head. "Does Fletcher want you back?"

I jerked and dropped my spoon. It clattered against my knife and nearly took a chip out of the soup bowl. Mom's frown was sharp, reprimanding me in her silent way before dabbing her mouth with her napkin.

"Kelly, for goodness' sake. What is wrong with you tonight?"

My eyes narrowed as coherent thought kicked in and helped me piece my brain back together. "You sent Fletcher?"

Mom raised her glass, her eyes twinkling. "He called me, darling, and wanted to know if he could speak with you. Of course I gave him your address. Did you manage to woo him back?"

"No." I shook my head, too confused and surprised to even show my annoyance. I wished my brain wasn't always so slow to catch up on Mom's deceptive antics. I should have been tearing into her, but instead I sat there like a dumb idiot, caught between the relief of her not finding out about Marcus and the horror that she had sent a cheating bastard to my doorstep.

She sighed and smoothed a lock of hair off her face with an elegant finger. "I guess the wedding is still on then?"

"Probably," I murmured.

"Well, that is a shame. I was hoping you'd be wearing the Echelon dress down the aisle on Valentine's Day, but *c'est la vie*, I suppose."

I frowned at her. "Mom, seriously, how could you—"

"But never mind. I have thought of another solution. Since you seem incapable of finding your own man, I've managed to procure you a lovely date for the wedding."

My mouth dropped open.

"His name is Asher Coburg. He's the son of Lester and Diane. Do you remember them?"

I shook my head.

"Lester and your father have been in business for years, and your father has agreed to take Asher under his wing this year, teach him a thing or two. He'll be perfect for you, darling. He's tall, handsome, far better looking than Fletcher. You'll look amazing together."

"Mom, I can't." I closed my eyes, trying to take control of whatever the hell was going on inside of me. It felt like an earthquake was splitting my body apart.

She sat back with a perplexed frown. "You have

someone better? Please, do tell."

My mouth opened and closed, my voice box straining to work.

But my brain wouldn't let it.

The name 'Marcus' was crashing from one side of my head to the other, but I couldn't form the word.

"Kelly, stop doing that with your mouth. It makes you look like a goldfish." Mom's expression was sharp and disapproving. "Now, pull yourself together. They'll be here any minute. You can meet him tonight, and I've arranged for him to take you out tomorrow evening on a proper date. You need to look familiar before the wedding. We don't want Fletcher thinking you've been pining for him this whole time." Her steely gaze assessed me. "I certainly hope you didn't give him that impression when he came to visit you."

Her right eyebrow peaked and I shook my head. "I sent him away."

She tutted like I was an idiot then muttered something about at least having a back-up plan. "I don't know what you'd do without me, darling." She snickered, still looking gorgeous even though I hated the sound coming out of her mouth.

I pressed my lips together, trying to form the letter M. I just about had it when she opened her mouth and more vile toxins spilled onto the table.

"You know, it's probably a good thing that you haven't gone ahead and done this on your own. With that Bryce person not working out, it's a relief that I can set you up with someone I know will be appropriate. We can't have you ending up with someone who doesn't fit, so to speak. You're a DeMarco. I know that makes it difficult to find the right person, but you need to be proud of your name. Your father and I are so excited for your future. You have so many wonderful things ahead of you. Maybe Asher will help you to see the light, and you can quit that silly job and get on with being the woman you were born to be."

I didn't have time to respond. The front door clicked open, and my father arrived with a drop-dead gorgeous man. My mother was right—Fletcher had nothing on the guy. He strolled into the dining room, unbuttoning his jacket and giving me a suave smile. I looked into his bright aqua eyes and tried to smile back, but all I really wanted to see was a playful, hazel gaze that made me feel warm and complete.

I imagined Marcus standing where Asher was, trying to impress my parents with witty conversation.

My spirit deflated.

My "Marvin Gaye" dance was done, and I was back to holding a needle, aiming it straight at a bubble I never should have blown.

THIRTY-NINE

MARCUS

I sat in my mother's office and fiddled with the stethoscope resting on the corner of her bright yellow desk.

"You can play with it if you want." She walked in and winked at me. Shrugging out of her white coat with the Disney character badges all over it, she grabbed the purse from under her desk then gave me a knowing smile.

I shook my head and stood. "Should we get going?"

"Sure." She grinned. "Thanks for picking me up."

"No problem." I tipped my head toward the door and stood back so she could go through first. She stopped at the nurse's station to say goodbye before heading out of the private clinic and into the sunny parking lot.

She looked over her shoulder as I caught up with her. "My car should be done, so if you could take me straight to the garage, that'd be great."

"Cool." I kept my words short. I wasn't really in the mood to talk. It'd been a weird, frustrating day.

I unlocked the passenger door and held it open for my mom. She reached for her seatbelt as I closed it and wandered around the front of the car. Her eyes were on me the whole time, assessing me, reading me even though I didn't want her to.

She waited until I'd started the engine and pulled into traffic before saying, "What's up, Scruff?"

I shrugged.

"Oh, so you're gonna make me guess." She rubbed her hands together, a gleeful smile flashing over her face. "Is it…"

"Please don't." I stopped at the traffic light and scrubbed a hand over my mouth. My whiskers were sharp and bristly. I'd forgotten to shave after the gym. Kelly hadn't been there. In fact, I'd barely seen her, because she'd gone out of her way to avoid me all day. I caught her at one point and tried to ask her what was wrong, but she mumbled, "Not at work," and fled the room.

After the way we'd ended things the night before, I'd returned home feeling elated, but an early morning call from Caris's mother and an elusive Kelly had set me in a foul mood and only reignited all my insecurities.

I wasn't cut out to be a manager, and I sure as hell wasn't cut out to be Kelly's boyfriend. The sex may have been crazy good, but it wasn't enough for her to fall in love with me...let alone claim me as her own. I didn't know how to make her do either.

"Has she broken up with you?" Mom's soft question made me wonder if I'd been talking aloud. I gave her a weird look and she just smiled. "The only time you've ever worn that forlorn expression is when things aren't going well with Kelly DeMarco."

I sighed, accelerating through the intersection and keeping my eyes on the road. "We're not really together, I guess. I mean, I'd like to be, but she's...something keeps holding her back."

"Is she worth it?" Mom's gentle hand on my arm stopped me from snapping at her.

I swallowed back my angst and murmured, "She's always been worth it."

Mom went quiet then, never a good sign. She was no doubt formulating some speech that would cut me to the core and make me re-examine my life. She was the reason I broke up with Allison when I easily could have settled for some long-distance drama. She was the reason I applied for a job I wasn't really capable of. She was the reason I purchased a house for my twenty-third birthday, believing I had it in me to pay it off.

"Marcus." Mom cleared her throat.

Here we go.

"Honey, all your life you've made it your mission to bring people joy. You only have to be you and you're making people laugh and feel better about themselves. As a kid, you were so good, always trying to keep everybody happy." Her tone was so warm it was hard not to smile at the compliments. "The only problem with that is you often sacrifice what you really want and end up compromising all the time. I worry you're selling yourself short."

"Kelly DeMarco is not selling myself short, Mom. She's completely out of my league!"

"No." Mom shook her head. "No, you see, that's where you're wrong. She's lucky to have *you*. Just like Everett Torrence and Caris are lucky to have *you*."

I snickered and shook my head. "You're only saying that because you're my mother."

"No, I'm saying that because you are an amazing man, and I don't want anyone to ever make you feel otherwise. You are a catch, Marcus Chapman, and you deserve a girl who wants to claim you as her own and let the whole world know about it. Now, I don't know exactly what's going on, but I do know that she shouldn't be messing with your head playing hot fish, cold fish."

I shrugged, about to say it wasn't that bad, but her stern look told me not to go there. Instead, I ended up admitting in a broken whisper, "I've wanted her for so long. I don't want to lose her."

"I know." Mom's voice quivered with empathy.

"I'm worried if I tell her everything I'm really feeling that she'll run the other way. I can't make her fall in love with me."

"That's true, but you *can* give her a choice. You're in love with this girl, and for the sake of your heart you need to tell her that you're all in or all out. You deserve to be treated with respect, and respect without honesty is worthless. You owe it to yourself to lay it all out on the table." Mom nodded then mumbled, "And I'm not just talking about her, either. I'd like you to stick it to that Caris girl."

I cleared my throat and gave her a wry smile. "I think I tell you and Dad too much."

She giggled. "I love you, Scruff."

I pulled into the garage and spotted Mom's car waiting for her. She unbuckled her seatbelt and leaned across to peck my cheek. Holding my face with her hand, she looked me in the eye. "You're the kind of guy who will give his all to get the things he wants. Just make sure you're fighting for the right stuff. Don't destroy yourself for something...*someone*...who isn't going to fight just as hard for you."

She left me with that nugget. It clunked and rattled around, torturing me as I drove to Kelly's apartment. She didn't know I was coming, but I didn't think I could handle a sleepless night composing all the things I wanted to say to her. It was better that I just showed up and we had it out—an open, honest conversation that would either save us or sever what we had.

FORTY

KELLY

I pushed the last pin into my hair then stepped back, turning my head from side to side to make sure my French roll was secure. My glittery drop earrings shimmered as I shook my head. My glossy red lips rose into a tight smile. I looked good. The dress had been waiting at my door when I got home with a note from Mom attached.

This will look perfect tonight. Wear your diamond drop earrings and necklace and go for a French roll in your hair. Let me know if you want me to come over and help you get ready ~ xx Mom.

I opened the lid to find a stunning midnight-blue dress that dipped low at the back and accentuated my curves. My mother always knew how to pick 'em. I slipped my feet into my high silver pumps and clipped to the door when I heard the bell.

Grabbing my clutch purse, I opened the door and stopped short when I saw Marcus standing there with a bottle of my favorite wine and a bright red gerbera. Typical Marcus—a rose would have been too cliché. Why did I love that about him?

The sweet smile on his face faded to confusion when he saw my dress, but then he smiled and whistled. "Wow, you look amazing."

"Th-thanks," I stammered.

"Sorry to show up unannounced. I should have called." He lifted the wine. "Things were kind of weird at work today, and I wanted to stop by to make sure everything was okay."

My head bob-bob-bobbed as I tried to form a coherent sentence. What the hell did I say? Any lie I came up with would be lame, and the truth was a bitch-slap in the face.

I ended up going with evasion, a standard tactic that tended to work with anyone but Marcus. "It's not a great time for me. Maybe we can talk about this later?"

His eyes tightened at the corners as he took stock of my appearance again. "Are you…?" He clenched his jaw, his lips pursing before he looked me in the eye and murmured, "Who's the lucky guy?"

I rested my forehead against the door. "It's not what you think."

"Really? Because right now it looks like you're about to go out on a date with someone. Someone who isn't me." The green flecks in his eyes sparkled, a hard glitter that made me antsy.

My mouth trembled as I licked my lower lip. "You're not my boyfriend."

"No, I'm just the guy you're sleeping with. No big deal, right?" His sarcastic tone was strained yet brutal enough to make my chest deflate.

"What do you want me to say?"

"I want you to tell this guy that you're with me and you don't want anyone else!"

Marcus didn't usually raise his voice. The fiery look on his face was hard to take in. I stared at the floor instead. "You don't understand. I can't...I can't do this. I have tried to tell you so many times, but you just won't listen. We can't be together."

"Yes, we can. We just both have to want it. I don't know what's holding you back, but whatever it is, we can fight it together."

"You don't even understand the fight!" I raised my arm, tears glassing over my eyes. "It's too hard. It won't work. I'm not saying this for myself, okay? Trust me. You don't want in."

He leaned forward, his expression emphatic and honest. "I know that all I've ever wanted is to be with you. You finally let me in, and it was better than I could have hoped for."

I gripped my temples. I needed to shut the door

in his face. Make him stop. But a stronger part of me had to stand there and listen.

"I've been working my ass off trying to make you love me, and the thing that kills me is I know you do. You're just too proud to admit it."

My hand dropped to my side and I stared him.

He gave me a sad smile and shook his head. "I can make you happier than any of those stuck-up pricks. I see the real you. I know you...and I can be the guy you need. I'd love you with everything I had...but you just won't let me, will you?"

I couldn't move.

His mouth dipped, his sparkling gaze muted by a heartbreaking disappointment. "I can't do this. I can't watch you date other guys." His voice broke and he held out the bottle of wine for me.

It took all my control to reach for it. I hugged it in the crook of my arm and didn't know what to say.

His gaze dismantled me as he held out the flower. "I'm all in if you want me, but I'm not gonna be begging at your door like some homeless puppy."

My heart started aching, each beat a painful, pitiful warning. Footsteps sounded down the end of the hallway, and Marcus turned to catch a glimpse of Asher. His eyes rounded before he looked to the floor then his jaw worked to the side, and a soft sigh came out his nose.

"I may not have anything on that guy, but I'm still a catch," he whispered with a dejected smile. "And I don't deserve this shit."

He walked away before Asher reached us. The tall Coburg son gave him a polite, friendly greeting and, in true Chapman style, Marcus found it in himself to respond with a soft, "Have a good night."

As he disappeared down the stairs, I held the flower to my nose and felt something inside of me break off. I didn't know what it was, but it hurt worse than anything I'd felt before.

FORTY-ONE

MARCUS

Life sucked.

I was so riled after leaving Kelly's place. Having to walk past that tall prick with his charming smile made me want to puke. I stumbled down the stairs and raced home, locking myself away for the weekend. I slumped around in my sweats, ignoring the world and watching the entire *Lord of the Rings* trilogy, plus the *Hobbit* movies.

Thankfully, Caris didn't do anything stupid, so I was able to pretend the only three beings in the world were me, Pumpkin, and Flash.

But then Monday morning came and I couldn't

hide anymore.

I arrived before everyone else and got stuck into work, dreading the moment when she would walk in. I didn't want to look at her. Acid had been sizzling my guts all weekend, and I knew it would flash up my throat the second I laid eyes on Kelly.

It pissed me off just thinking about it.

A knock at the door made me flinch.

I looked up to see Justin walk in with a nervous smile.

"All good?" My stomach knotted. What the hell had Caris done now?

He nodded. "She apologized."

"Really?" I jerked in my seat. "When? I thought I had to take her this week."

Justin shrugged. "I g-guess she decided to get on with it o-on her own."

"Okay, then." I snickered. "Suits me. Did she say anything about singing at a birthday party?"

"Apparently, she's doing it th-this evening. They've already dropped the suit against us."

I closed my eyes and scrubbed a hand down my face. "Thank God."

Justin grinned.

"Thanks for your help, man. You've been amazing."

He shrugged, his twitchy smile kind of shy as he rubbed the back of his neck. I glanced at his wedding ring then looked back at my computer.

"Well, let's hope she doesn't do anything that stupid again." I scratched the corner of my mouth, wondering if I should attend the birthday party with her.

"I sure hope not." Justin chuckled. "I-I don't need the extra w-work."

"Me too, brother." My smile faltered as I glanced at him. He looked exhausted. I frowned. "I hope this extra work hasn't put you too far behind on your studies or anything."

Justin brushed the air. "No, I mean, I study at night, so…"

My eyes narrowed. "Do you ever take time off? Your wife must want to see you."

"I-I haven't re-re-re…" He sighed, closing his eyes and punching out the words, "I haven't had the time."

His lips pulled into a grim line while his eyebrows dipped together. He looked like he'd had this argument before.

I picked up my pen and tapped it against my day planner. "Work life getting the better of you, huh?"

His shoulders slumped. "It's hard to fit it all in, you know? H-how do I keep S-Sarah happy and my b-boss happy and-and-and study. I d-don't…" He sighed.

"Sarah's your wife?"

He nodded, scratching the back of his curls. "She's beautiful, and I feel like I never get to see her. We're both s-so busy."

A soft sadness swept over his face.

"At least you get to wake up beside her in the mornings, though, right?" My melancholy tone matched his expression.

His lips twitched with a halfhearted smile. He looked as though he wanted to say more but couldn't.

"How long have you guys been married?"

He swallowed. "Not even a year. We got married a week after graduation then moved here and both started working. It's...sh-she got her dream j-job and she's really happy."

"How about you?"

"Sh-she's my college sweetheart. The only girl I've e-ever loved."

I didn't miss the way he avoided my question, but I didn't have time to ask for more. Kelly appeared in my doorway looking so damn beautiful it wasn't fair. Justin quickly took his leave, and I had to force my eyes away from Kelly's hips as she clipped toward me in her black heels.

"Morning." She nodded, all professional, like we'd never seen each other naked. Her long finger tapped on the edge of the iPad while she gazed at the floor. Her hair was up in a high ponytail, draping over her shoulder like a silk scarf.

I couldn't talk so I just beat my pen on the desk.

"I, uh, was wondering if you had anything specific you wanted me to do for you today or this week. You usually email me a list, but..."

I ran my tongue over my bottom teeth and turned to my computer. Opening a new message, I checked my planner and quickly typed up a briefly "to do" list. Turning back with a deadpan stare, I murmured, "It's sent."

Her expression crumpled. "Marcus, I..."

I cleared my throat and sat tall before she could finish. "So something's come up for Chaos. I'm going to be flying over to help them out for a few days. If I need anything more from you, I'll email it over."

It was a total lie. Chaos was doing fine, but I needed out. Caris would just have to manage the birthday party on her own. I had to think about my own survival.

Kelly was far too gorgeous for her own good, and being around her made me want to impale myself. I'd had a taste of life with her, loved every second of it, and it was being ripped away from me, because she was scared or proud or...I don't know! Whatever bullshit story she wanted to spin, I wasn't interested in listening to it.

The idea of her date with Mr. Tall and Handsome had brutalized me all weekend. Had they ended up in bed together? A cruel image flashed through my brain. I clenched my jaw and swallowed, still unable to look Kelly in the eye.

She nodded at my abrupt tone, her nostrils flaring slightly as she blinked. "I didn't mean...it's so hard to explain this to you. I just..."

"I'm not your type, I get it. I don't meet the extensive criteria." I stood up, sliding my hands into my pockets to hide the fact they were shaking. "I don't want to talk in circles or anything. You know I think you're wrong." I looked down with a heavy sigh. "But I guess it doesn't matter what I think."

Her jaw worked to the side while her eyelids

fluttered. Gripping the iPad to her chest, she turned for the door. "Have a nice trip, Marcus. Travel safe." She paused before leaving, drumming her nail on the frame and looking back at me. "Marcia asked me to remind you to send the morning song, but I can do it on your behalf if you're not up for it."

I raised my chin and smoothed down my tie. "No, that's cool. It's my thing. I can do it."

Like hell I was letting her know just how much she was killing me.

She nodded and clipped out the door. I plopped into my chair and snatched up my phone, dialing the airline and booking a flight before looking through my playlist and selecting a song.

It was tough going. I wasn't in an upbeat mood. I flicked my finger to scan down the list then paused as an old song from the nineties caught my eye. My lips twitched, and I sniffed out a sad sort of chuckle.

Pulling up a new email, I attached the song to my usual bunch of morning listeners and pushed SEND. I collected up my stuff and headed out the door before it arrived in her inbox. I didn't even turn to wave or smile as I left the building. I wasn't interested in any kind of goodbye…I just wanted to get the hell out of LA and as far from Kelly DeMarco as I could.

FORTY-TWO

KELLY

The earplugs felt like nails as the song played.

"Everything You Want" by Boyce Avenue. I hadn't heard the version before, and the acoustic style was a million times louder than the original Vertical Horizon release. The words were so clear and bullet-like. They peppered my chest—little bee stings that made me cross my arms and slump down in my chair. I stared at the screen until my vision blurred.

I couldn't believe he'd sent the song to everyone in the office.

I wanted to be mad, but I couldn't feel anything

more than tragic emptiness.

The final chorus started with the singer changing the words from *he* to *I*. It was Marcus's way of singing straight at me, making sure I felt his confusion and pain. I wanted him to understand, but there was no way to explain my warped, emotionally deficient family. He'd never get the idea of marrying for security. He was too romantic.

He wasn't cut out for my kind of life—media, parties, social appearances. He didn't know the first thing about running a fashion company. He had no asset to bring into the relationship...except the fact that he was amazing in bed and could make me laugh like no other.

Aching sadness swept through me as I stared toward his empty office. I had no idea how long he'd be gone for. I didn't know what the Chaos emergency was and I didn't even care. I just knew that I'd miss Marcus. Even though it was easier not having him around, I'd miss him anyway.

Marcia nudged me with her elbow.

I yanked out the plugs and frowned at her.

"Are you okay?" Her voice was so tender my eyes glassed over before I could stop them.

"I fucked up," I whispered, leaning my head into my hand and trying to hide my face.

"What do you—?"

The phone rang, cutting her question short. I snatched it up before she could delve any further. "Torrence Exec, Kelly speaking."

"Kelly, *what* is going on?" Mom's voice was sharp. "Why did you cancel on Asher? I assumed when I couldn't reach you this weekend it was because you were spending time with him, but I've just had a call from your father and apparently you sent him on his way."

I opened my mouth to respond with the speech I had rehearsed while moping around my darkened apartment all weekend.

"And what's this about a man at your door? Who was that?"

My stomach knotted, pulling the words back down my throat and replacing them with a little squeak.

"Are you seeing someone I don't know about?"

"No?"

"Why did you just say that like a question?"

I squeezed my eyes shut.

"Kelly Rosina, you better start explaining yourself."

Swallowing down the bile that was tickling the back of my throat, I forced a smile. "I'm not seeing anyone. I had really bad period pain on Friday night, and I didn't think Asher would appreciate those details, so I told him I had a headache."

I held my breath while I waited out my mother's deliberation. I couldn't believe I was twenty-two and still afraid of my mother. It was ridiculous! But I couldn't seem to do anything about it. The woman was damn intimidating, and I'd spent my entire life trying to make her happy.

When was I going to realize that I couldn't?

"Well, I hope you're feeling better now, because Asher has kindly agreed to take you out tonight.

He'll collect you at seven-thirty. I'm sending over a new Echelon dress. Wear the Christian Louboutins I bought you for Christmas, they'll match perfectly. And go for pearl drop earrings, no necklace. Got it?"

"S-sure."

"Don't stutter, Kelly. It makes you sound obtuse."

I gripped the phone so hard I thought my knuckles might punch through my skin.

"Now, you have a good time tonight. I'm hopeful this will go well. A Coburg-DeMarco union would do wonders for Echelon. We're counting on you, Kelly."

She hung up, but I kept the phone pressed against my ear, too dead inside to even move. Marcia bustled into reception and placed a mug of steaming coffee beside me.

I hadn't even noticed her leave. Slipping the phone into the cradle, I wrapped my fingers around the hot mug.

"Hey." Marcia nudged me again.

I couldn't turn to face her when I snapped, "What?"

She paused then let out a soft sigh before murmuring, "I'm here if you need to talk."

I didn't. I couldn't.

What the hell was there to say anyway?

Gripping the mouse, I dragged the arrow across my screen and highlighted Marcus's email, punching delete on his damn song and trying to make myself believe that Asher would be easy enough to fall in love with. A Coburg was what my family needed, not some no-name Chapman.

My heart beat with a thick, aching tremble that hounded me for the rest of the day, making it hard to function and nearly impossible to breathe when I opened the door and greeted my hot date.

He took me to Chiffon's, a classy French restaurant decked out in shimmering fabrics and the top tier of society. Asher placed his hand on my lower back as we were led past the stage to a table in the corner. The lady singing had a sexy, pert voice that was soothing, yet entertaining. I sat down and waved to a model and his actress girlfriend that I recognized from a fashion event a few months back. Their smiles told me they were trying to place where they'd seen me before. Asher nodded to a businessman I didn't know, but it was obvious from the lavish jewelry his wife wore that they were loaded.

I slipped into my chair and tried to focus on what Asher was saying. He chatted about business mostly, waxing on about how wonderful my father was and how much he was enjoying collaborating with him.

I smiled and nodded where appropriate, sipping my wine and trying not to check my watch every two minutes. By the time dinner was served, I was bored out of my brain. I admit, I wasn't putting in much effort, but I could tell that Asher wasn't my cup of tea. I couldn't imagine taking him dancing.

My mind flashed with memories of mouthing words with Marcus as we danced at the club, and then shot forward to him touching me while we swayed to "Marvin Gaye." The wineglass slipped in my sweaty fingers. I fumbled it onto the table before I could spill red liquid across the white cloth.

"So, that's my five-year plan, but I know things can change." Asher smiled at me, reaching across the table and lightly brushing my fingers. "Unexpected people can come into our lives."

The lady on stage was singing a tune I recognized. I glanced her way. The song was "No Good For You" by one of my favorite artists, Meghan Trainor. I couldn't help a smile—I loved every one of her songs. Asher obviously thought my light smile was for him. He gathered my fingers in his, rubbing his thumb across my knuckles before raising them to his lips.

I gazed at his smiling face then forced myself to look directly into his blue eyes. They reminded me of Fletcher's. They held that same high-end contempt. Most people wouldn't notice it. They'd be too wowed by the dazzling charm and appearance, but I'd been born and bred with people just like the Coburgs, and since hanging out with Marcus, Mr. No-Fuss Humility, it was screamingly clear to me.

The words to the song caught my ear. I knew them by heart, and it was hard not to sing along in my head. As I gazed at my date, he morphed into Fletcher, and the song was so damn appropriate it made me snicker.

I reclaimed my hand and tucked it beneath the

table. Dipping my head, I pressed my lips together and tried to bring my rattling insides under control. I wasn't sitting opposite Fletcher. I was sitting opposite Asher, but I honestly could not tell the difference.

Pulling my shoulders back, I gazed at the Coburg millionaire. He was still smiling, a triumphant little smirk. If only he knew what I was really thinking.

I wanted to tell him, but my mother would freaking kill me.

The waiter arrived to clear our plates. "Would you like the dessert menu?"

"Not for me, thank you." I raised my hand and shook my head, thanking him as he took my plate away. Asher asked for the check and sat back to gaze at me.

"Would you like to go for a walk before I take you home? The lights are beautiful down this street."

They were. Chiffon's was located on a gorgeous, quaint walking street where evening shoppers strolled and buskers played. Businesses lit their storefronts and restaurants with fairy lights that made the cool winter nights magical.

I nodded and clipped, "Sure. I'd love to."

Too busy signing off his credit card slip, he didn't notice my lie. When he stood and offered me his arm, I slipped my hand in the crook of his elbow and let him lead me down the street.

We looked like the perfect couple, both tall and beautiful. The wind ruffled my hair as I glanced up at him. He was smiling and talking about tickets to the opera. His mother was a huge fan and they went at least three times a year.

"I'd love for you to join us some time."

My mother would love that.

I smiled tightly and continued strolling, picturing myself in a stuffy theater, fighting sleep as the voices trilled and echoed around me. I'd been to plenty in my time…and the ballet. It was so sophisticated and mature…and boring! I'd endured it all to please my parents, and Fletcher, and where had it gotten me?

A group of teenage girls caught my eye. They were standing on the side of the street busking. One had a guitar in her arms, her eyes dancing as she brought her giggling girlfriends into line.

Two of them clapped a steady rhythm and then she came in with her guitar. The fourth one stepped forward and started singing "Next To Me." They sounded amazing, so I stopped to listen, leaning my head to the side as I watched them.

They looked so happy and carefree, singing about their perfect man. I listened to the words, letting them soak in as Asher stood by my side, obviously growing impatient. The longer the song went on, the more my insides shredded.

I'd had a man who could be everything I needed. He'd stand next to me no matter what. I glanced up and glimpsed Asher's perfect profile. Who the hell was I standing next to? Some guy my mother picked out for me?

My forehead creased with a deep frown as I

spun on my heel and faced him.

"Would you rather own a house full of cats or one donkey?"

"Excuse me?" His comical frown made me smirk.

"It's a game. Would you rather..." I spun my hand in a circle.

"I see." His eyebrows dipped together before he gave me a smooth smile. "Don't you think you're a little old for games?"

"Is there such a thing as being too old to have fun?"

"We are having fun." He grinned. "We had a delicious meal, interesting conversation..." His arm snaked around my waist. "And I'm sure we can find some more 'fun' things to do, if you wanted."

I rested my hand on his arm and gazed into his eyes. "I'm never going to be able to wear my slouchy sweatpants around you."

"What?"

"I'll be too self-conscious...and you don't make me laugh. We've been together nearly two hours and I haven't laughed once. There's no way you'd be cool with me dancing barefoot in a club. Would you?"

"You? ... I don't really like dancing, and this conversation is confusing me."

I pushed out of his grasp and shook my head. "I have to go."

"What?" Asher looked mildly insulted, but I couldn't care.

Turning on my heel, I stalked away from him,

my mind exploding with one repeated thought.

Marcus.

I wanted Marcus next to me…and no one else.

FORTY-THREE

MARCUS

I saw Kelly's name flash on my screen and rejected the call. I didn't have time for her bullshit, not when I was set to head back to LA so quickly. I had touched down in Denver, Colorado and was halfway to the hotel where Chaos was staying when I got a call from Caris's mother.

Her daughter was in jail.

Sweet Caris had shown up to this birthday dinner as promised. The only problem was, she'd shown up drunk off her ass and ended up puking in the birthday girl's lap, but not before coming on to the girl's cousin. The hotel owner had caught them half-naked in a darkened bedroom while the birthday candles were being lit. He'd hauled them both out of there and pushed her into the dining room to sing...but instead she'd puked.

Caris's mother had no idea how it happened and was accusing the birthday girl's father of spiking her drink then having the audacity to manhandle her.

It was inconceivable to think her precious baby girl could be responsible.

I was ready to kill something, and I didn't want Kelly in my warpath.

My phone had been buzzing nonstop since the incident. Everyone wanted a piece of me—the hotel manager, Caris's mother...Caris herself even called to bust my ass about making her do the stupid gig in the first place. And finally Everett Torrence called. I was due in his office first thing the next day for a meeting that would decide my fate.

I was waiting for the "You're not cut out for this" speech, which I no doubt deserved. I couldn't control Caris.

I couldn't control anything!

My phone buzzed again. I ripped it out of my pocket and saw Justin's work number.

"What the hell are you still doing at work?" I barked.

"St-studying. I-I-I just heard about C-Caris. What do you need me to do?"

I sighed and tipped my head back against the airport glass. "Go home. You've got someone who actually wants to share a bed with you. Don't take it for granted. Go be with your wife, man."

I hung up before he could reply, slipping the phone back into my pocket and willing the night away. I wanted to get it over with as fast as humanly possible.

"Flight UA29 leaving for LAX is now boarding."

I snatched my bag and strode toward the counter, flashing the hostess a tight smile as I barreled past her. I didn't want to head back to California and all that awaited me. But I had no way of getting out of it. I should have been at that birthday party.

I needed to get my shit figured out, but it was damn nerve-wracking. I'd stood up to Kelly on Friday night, and although it felt good to get it off my chest, I'd left her place empty-handed. Did I risk standing up to Everett Torrence in the morning only to suffer the same fate? It would only take a three-word statement from him and I'd be left on the street, jobless.

I slumped into Seat 23B and squeezed my eyes shut. How much did I bend over backwards to keep someone happy? How much did I compromise?

Caris didn't deserve to be with Torrence Records anymore, but she was the pot of gold and I was a nobody. It wasn't hard to guess who'd win the battle in the morning. The only decision I had left to make was—what kind of man did I want to be? Did I stick around and put up with the bullshit or did I stand up for myself?

FORTY-FOUR

KELLY

I strode into work, still restless and antsy, hoping my early morning email to Marcus had gotten through. He'd ignored my call the night before, and I hadn't bothered leaving a message. I figured he'd call me back when he had a chance...but he didn't, and then I started thinking he was ignoring me.

I hadn't slept all night. I'd lain awake staring at the ceiling until I couldn't take it anymore, then paced the dining area for a while. Finally at 4 a.m., I'd pulled out my laptop and trawled through my song list, looking for the perfect message to send him. I wanted to redeem myself and let him know that I was in. No more tall, dark, and handsome for me. I wanted Marcus and no one else.

I'd attached the song "Happy" by Never Shout Never and pressed SEND, nervously jittering around my apartment until the sun rose.

As soon as I got to work, I opened my inbox and scoured my mail for a reply message, but *nada*. Colorado was in a different time zone, so he might not have seen it. He was such an early riser, though. I couldn't think anything other than *he's ignoring me.*

My spirits deflated slightly, but then I thought about how tenacious he'd been in winning me over. I didn't have my personal computer with me, so I went to my online sent folder and re-sent the song "Happy." I figured I'd just keep doing it until he replied.

The sound of the email swooshing from my outbox coincided with the ding of the elevator. I looked up with my work smile, and my mouth dropped open as an exhausted Marcus strode past me.

"Hi," I squeaked.

He gave me a polite nod and headed straight to his office. His pallor was basically gray. I jumped up and followed him.

"Are you okay?" I closed the door behind me and hurried to his desk.

"What do you want, Kelly?"

I crossed my arms and scowled. "I want to check you're okay."

He dropped his bag on the floor and glanced at me. "I'm fine."

"What happened? I thought you'd be gone all week?"

"Caris happened." He slumped into his chair and switched on his computer. The machine buzzed and whirred. "So I'm back to deal with more bullshit!"

His angry tone made me flinch. I gripped my arm and gazed at him. "I sent you an email last night."

"Yeah, I saw it this morning." He scrubbed his face then stared at the screen as it dinged with incoming mail. "And I see it now, as well."

I grinned.

"Why did you send it to me?" He spun his chair to face me. His glare and harsh tone matched perfectly.

I looked to the floor and lamely muttered, "Because I wanted you to know that my date was a waste of time. I spent the entire evening thinking about you and wanting to be with you." I forced my eyes off the floor. "I wanted you to know that I'm in."

My chest shuddered and I squeezed my folded arms against myself.

He must have noticed the gesture, because the flash of joy on his face was stolen by a narrow-eyed skepticism. "You're *all* in?"

"Uh-huh." I swayed my hips as I walked around his desk then perched my butt on the edge. Grabbing his tie, I threaded it through my fingers with a little grin. "I was thinking after work we could head back to your place and, I don't know, enjoy really good make-up sex?"

His cheeks flushed and he smiled, swallowing loudly before gently taking the tie out of my grasp.

"So you love me then?" He leaned back and scrutinized my face with his keen eyes.

"Of course." I smiled, trying to hide the rattling effect the L-word always had on me. "I just want to be with you."

"And you're ready to tell the world? Your parents?"

My expression fell before I could stop it.

His snigger was all-knowing as he pushed his chair away from me and stood, pacing around to the other side of the desk. "I'm not after a love affair, Kelly. Yes, we're great in bed together, but that's not why I fell for you. I want something real…an actual relationship."

"We… We can have that." I threw my arms wide, hating the course of the conversation. I was expecting him to be touched by my email gesture. Hell, I thought he might even take me on his desk when I admitted I was all in, but he was fighting me on it, pressing me to make all these dramatic statements.

"I don't want to be with someone who's embarrassed to have me around. Admit it, you have every intention of hiding me away. I'm going to be your quiet little fling. The guy you flirt with at work. And the second you head home for your Thursday night dinner, I'm going to cease to exist.

You want me in this world, but you won't bring me into yours."

"I'm not emba... You're making me sound like some kind of rich floozy who has a man on the side."

"But that's what I'll be, right? I'll be the guy who keeps you happy and entertained, like some place holder while you keep your eye out for Mr. Perfect...the one Mommy and Daddy approve of."

"I don't want to date anyone else, that's what I'm saying to you."

"But you don't want anyone from that part of your life knowing about me!"

I pinched my lips together, holding back my frustrated scream. "You don't know what she's like, Marcus! I am doing you a favor. You do not want to come into my warped world!"

His face bunched with sad confusion. "Then how are we ever supposed to be together?"

"I—I..." A heavy sigh was my only answer.

Marcus gave me a glum smile and walked back around to his computer. Double-clicking the mouse, he started "Happy" playing.

The words filtered into the office—bright and cheerful.

Marcus's gaze penetrated me as he softly said, "This song is just words, unless you're willing to act. I make you happy? Then show the world. Let them hear you say, 'I love you, Marcus.' Tell your mom your boyfriend's coming over for dinner."

My lips trembled as I blinked to fight the tears building in my eyes. Clenching my jaw, I broke eye contact and stood tall, smoothing down my skirt before heading for the door.

"Good luck with Caris. Let me know if you need anything."

Marcus didn't make a sound, and I couldn't look back to see what his face was doing. All I knew was that he was asking too much.

FORTY-FIVE

MARCUS

I hated myself for the way I spoke to Kelly. What the hell was wrong with me? She'd offered to be with me again and I'd rejected it.

I was an idiot.

But unlike her, I knew what I wanted and I was done compromising.

I pulled in a lungful of heavy, suffocating air and dragged my butt up to the top floor. Everett's secretary sent me into the boardroom where Caris and her mother were waiting with Justin and his boss, Clay. Everett Torrence sat at the head of the oval table.

"Sorry, I'm late." I smoothed down my tie and took a seat beside Justin, who immediately slid a file into my hands.

He gave me an encouraging smile that did nothing to settle my nerves. When I'd arrived home in the early hours, I'd spotted Kelly's email and gone to bed giddy, but I hadn't been able to sleep, and the more I thought it through, the more I realized I couldn't fall back into bed with her unless we were both doing it for the right reasons.

After winning that argument in my head, I then decided that the same thing had to apply for Caris and Torrence Records, which was why I'd called Justin at six in the morning and asked him for a favor.

I gripped the file in my hand.

"So, let's see if we can't problem-solve this together." Everett pressed his palms into the table and looked to his favorite lawyer, Clay. "Are we going to have a continued problem with this man, or can we avoid a second suit being filed?"

My nerves were skittish as I glanced at my boss. Unfortunately, it came through in my voice when I interrupted.

"Sir," I squeaked then quickly cleared my throat. "Sorry." I covered my mouth with my fist and cleared my throat again. "Mr. Everett, sir. Do you mind if I share a few thoughts before we proceed?"

He looked cynical but gave me a short nod.

I flipped open the file and skimmed down the page, noting the multiple highlighted sections.

"Before I share what I really want to say, I'd like

to apologize for not attending the birthday party with Caris last night. I should have been there to monitor her behavior, but I didn't think she'd need a babysitter for a one-hour gig. It was my error, and I take full responsibility."

I held my breath as I looked at Everett. He gave me nothing but a blank-faced stare, so I kept going before I lost my courage.

"I have here a copy of Caris's contract with Torrence Records, and we've taken the liberty of highlighting all the areas that she has breached or is currently in breach." I slid it across the table. "Some of these you may not be aware of. As her manager, I've tried to deal with most of them quietly and do the job you requested of me."

Everett's eyes bulged as he noticed the amount of fluorescent color on the pages.

"I think it's clear that myself and many of the staff here are bending over backwards to accommodate behavior that should not be tolerated."

Out of the corner of my eye, I noticed Caris stiffen. Her mother patted her arm while shooting me a vicious glare. I met it head-on and started listing the things I'd memorized.

"Defacing public property, underage drinking, socially disruptive behavior, stealing."

"She never—" Her mother tried to interrupt me, but I raised my hand and kept going.

"Attempting sex with a minor."

Her mother swallowed and lifted her chin. "That boy lied about his age."

"According to your intoxicated, fabulist daughter?" I raised my eyebrows. "I know who I'd be more inclined to believe. The truth of the matter is, Caris, I don't think you're worth it."

She bristled at my words, her eyes flashing with warning. She opened her mouth to give me her "pot of gold" speech, but I spoke over her.

"You may have an amazing voice, and you can draw a huge crowd. But you have no respect or integrity, and according to Torrence Records' mission statement, those are the kinds of artists we want to be working with. You're not the only pot of gold in this world, and we can do better."

Her eyes flashed. "How dare you speak to me that way. Any record company would take me like that." She snapped her fingers. "But I was nice enough to come here and see if we could work together. Now you're trying to back out on me? Oh, I don't think so. You want to know what being sued *really* feels like?" She spun to face Everett, pointing her long fingernail at me. "Torrence, you fire his ass or I am gone. And believe me, if I go I will be getting the best lawyers in this town to sue Torrence Records for all it's worth. By the time we're done, you'll have nothing left."

I looked to Everett who was gazing at the file with a grim frown. His lips pursed to the side before he glanced up at me then slowly tracked his eyes to Caris. Her angular face was highlighted by her threatening expression, but the big-boss seemed completely unfazed as he flipped the file closed.

"Well? Get on with it." Caris tipped her head at me. "I've got an album to finish recording."

Everett took a slow breath in through his nose and tapped his finger on the top of the file. "I'm sorry to inform you…" He gazed at me and my gut sank.

Great. So standing up for myself and my ideals was complete horseshit then. I lost the girl and my job.

"That I will not be firing my best manager. The way he has handled all your messes is well above and beyond the call of duty. You want to sue my company?" He stood, pressing his fingers into the table and leaning over her. "You go right ahead. As of now, you no longer have a contract with Torrence Records."

Caris shrunk away from him with a small gasp.

Her mother's chest puffed out as she tried to counter the intimidating man. "You can't—"

"Ma'am! I wouldn't say anything if I were you." He buttoned his jacket and pulled it straight then looked to his lawyer. "Get this finalized for me, will you? I want the paperwork completed by the end of the week."

"You got it." Clay and Justin started scribbling notes as Everett walked from the room. Just before leaving, he turned and gave me a subtle wink. My face bloomed with a smile before I could stop it.

*****

Kelly stepped into my office. Since our final fight, she'd gone into professional mode. We only spoke about work and kept our sentences short and clipped. As triumphant as my Tuesday meeting had been, the rest of the week had been total crap.

Finalizing Caris's dramatic exit from the company turned out to be hours of paperwork, which I had to meticulously read and sign. Her being in major breach of contract had been great for us, but it didn't stop us from having to cross every T and dot every I. We had to sew everything up tight so that if she *did* sue, we were ready for her. That had been a time and brain suck, leaving me with no spare energy to deal with my Kelly issue.

I'd let her go and it hurt like nothing else, but I couldn't bend.

I wouldn't be her love affair. I wanted more. I'd always wanted more from her, and this time I was willing to hold out for it.

Her smile was tight and sad as she walked to my desk. She stopped short when she heard the song playing softly out of my speakers, "Let Her Go." It was a haunting version by Jasmine Thompson and, for some warped reason, I'd been listening to it a lot. It was so freaking sad. I didn't know why I tortured myself, but it kept coming up on shuffle play then getting stuck in my head, so I had to listen to it over and over until I thought I'd drown in the melody.

She cleared her throat and gripped her hands together. "Is there anything else you need before I leave?"

I looked at my computer screen to check the time—11:25 a.m.—then frowned at her.

"I have a wedding." Her smile was weak and unenthusiastic. "I have to be there. Bryce gave me permission, but he's not here right now. If it's okay with you, I'm going to sneak away at midday so I can get ready and be there for the three o'clock start."

"Family wedding?"

Her skin blanched and she swallowed. "Something like that."

"Weird that it's on a weekday."

She shrugged. "It's Valentine's Day."

"Of course it is." I'd been walking past the cacophony of red all week, trying to ignore the love hearts and roses.

I pulled off my reading glasses and looked at her, drinking in her stunning face and wishing she'd ask me to go with her. I'd say yes in a heartbeat. It was all she'd have to say and I'd be hers forever.

But she wouldn't ask.

She wouldn't let me in, so I had to force my lips together to stop any kind of sentiment spewing out of them.

Wriggling in my seat, I slipped my glasses back on and gazed at my computer screen. "I don't need anything. You head off when you're ready. Hope you have a good time."

"Thanks," she whispered.

I couldn't watch her leave, but as soon as the door clicked shut, I threw off my glasses and slammed back into my seat. The music was still wafting around me, a sad, melancholy reminder that I was a stubborn idiot and my high school self would be absolutely horrified by my behavior.

FORTY-SIX

KELLY

The cathedral was cool and drafty. It didn't help that LA had put on a blustery day. Red, heart-shaped balloons had blown past me as I stepped onto the street and clipped up the concrete steps. I was in the strapless dress Mom had chosen weeks ago. It was a long, luscious wine-red number that hugged my torso so damn tight I could barely breathe, then at mid-thigh fell in waves of fabric that floated down to my ankles. I had sticky tape on my breasts, holding the fabric in place and making me look perfect...just the way my mother wanted.

I walked into the stunning church, gazing up at the intricately carved pillars to the high ceiling. The cavernous building smelled like roses. The wedding designers had decked out the space in extravagant blooms of red and white.

A camera clicked behind me, and I did a double-take over my shoulder when I spotted Charlie. I grinned and she snapped my image again. Mom had mentioned Charlie volunteered to take some photos at the wedding. She was mortified that her niece had boldly approached Evangeline's parents at the party to offer, but Evangeline's mom had been taken with my quirky cousin and said yes on the spot.

It was pretty impossible not to love Charlie.

Holding the camera against her shoulder, she looked me up and down.

"Okay, I've totally heard of *spank me* jeans, but never a *spank me* dress. Hot damn, woman, that thing looks so good on you. I just want to give that tushy a tap."

It was impossible not to laugh. I loved Charlie. She could always make me smile...just like Marcus could.

I ran a hand down my stomach and pulled a face.

She giggled. "The things we do for hotness, right?"

I ran my eyes down her burnt-orange dress, mismatched with a pair of knee-high boots with big silver buckles. My mother would die if I walked out of the house like that. Charlie got away with it, though, because she was, well...Charlie. She had a multicolored scarf holding her hair in a reckless knot at the back. The silky strands rested on her shoulder, one of them tangled within her spiral earring. I reached forward to correct it.

"I want to grow up to look just like you." She sniffed. "Ooo, and smell just like you, too."

I stepped back with a doleful smirk. "You don't want to be like me, Charlie."

"When you find your happy, I will."

Her statement stumped me, so I let out a confused chuckle. "I am happy."

"No you're not." Her nose wrinkled.

I sputtered a couple of times then eventually sighed. "Okay fine, so how do I find my happy?"

A dimple scored her right cheek as she gave me her classic half-smile. "You stop worrying about what everyone else thinks and listen to your heart. It gives you the freedom to go after the things that really matter to you. Totally works for me." She winked and turned at the sound of her name. Scampering through the incoming guests, Charlie headed to the door to snap shots of the arriving groom and his men. I stood in my place, the air in my lungs stale and thick as I tried to figure out what my happy looked like.

The truth was, I knew...I was just too afraid to stop worrying about what everyone else thought.

"Kelly, what are you doing just standing there?" Mom bustled up behind me in her ankle-length chiffon dress, flicking her gloved hand for me to follow her. I shuffled down the aisle as she prattled on. "Asher just called me to say he's standing outside your apartment ready to collect you and you're not there. You were supposed to come together. That was the whole point!"

"I decided to come on my own," I mumbled, still dazed by Charlie's simple comments.

"I don't know what is wrong with you at the moment. I set up everything to work perfectly, and you will not comply. Honestly, Kelly. Asher is the perfect match for you, why are you being so reticent?"

"He's not my perfect match," I countered softly.

Mom sighed and gave me a sympathetic arm squeeze. "I understand today is hard for you. I wouldn't want to see my ex getting married either, which is why I was trying to soften the blow by providing someone for you."

I wriggled out of her grasp. "You don't need to do that."

"Well, it's not like you're finding anyone on your own." She bulged her eyes at Dad, who was sitting there quietly assessing my outfit. I could tell by the slight smirk that he was happy with the design but may have gone for a different hairstyle.

I stepped back from both my parents, their judgment feeling like a ten-ton wrecking ball. It pissed me off, so I let out a huff and snapped, "But I did find someone."

"Excuse me?" Mom placed her gloved hand on her hip and looked at me. "You asked someone to come with you and they said no?"

I shook my head, suddenly realizing that

Marcus never would have denied me. I could have asked him to walk through fire and he would have. All he wanted me to do was claim him, that's it, and he'd do anything for me. He'd love me through my bullshit and kiss me when I was sick. He'd listen to me rant and yell then try to make me laugh with some ridiculous game or joke. He hadn't met my parents yet, but he'd stand his ground and do whatever it took to be with me…if I was only willing to stand with him.

My eyes glassed with tears as a goofy smile spread across my lips.

"Kelly, stop grinning like a chimp, you look ridiculous." Mom squeezed my wrist then saw someone over my shoulder. "Oh, here comes Fletcher. He's just noticed you…and he looks like he's drooling." Mom's smug smile made her lips purse into a repulsive kind of duck face. Her cheekbones protruded more than usual, and for the first time in my entire life, I saw all the way through her veneer and spotted the arrogant, uppity woman she thrived on being.

I snatched my wrist back and shook my head. "I don't care. He can look all he likes. He can be jealous or nonchalant, I no longer give a shit!"

"Kelly," Mom hissed, looking around her before whispering, "Mind your language."

"I don't want him. I don't want Asher. I just…" I huffed and looked between my parents. "I want Marcus."

"Who?" My father frowned.

I looked to the ceiling, willing my racing heart to

slow down enough to let me speak the truth. Sucking in a quick breath, I let it whoosh out my lungs before saying, "He's not the man of my dreams. He's not even a guy I ever thought I'd end up with, but he's perfect." I swooned, placing a hand on my chest as images of our time together flashed through my mind like treasured photographs.

"Kelly, what are talking about?" Mom's sharp voice made my eyes snap back to hers.

I shot her another goofy smile and gathered up the front of my dress. "I have to go."

"What!" Mom tried to snatch my arm as I turned, but I shook her off and started running for the entrance. "Kelly!" she called after me.

I brushed past Fletcher, ignoring his flirty greeting and scampering out of the church before anyone could stop me. My dress floated out behind me as I skipped across the road, nearly giggling with excitement as I raced to Torrence Records, hoping I hadn't missed the chance to claim the only man I wanted.

FORTY-SEVEN

MARCUS

Everett sat opposite me, his broad shoulders making him look like a defensive lineman. In spite of the fact he stood up for me with Caris, he still intimidated the hell out of me. I felt like a pipsqueak sitting on the couch across from him and trying on my best smile to a potential Torrence artist.

Maverick Glade.

He was a singer/songwriter who looked like Dean Martin and sang like Johnny Cash. He wasn't the style Torrence usually went for, but his super-hot looks had girls across the nation swooning, and the YouTube channel he started up six months ago had gone viral. It was called *Just A Man and His Guitar*. The ladies couldn't get enough of it.

A Torrence exec spotted him a few months back and had been tracking his progress. When rumors started circulating that he'd had offers from other record companies, Everett jumped on it immediately. He was looking at me to manage the guy. I hoped it would be an easier task than Caris, because I had some major redeeming to do.

Everett's thumb twitched on the armrest. "So, what do you think, Maverick? I can guarantee Marcus would take good care of you. He's one of the best managers we've got."

A languid smile pulled the right side of Maverick's mouth up, but he didn't say anything. With offers coming in from all sides, he had the luxury to choose, and Everett hated being in that position. He wouldn't want to pander like he had done with Caris, but a big client like this would make up for the Caris windfall.

I eyed them both carefully, wondering what his final decision would be. Maverick pursed his lips and was reaching for the contract again when my office door flew open.

"Marcus, I…" Kelly gasped and stopped in the doorway.

My mouth dropped open. She looked incredible, like she belonged on the red carpet at the Oscars or the cover of *Vogue*. That silk dress with her sultry red lips and those eyes looking straight at me.

I rose from the couch, drawn by some magnetic

force. Her gaze held me in place, and all I could do was stare at her. There was something about her expression that told me what she had to say was vitally important. I didn't want to miss a word of it.

Everett cleared his throat. Kelly and I both flinched at the sound. I glanced down to see my boss tipping his head at the door with an annoyed scowl.

"Um…" I smoothed down my tie.

"Sorry to interrupt." Kelly smiled at the two men opposite me, her eyes flashing with embarrassment when she noticed Everett Torrence sitting in my office. Yes, it never happened, but after I'd given Maverick a tour of the building, Everett had been waiting for us in my space. I still hadn't figured out why.

The two men nodded at Kelly, their eyes traveling down her body with appreciation. It was impossible not to check her out—she was drool-worthy in that dress.

"No problem." I smiled, my gaze flicking over the two men as I strove to be professional. "I don't actually need you for anything right now, so why don't we catch up after this meeting."

Kelly's head bobbed. "Okay, sure. I'll just…" Her sigh was soft, more like a shudder, as she turned out the door, but then she paused and spun back. Pressing her lips together, she looked at Everett. Uncertainty washed over her expression, but it was swept away when her eyebrows pulled together and she looked right at me. "Actually, you know what? I can't. I'm sorry to disturb…" She smiled at Maverick then pointed to me. "But I have something really important that I need to tell this man and it can't wait, because he does need me." Her eyes flicked to mine. The slick sheen coating them hit me right in the heart. "You need me…just as much as I need you. And I'm sorry I wasn't willing to fight for us. I was afraid. I couldn't fit you into my world. All I could see was one obstacle after another, so I gave up."

Her mouth curled down and she started blinking. Placing a trembling hand over her mouth, she lightly rubbed the edge of her lips before continuing. "But I realized today that it doesn't matter whether you fit or not, because I want you by my side. You make everything better. Being with you makes me so happy." She patted her chest, a stray tear wandering down her cheek as she sucked in a breath. "I love you, Marcus. I *love* you, and I'll tell anyone you want me to because I am all in."

A goofy smile spread my cheeks wide before she'd even finished. Tears glassed over my eyes before I could stop them, and if it hadn't been for more throat-clearing from Everett Torrence, I would have vaulted over Maverick and kissed my woman senseless.

"Maybe you two could finish this later?" Everett's thick eyebrows rose, his strong gaze emphatic.

"Of course." I nodded, gazing back at Kelly and giving her my best smile. "Are you free tonight?"

Her head bobbed rapidly. "I'm all yours."

My insides sizzled, and it was an effort not to giggle. I felt like Charlie after he'd unwrapped his Wonka Bar and discovered a golden ticket. "I'll pick you up at seven."

Kelly's smile took over her whole face. Her dreamy expression was radiant, and I swear my heart catapulted out of my chest for a beat before settling into a heady rhythm. Kelly DeMarco loved me, and she was willing to tell the world.

FORTY-EIGHT

KELLY

Walking to the elevator was impossible, so I floated there instead. I could feel Marcia's surprised gaze on my back, but I couldn't turn and tell her anything. Talking would have been hopeless. I could barely form a coherent thought, let alone a sentence. Bubbles were popping inside of me like a crazy fireworks display. I'd done it. I'd told Marcus the truth, and it felt so damn good.

I pressed the Down button and checked my watch. Only three hours until seven o'clock. Only three hours until I kissed my man.

The doors dinged open and I stepped inside,

smiling at the marketing exec and her assistant. Spinning around, I checked that the parking garage was highlighted and then…

"Hold the doors!"

My heart lurched at the sound of Marcus's voice carrying across the lower exec floor. I jammed my hand on the Open Doors button.

He puffed into view with a dopey smile. "You forgot something."

"What?"

Before I could blink, his hands cupped my face and he leaned up to kiss me. His firm lips touched me right down to my core before he opened his mouth and sealed the deal with a kiss that had Marcia cheering from behind her desk. I ran my hands around Marcus's solid torso and gripped his waist, noticing out of the corner of my eye a few curious onlookers popping out of their offices.

I shut my eyes against them all and lost myself in Marcus.

Marcus.

His name was a contented sigh in my brain, a promise of something more…a life I never knew I wanted.

He pulled away and brushed his nose against mine. "I'll see you later." His breath caressed my skin, his soft voice sounding like a sonnet. "Wear something…"

"Comfortable," I murmured.

"I was gonna say nice, but if you'd rather comfy, then…"

I snickered, stepping back into the elevator as it

started to beep in protest. I shone him my best smile and winked. "Most definitely comfy."

His grin was adorable. It carried me down to my car and all the way home where I floated through my door and found a very different face waiting for me.

"Mom!" I jerked, gripping the doorknob like it would somehow keep me upright. "What... How?"

"I own this apartment, I have a key." Her tone was acidic, the unimpressed glint in her eye making my insides shrivel. "Where have you been?"

"I, um..." I licked my bottom lip and stepped into the apartment, leaving the door ajar in case I needed a quick escape. Clearing my throat, I raised my chin and forced myself to look at her. "I had to pop into work and pass on a very important message."

"More important than Fletcher's wedding?"

"Most definitely." I grinned.

Mom's eyes narrowed, zeroing in on me and stripping the smile from my face. "You embarrassed yourself and your family today, running out of the church like some madman. Gossip was rife before the ceremony even started." Mom clutched her purse and pulled her shoulders back, her cheeks tinging red as she looked me up and down. "Now, you will make amends for your abhorrent behavior and join me at the reception. You will smile, you will converse, you will make people believe that you are in full control of your faculties, whether that be true or not."

I rolled my eyes. "Of course, I'm in full control of my faculties! My mind's never been so clear." I kicked off my shoes. They landed with a clunk on the wooden floor, making my mother bristle.

"Put those back on. We are leaving!"

"No." I shook my head. "I'm not going to the reception. I shouldn't have been asked to attend the wedding in the first place. I don't care about appearances. You can do this gig without me."

"Kelly, you are my daughter, and you will not humiliate me like this."

"I'm not trying to humiliate you!" I threw my arms wide.

Mom sighed, pulling in a slow breath like she was trying to keep it together. "I understand that you loved Fletcher. He hurt you, but you must rise above it. You can't let them win. To get the things you want, you must be steel."

"No, Mom, I must be open and willing to fight for the things that matter." I stepped toward her, gently placing my hands on her shoulders. "Fletcher doesn't matter anymore, and neither do any of the guys you try to line up for me. I don't want to get married for the good of the company. I'm not a business transaction, I'm your daughter. And I should get some say in my own life."

Mom rubbed her temples like I was giving her a migraine. "Kelly, this is bigger than you."

"It doesn't have to be. There's no law saying I have to marry a multimillionaire."

"But the company."

"I don't care about the company." I let her go,

my arms slapping down against my sides. "It's not even *my* company! I didn't ask for it."

Mom's eyes bulged, her face taking on an ashen quality before turning brittle. "Fine. You don't care about our family, what *do* you care about?"

"Marcus. I care about Marcus. I want to be with him, without any of your bullshit pressure or demands. I should be allowed to love who I want...and I want him."

A shuffling at the door made me spin. Yanking it open a little wider, I spotted Marcus. His tie was askew and his hair was mussed. From the way his chest was heaving, he looked like he'd been sprinting to reach me. I grinned at his beautiful, disheveled self and felt my knees weaken.

"I couldn't wait 'til seven," he murmured with a sheepish grin.

"Who is this?" Mom's sharp voice was a bucket of cold water.

"Hi there." Marcus stepped around me, extending his hand in greeting. "Marcus Chapman."

Mom's right eyebrow arched, and she looked him up and down then glared at me. "No. Absolutely not."

I made a fist and gave Marcus a tight smile. "Can you give us a second?"

"Of course." He lingered by the door looking sweet and adorable, while I snatched Mom's arm and pulled her into my bedroom.

"Let me go!" She flicked my hand off. Her horrified expression was so exaggerated it was almost comical.

"How dare you look at him that way!" I snapped. "You have no right to dictate who I fall in love with."

"Oh, Kelly, don't be insane. You know full well he's not marriage material. He couldn't possibly become a member of our family. One look at him and I can tell he'd be of no financial benefit, not to mention the fact he's a complete hobo. The media would have a field day. He's absolutely classless."

My insides were raging as she tore strips off my man. None of it was true. Marcus had more class than all of those stuck-up snobs.

"I'm not asking your permission." My voice had a cold, steely edge to it. Damn it felt good to finally tell her what I wanted to say. "Marcus is ten times the man Fletcher or Dad or any of your stiff-coat businessmen are."

Mom pointed an elegant finger at me. "Don't speak about your father that way."

It made me sick that she kept defending him.

"He's a highly respected businessman and makes us look damn good. Now, we have spoken about this. It doesn't matter how remarkable this *Marcus* might be, he's not suitable! You are a DeMarco, you don't have the luxury of choice!"

"Yes. I. Do!"

We stood less than an inch from each other, facing off like two mountain goats ready to lock horns. I couldn't let her win, but that ruthless glare on her face was chipping at my resolve.

Pissing my mother off was never a good idea.

Her voice dropped to a soft timbre, a red flag for the blow she was about to strike.

"May I remind you that your father and I own every aspect of your life. We pay for this apartment, your cleaner, your clothes and makeup. Your credit cards, how do you think they get paid off?"

I stumbled back from her, my heel bashing into the base of the bed. I winced but locked my jaw, refusing to pull a *that hurts* face.

"I would advise you, very strongly, to consider what might happen if you refuse to comply with my one simple request." My mother's tone was sharp and cutting.

Simple request, was she kidding?

"You're forcing me to give up someone I love so I can live your plastic-coated, empty life. I don't want that." My voice shook. "I want to be with someone who's going to be faithful to me, and respect me. Someone who will treat me well. Not for show but because they actually want to see me happy. I can't do what you do. I don't know how you cut off feelings so easily."

Her fine nostrils flared while a tendon in her neck pinged. She looked away from me like I'd just slapped her across the face. "You'd give it all up for some short, mussed-up mess? I don't even know what he does!"

I looked to the floor and mumbled, "He's a band manager for Torrence Records."

Mom scoffed as if I'd just said he was a street cleaner.

I pointed toward the living area where Marcus was lingering, no doubt hearing every word shouted about him. "He's a good guy, and he loves me."

"If you think that's going to carry you through, you've got another think coming. You don't even know what it is to work for a living. You've had a silver spoon life, and I can tell you that you will *hate* getting your hands dirty!" The venom in her tone made each word come out sharp and snappy. "Don't let your foolish heart override common sense, Kelly. You're smarter than that. I will strip every last penny out of your life if that's what it takes to teach you."

My lips trembled when I tried to press them together.

"No more nice clothes, no more fine dining. You can live like the rest of the working class and know what it's really like to worry about paying your bills on time."

My insides were about to concave. I could feel the inner earthquake brewing. I crossed my arms over myself and gripped the edge of my waist.

"I don't think she needs to worry about that." Marcus stepped into the room, his calm voice contradicting the fury in his gaze. The tight knot in my belly unraveled when he smiled at me and stepped to my side. He placed his hand on my lower back and gave it a gentle rub. "I know this isn't my fight, Mrs. DeMarco. I hope you don't mind the interruption, but I just couldn't handle you yelling at my girl that way."

Mom's neck rose high, and she pulled in an indignant breath.

Marcus remained calm and unflappable, his voice steady and even. "I know what you're trying to do—scare her into compliance. But the thing you're forgetting is that Kelly has a job. One she's very good at. She can pay her own bills now, and as for an apartment, she's welcome to move into my house any time she's ready."

I flinched to look at him, my heart melting into a puddle as I imagined waking up each morning in his bed with Pumpkin and Flash sleeping at our feet. I pictured myself walking in the door after work and kicking off my heels, puttering around in his little kitchen then slouching on the couch with him.

A watery smile spread across my face.

Mom's irate tone tried to steal it from me. "Really, Kelly? You'll give it all up for *him*?"

I turned to face my lover, draping my arm over his shoulder and gazing into his eyes. "No. I'll give it all up for us."

He grinned back at me and mouthed, "I love you."

"I love you, too," I whispered, running my fingers into his hair and brushing my lips against his.

I was aware of my mother still standing there in her finery, but she didn't say anything. She just kept staring at us with a lost kind of longing on her face. Marcus wrapped me in a hug, and I rested my chin on his shoulder, giving her a smile I hoped she'd understand.

I didn't know whether she did or not.

She walked out of the room, and I was left with Marcus.

As much as it hurt to see her leave, it couldn't dampen the happy bubbles popping in my chest. I had Marcus...and that was all I really needed.

EPILOGUE

MARCUS

"Dude, you look exhausted. Would you go home already?"

Justin scrubbed his face and yawned. The bags under his eyes were black and blue, his skin a pale cream color that looked awful on him.

His shoulder hitched as he yanked his tie and pulled it off. Checking his watch, he hissed and reached for his phone, sending a quick text before pushing his half-eaten Subway lunch aside and hunching over a legal textbook that looked like hard work.

I leaned against his office door and eyed him.

"Maybe you should take tomorrow off. Have a catch-up study day or something."

"I-I can't, man. I've got t-to finalize contracts for the n-n-ne-new..." He huffed and took a breath. "For the new guy tomorrow, and I-I have a test in the afternoon."

"Okay, I'm just saying. When was the last time you saw Sarah?"

He closed his eyes and banged his head on top of his textbook. "I don't want to talk about Sarah."

My stomach knotted. "Something happen?"

He shook his head and sniffed. "Can you just go, man? I've got work to do."

I pushed off the doorframe and stood my ground, wondering how much pressure I should put on him. He looked ready to fall apart.

"Just go," he croaked.

Easing quietly away from his office, I walked down the corridor while worry ate me alive. I had no idea what was going on with the guy, but for someone who was supposed to be celebrating his one-year anniversary in a few weeks, he wasn't looking too enthusiastic about it.

I'd always imagined marriage to be the easiest thing in the world. My parents made it look like a dream. Although, Kelly's parents made it look like a nightmare. Correction: Kelly's parents made it *look* good, but the truth below the surface was a frosty nightmare. I cringed as I headed down to my girl, reliving our most recent dinner at their place. It had been a quiet, secretive affair—the first time I'd been invited to their house. Awkward was the understatement of the year, and we'd only stayed an hour. Kelly cried on the way home, which broke my heart. I wanted to slap her parents senseless. Could they honestly not see how happy we were together?

It was obvious the dinner invite was a ploy to break us up. I could tell they missed their daughter, but not enough to welcome me into the fold. They still hadn't offered Kelly a dime since she moved in with me, but she didn't seem to mind. She'd picked up a few classes at the gym, which Logan was paying her for, and that had become our entertainment budget. Between our two incomes, we were covering all the other expenses. My comfortable little bungalow suited us just fine, and so far she hadn't curled her lip at anything. Kelly was the most happy and carefree I'd ever seen her. Life was bliss and the only thing I wanted to change was to make her my wife.

I couldn't ask her, though.

She never spoke about marriage, but I got the impression that she was kind of anti the idea. I understood why after she told me the truth about her womanizing father. No wonder she'd had such a hard time trusting men. I wouldn't let her down, though. I was determined to be the best boyfriend the world had ever seen.

Sauntering into the main office, I raised my hand in farewell to Marcia, who was skipping to the elevator with an excited grin.

I looked at Kelly, and she smirked at her animated friend. "Date night," she told me when the elevator doors dinged shut.

"Nice." I came around the counter and perched my butt on her desk.

"You nearly ready to go?"

"Yeah." I nodded, still feeling a little unsettled about Justin.

Her long fingers brushed against my thigh as she gazed up at me. "Everything okay?"

"Yeah, I just had a weird conversation with Justin. Something's going on with him and Sarah." My suit jacket rustled as I crossed my arms.

"Oh hey, did you know I found out that she works for my dad. She's one of his designers."

"Small world." I raised my eyebrows. "I wonder what's up with them?"

"Hey." Kelly squeezed my chin and made me look at her. "It's not your marriage, which means it's not your problem. And I'm not saying that to sound bitchy, but you and I have been living together for over four months now, and I've seen your weakness for taking on everybody else's burdens. Don't carry this for him. They have to work out their own problems."

I leaned forward and kissed her. "I'm so glad being with you is so easy."

She grinned.

"Do you think we'll ever get married?" The question just popped out before I'd thought it through. I swallowed and gave her a casual smile, hoping she wouldn't make a big deal of it.

She leaned away from me, her eyes searching my face before she shrugged and murmured,

"Maybe."

I stilled. "Maybe?"

The corner of her mouth twitched. "Maybe."

My insides bubbled with glee, which I did my best to hide as I stood from her desk and slid my hands into my pockets. "So if I asked you, you'd say yes?"

"I guess you'd have to buy a ring and ask me to find out." She pressed her lips together, her sparkling gaze brushing over me.

I narrowed my eyes at her teasing expression. "So let me get this straight. You're expecting me to spend a month's salary on a ring you'll no doubt want to switch for something else, and then you want me to go down on one knee on the off-chance you *might* say yes?"

"Uh-huh." She giggled, her head bobbing.

I brushed the air and stepped away from her desk. "Forget it. You want to marry me, you can ask me yourself."

"Oh! So romantic!" She scoffed.

With a chuckle, I headed for my office, ready to collect my stuff and head home. She had no idea how badly I wanted to do everything I'd just teased her about, but I knew Kelly...and that kind of thing made her nervous. Putting her in the driver's seat may have seemed unromantic to some, but it would make Kelly feel safe and secure, which was all I really cared about.

I pulled out my chair and sat down with a grin. Wiggling my mouse, I lit up the screen and was about to close down my computer when a message dinged into my inbox. I saw it was from Kelly and double-clicked it immediately.

Meghan Trainor's voice filled my office at the same time Kelly appeared in my doorway, mouthing the words to "Dear Future Husband." She rested her hand high on the frame, looking like a siren with her hip jutting out to the side.

A soft chuckle escaped my lips when the beat kicked in and she swayed into the room. She was still mouthing the words, looking sexy as hell as she started dancing around my office and flirting with me.

I was mesmerized.

She shimmied up to my desk, her hands sliding down her thighs before she perched on my lap and gently tugged my tie. She pulled me an inch from her face and kept singing the words at me, telling me exactly what she expected of our future marriage.

I couldn't wipe the smile from my face. I was the happiest man on the planet.

I'd finally won my girl and she'd won me.

The song finished and I cupped the back of her head, forcing her to kiss me. She melted against my mouth with a sweet moan. Pulling back, I looked her in the eye and with a slow smile, whispered, "Okay, I'll buy you a ring."

THE END

Thank you so much for reading *Troublemaker*. If you've enjoyed it and would like to show me some support, please consider leaving a review on the site you purchased this book from.

KEEP READING TO FIND OUT ABOUT THE NEXT SONGBIRD NOVEL...

The next Songbird Novel belongs to:

Justin & Sarah

ROUGH WATER
Due for release in spring 2016

But while you're waiting for their story, keep an eye out for the first Chaos novella…

RALPHIE

He kept it a secret.
He sold the lie.
No one would ever know how much he loved Nessa Sloan.
To him, she was perfect. But she loved another, and so he had to watch in aching silence as his best friend, Jimmy, fell in love with the only girl who'd ever mattered.

But there is another…

A Sloan sister is on her way with an unwanted message that will rock Nessa's world and split the band apart. Sides will form and for the first time, Ralphie will find himself opposing his little Nester and standing up for a girl who might have the power to win his heart.

This novella is an exclusive story for my newsletter subscribers only. If you'd like to receive the story in March 2016, then please sign up to become a Songbird Novels Reader.
You'll also receive a free e-copy of Home (A Songbird Novel) when you sign up.
http://eepurl.com/1cqdj

You can find the other Songbird Novels on Amazon.

FEVER
Ella & Cole's story

BULLETPROOF
Morgan & Sean's story

EVERYTHING
Jody & Leo's story

HOME
Rachel & Josh's story

TRUE LOVE
Nessa & Jimmy's story

.

ACKNOWLEDGEMENTS

As always, I have a wonderful team of people helping me create, refine, and promote this next Songbird Novel.

Thank you so much to:

My critique readers: Cassie, Rae, Marcia, and Anna. Your feedback and insights are always spot on.

My editor: Laurie. You're the best. I love working with you.

My proofreaders: I so appreciate your time and attention.

My Advanced Reading Team: Thank you for your thoughts, opinions, and reviews. Your help is so vital to my work.

My cover designer and photographer: Regina. Woohoo!!! This cover is so amazing. Thank you!

My fellow writers: Inklings and Indie Inked. Thanks for your constant support and encouragement.

My Fan Club and readers: THANK YOU! I love and appreciate you guys so much.

My family: You are my constant source of love and encouragement. Thank you.

My savior: Thank you for showing me that the best things can come in unexpected ways. You are a God of surprises and I love you for that. You always know what's best for me.

OTHER BOOKS BY MELISSA PEARL

The Songbird Novels
Fever—Bulletproof—Everything—Home—True
Love—Troublemaker
Coming in spring 2016: Rough Water

The Space Between Heartbeats
Plus two novellas: The Space Before & The Space
Beyond

The Fugitive Series
I Know Lucy — Set Me Free

The Masks Series
True Colors — Two-Faced— Snake Eyes — Poker
Face

The Time Spirit Trilogy
Golden Blood — Black Blood — Pure Blood

The Elements Trilogy
Unknown — Unseen — Unleashed

The Mica & Lexy Series
Forbidden Territory—Forbidden Waters

Find out more on Melissa Pearl's website:
www.melissapearlauthor.com

ABOUT MELISSA PEARL

Melissa Pearl is a kiwi at heart but currently lives in Suzhou, China with her husband and two sons. She trained as an elementary school teacher but has always had a passion for writing and finally completed her first manuscript in 2003. She has been writing ever since, and the more she learns, the more she loves it.

She writes young adult and new adult fiction in a variety of romance genres—paranormal, fantasy, suspense, and contemporary. Her goal as a writer is to give readers the pleasure of escaping their everyday lives for a while and losing themselves in a journey...one that will make them laugh, cry, and swoon.

MELISSA PEARL ONLINE

Website:
www.melissapearlauthor.com

YouTube Channel:
www.youtube.com/user/melissapearlauthor

Facebook:
www.facebook.com/melissapearlauthor

Instagram:
instagram.com/melissapearlauthor

Twitter:
twitter.com/MelissaPearlG

Pinterest:
www.pinterest.com/melissapearlg